STRANGER IN A STRANGE LAND

Sammy looked around and scratched his head. "This place really looks familiar, but it's certainly not California." He peered at Brianna, squinting. "Am I in Ireland?"

"Eire?" she questioned back.

"Yeah, Eire. Ireland."

She nodded.

His tanned face went pale, his eyes widened in shock. His breath caught in a gasp. He stumbled and sat down on a block of stone just outside the hut.

"Sammy?"

He looked at Brianna in a dazed way that frightened her. She took his hands and he held on to her tightly.

"How did I get to Ireland?" he asked.

"I called you here," she admitted, certain now that the singing spell had worked. "Across the sea to me."

Also by Susan Sizemore

Wings of the Storm
My First Duchess
My Own True Love

Available from
HarperPaperbacks

Harper
Monogram

In My Dreams

SUSAN SIZEMORE

HarperPaperbacks
A Division of HarperCollins*Publishers*

HarperPaperbacks   *A Division of* HarperCollins*Publishers*
10 East 53rd Street, New York, N.Y. 10022

Copyright © 1994 by Susan Sizemore
All rights reserved. No part of this book may be used or reproduced in any manner whatsoever without written permission of the publisher, except in the case of brief quotations embodied in critical articles and reviews. For information address HarperCollins*Publishers*,
10 East 53rd Street, New York, N.Y. 10022.

Cover illustration by John Ennis

First printing: October 1994

Printed in the United States of America

HarperPaperbacks, HarperMonogram, and colophon are trademarks of HarperCollins*Publishers*

❖ 10 9 8 7 6 5 4 3 2 1

This book is dedicated to Carolyn Marino, who encourages me in my writing, and Karen Solem, who lets her. In all other ways they are responsible adults.

Acknowledgments

For technical assistance on this book I want to thank
Jody Lynn Nye, who knows Irish history; Jane Kauf-
fenberg, who knows how to break bricks with her
bare hands; Marguerite Krause, who rides motorcycles and plays French horn (not usually at the same
time); and Susan Kay Law, who owns a laser printer.

Prologue

Los Angeles, A.D. 1993

"My last girlfriend said I'm more like a golden retriever than a pit bull. What do you think she meant by that?"

The tattoo artist didn't reply but kept on working on the white crane he was putting on Sammy's bicep. Sammy thought maybe he better keep quiet rather than distract the man. He wouldn't want to end up ruining a masterpiece he was going to be wearing permanently on his skin.

Still, he was puzzled about why Cary had said what she did, and then smiled, kissed him, and rode off up Highway 1 with another guy. He wasn't upset, just puzzled. Having ex-girlfriends was standard operating procedure for Sammy. He liked it that way. Once he thought he'd met a girl he could settle down with, but that had been a big mistake. He knew now that he was meant to be a loner.

"You're nice, that's what she meant," Joe, the tattoo artist, answered after a few minutes. "Nicest guy I ever met. You have this way of taking in birds with broken wings."

Sammy laughed. "Right."

"You do. You fix their wings then they fly away."

"That's for sure."

"Every girlfriend of yours I've ever met says you're the best thing that ever happened to them. You've been the best man at lots of their weddings."

"I was asked to be maid of honor once, too."

"I remember that. Well, you were Lois's best friend. Like I said, you're nice. Everybody likes you. Women love you, guys like you. I even like you. You're disgusting."

Sammy snorted. "Nice isn't good for my image."

"So you're a fourth *dan* black belt," Joe said. "A fourth *dan* black belt in karate can afford to be nice."

"Yeah, I guess." Sammy would have shrugged but that really would have messed up the design of the tattoo. "This hurts like hell, you know."

Joe was covered in colorful tats from head to toe; of course he knew it hurt. He just chuckled.

This was Sammy's first tattoo, and he'd been putting it off for years because he decidedly did not like needles. Just about everybody he knew had tats, all of the guys and plenty of the women. Sammy'd always intended to get one but kept putting it off, waiting for inspiration.

The only reason he'd finally come to his friend's Sunset Boulevard hole-in-the-wall shop as a customer was the dream. He'd been dreaming about this big white bird off and on for weeks. Sometimes the bird changed into a woman, but he could never quite make out what she looked like. So finally he'd decided it was a sign. Cary, who was into shamanism, had taught him about spirit guides. His way was more Zen than Native American, but he could get into the idea of a totem animal. He'd figured the white crane was his totem. Besides, the design Joe had come up with when Sammy told him what he wanted was fantastic.

"This is going to be sore for a few days," Joe said when he finally put the needles away.

Sammy rolled his shoulder while he looked at his arm in the wall mirror. "Looks good." He could deal with pain, it was just a matter of training and concentration. And pure dumb endurance. "Looks real good." He stood up, pushed his heavy blond curls out of his face, and reached for his motorcycle helmet. "Gotta go," he said. "Got a class to teach."

Joe just nodded, not mentioning a bill, and Sammy left the shop with a wave and a grin as he went out the door. When he reached the Santa Monica Freeway, riding his Harley toward Venice Beach, he heard the singing.

Again.

Above the roar of the engine and the heavy traffic, a haunting voice—a clear, sweet soprano—did just that: it haunted him. He didn't get it. It worried him a lot.

The voice sure was pretty.

"You ever been to Ireland, Brother Bill?" Sammy asked the question out loud but also with his hands, since his friend was deaf. Sammy also knew the answer even before he asked his burly, bearded, and bald drinking buddy. The farthest Bill had ever been was Milwaukee, Wisconsin. And, of course, Sturgis. Bill and his club, Holy Thunder, went to the August biker gathering in South Dakota every year to preach the Good Word to other bikers.

Sammy usually went with them, but he wouldn't be going this year. Not with Jerry Park's trial scheduled for August, which was only three weeks away. The rally was important to Sammy, but not as important as seeing justice done.

"Ireland?" Bill asked, his hands moving in the elegant motions of American Sign Language. "Why would I want to go to Ireland?"

"It's pretty there," Sammy signed back. "Rains a lot, but that makes it real green and moody. I like it there."

Sammy leaned back and propped his big feet up on Bill's battered old desk. Every piece of furniture in this warehouse converted into a mission was bruised and beaten up but comfortable. Brother Bill believed the folks he took in should be comfortable.

"I spent a month in Ireland right after I got out of the marines. Did I ever tell you about Mary? She was an archaeologist."

Brother Bill chuckled. "Another girlfriend."

"Yeah. I rented this tiny little car and just drove around, you know? You wouldn't believe what passes for roads over there." Sammy smiled at the memories. The driving had been a challenge, and he liked challenges. "My car broke down just as I got to this old village some archaeologists were digging up. That's where I met Mary. She was a graduate student. She taught me a lot."

Bill snorted. "I bet."

"Yeah, we spent a couple weeks together, but I meant

she taught me about Irish history. This village, it had all these little stone houses people lived in over a thousand years ago. I helped them dig up this old church that had been burned down." Sammy traced his fingers over the Harley-Davidson logo on his wide silver belt buckle, and then resumed signing. "It was ugly, the way the Vikings destroyed that place. A real shame. You know, I've always wished there was some way I could have helped those people."

"You can't change the past, son."

"I know. But working the dig taught me that nothing's really new. I remember we found this carving—it was all full of curlicues and stuff—but I swear it was the Harley eagle all done up to look Irish."

Brother Bill savored another sip of beer before he signed, "There's nothing new under the sun, says so in the Scriptures."

"Yeah, I guess." Sammy ran a hand through his unruly hair, which was still damp. He'd taken a shower after teaching a self-defense class to some battered women who'd run away from their old men and ended up at Bill's warehouse.

Bill leaned forward. "You have the look of a worried man under that dumb I-don't-need-nothing-or-nobody act of yours. What's the matter, son?"

Sammy didn't like to think of his attitude as a dumb act, he just liked to leave himself cheerfully open to whatever came his way without any needs or wants getting in the way—it was a Zen thing. Brother Bill was perceptive, and he never judged anybody.

Sammy considered just saying that he was pissed off about what the women he was teaching had gone through. He was, but that wasn't his immediate concern. He had to talk to somebody about this, though.

"Okay," Sammy admitted, "I think I'm losing it. Big time."

"Losing it?"

"My mind. I'm goin' crazy, man." Sammy slapped his feet down off the desk and stood; years of martial arts training made his movements economical and graceful. He wanted to pace, but he didn't want to let the anxiety get to him. He'd been cultivating stillness for a long time.

Samuel Bergen didn't do mental demons, that kind of nonsense was not his style at all. Okay, he admitted to himself, he did do demons—everybody did—but the point was to face them and get rid of them. Emotional baggage was not good for you. The point was to be whole inside yourself, without needing anyone or anything. This singing thing was just a little too weird for him to handle yet, that was all.

"It's—the music," he finally said.

"Music?"

"Yeah. Singing." He pointed to his head. "I keep hearing it, in here."

"What?" Bill asked with a smile. "All that Metallica finally get to you?"

"No way!"

"You hear music in your head? So? Everybody does. I have this old Righteous Brothers song rolling around in my mind all the time even though I can't hear it out loud."

"This is different. What I hear—it's kind of like Clannad or Enya—"

"What?"

"Irish folk stuff, sort of. I've got a couple of Clannad CDs. I bought one cause of this song they did that was used as background in a Volkswagen commercial. It's called 'Harry's Game.' It's kind of wussy music, but I like it. What I hear in my head is kind of like that, but it's not. It's this girl."

"Sammy, with you there is always a girl."

"Yeah, but there's this girl in my head singing to me. Different stuff all the time. She sounds lonely. It's driving me crazy."

"A girl. Singing in Irish to you. In your head."

"Yeah," Sammy said and waited for Bill's assessment.

Brother Bill looked steadily at him. "Yep," he signed. "Sounds like you're going crazy to me."

1

Ireland, A.D. 805

"You were singing in your sleep again," Donal told her.

From the dry way her throat felt, Brianna knew her twin brother spoke true. She sat up slowly, keeping the rough woolen blanket tucked around her shoulders. Though it was summer, the air just before dawn was uncomfortably cool. Especially to one who'd been dreaming of stony mountains covered in sun-seared scrub brush.

"In the dream it was hot," she said, though not to Donal, because he was paying her no mind as he stirred up the banked peat in the room's central hearth. She could hear their father still snoring behind the leather curtain separating his room from the rest of the little house.

"I'm hungry," Donal said, his tone suggesting strongly that she needed to do something about it, and soon.

Brianna smiled and gave a jaw-cracking yawn. She'd spent most of the night tending a feverish child, humming lullabies mixed with healing spells. As soon as she'd laid her head down to rest on her pallet in her father's house the dream had come. She knew she had only a few more moments to herself before her day's work began, so she stared into the room's deep shadows and savored the memory of the dream. Donal would have his meal soon enough, but she wanted a few moments to herself first.

She often dreamed of the hot, sunny place where the smoking city lay. Mountains loomed on its horizon, and a green ocean stretched to the west. The city itself spread across brown hills and into twisting valleys. She had no idea where in the world the smoking city existed, perhaps only in her dreams.

She dreamed too much, she knew, and her dreams often turned into true visions. She had no idea whether the city was real, only that it haunted her. Sometimes the haunting was frightening, sometimes comforting. Sometimes she caught shadowy glimpses of a man, but she could never make out his face.

Her dreams always filled her with longing, but for what, she knew not.

Last night her dream of the city had been a good one. This time she had almost made out the meaning of the great white standing stones that stood high on one of the city's hills.

Donal's hand landed on her shoulder just as she heard the rattle of brass rings as her father pushed the curtain aside. Her father came into the room, coughing.

"So much for time to myself," Brianna said as she threw off the covers and got to her feet.

The contact of her bare skin against the cold earthen

floor helped bring her fully awake. The time for dreaming was over. She straightened her sleep-wrinkled linen chemise and hurried to pull on a tunic. She would worry about bathing and braiding her hair later.

"I got the fire going for you. Time we broke our fast," Donal said.

Her father glanced into an earthenware jug, then turned a mildly reproachful look on her. "You forgot to bring in fresh water last night, my darling."

She'd asked her foster brother, Ailill, to fetch the water before he spent the night out in the sheep pasture. Of course the lad had forgotten. She did not tell her father so. It was her responsibility to see to the needs of the house. Right now, that meant getting the men fed. It would not do for her father to be late for morning mass, since he was the abbot of the monastery of Ban Ean. Father would not eat before saying mass, but she knew she could persuade him that a bit of warm milk mixed with honey would do him good.

Brianna snatched up a bucket and headed for the door to fetch fresh milk from the community's dairy. Dawn was still only hinting at putting in an appearance as she crossed the village square. She gave a quick look at the sky and began to sing as her long day began.

At mass Brianna sang under her breath while everyone else in the church prayed. She knelt on the gray stones of the ancient church floor, easily ignoring the well-known chants to the Lord and saints that the people around her intoned together. It was a pleasant, comforting sound.

It was harder for her to block out the beginnings of one of her visions as she sang snatches of bardic verse, looking for a healing spell to help the child she'd sat with the night before. Her mind wanted to tell her something, but she forced it to leave her alone for now. She couldn't care about the future when she had this problem to deal with in the present. Though little Murcha's fate was in God's hands, she knew it was her duty to do what she could to help cure the wee one's fever.

When her grandfather left for Rome he had taken her and Donal aside and charged them to mind the health and happiness and safety of everyone in Ban Ean. "Your father's duty is to see to souls," he had told them. "Yours, children, is to see to everything else."

Her grandfather was a wise and formidable bishop, and Brianna took his instructions seriously. The problem was, there were forty people left in Ban Ean after the bishop took his chosen companions off to Rome, and there was only one of her.

Brianna had lost her dearest support when her mother died. She missed having someone she could talk to. When the loneliness struck at her so hard, prayer did no good. Instead, she did her best to sing the pain and longing away.

She'd been singing for someone almost all the time of late.

As the mass ended Brianna said a quick prayer for the repose of her mother's soul, then hurried from the church. She could feel a vision wanting to have its way with her, and she needed to be alone. She knew she couldn't concentrate on how to help the feverish child with her thoughts clouded. She should have known better than to try to fight her magical gift in the first place. The villagers were heading to their work, most to tend the fields and fishing boats. Her father, her brother, and many of the monks would spend the day in the scriptorium where they copied and decorated sacred manuscripts. Brianna stopped at her house long enough to snatch up a basket, then headed across the sheep pasture toward the oak grove on a hill overlooking the sea. There she could gather herbs and have some time to herself to see what the future would bring.

Los Angeles, A.D. 1993

Even though it was nearly midnight, Sammy wasn't surprised to see Brother Bill's Harley waiting in the driveway when he drove up. Bill was sitting on the top step, next to an overgrown hibiscus bush. Sammy lived on the bottom floor of a three-story apartment building he owned on the edge of West Hollywood, just down the hill from the grounds of the Mormon temple.

"So," Sammy gestured, coming up to his friend waiting on the stoop, "whatcha doin'?" He pulled off his helmet and leather jacket and put them down on the porch. He was wearing a sleeveless orange T-shirt, high tops, and a pair of loose-fitting orange and white striped Zubaz pants. A fanny pack was strapped at his waist. He waited for Brother Bill to lecture him on riding a motorcycle in nothing more protective than the jacket, but a lecture wasn't forthcoming.

"Just watching the police helicopters circle," Bill signed, and pointed up at the sky. Bill looked old and tired in the glow from the amber glass porch lamps. He stood up. "Didn't come to stay. I came to say I'm sorry."

"Sorry for what?" Sammy asked.

"For not taking you seriously this afternoon. If you hear voices—"

"Singing." As Sammy spoke the singing started in

his head again. He listened for a moment before focusing his attention on his friend. It was a new song, and very compelling.

"Singing," Brother Bill repeated. "Voices, whatever. If you're in trouble, I want to help." He patted Sammy's shoulder. "I just wanted to let you know that I'm here for you, whatever you need."

Sammy smiled. "I appreciate it."

"Me and everybody in Thunder will do anything for you, Sammy. I mean that, anything. Anytime you need us, you just call."

Sammy nodded, but the voice in his head was growing louder. Was it even in his head? It seemed to be coming from everywhere.

It was coming from up the hill, wasn't it? Calling to him from the top of the hill. From the garden up by the gold Los Angeles Mormon Temple spire. She was waiting for him up in the garden, wasn't she?

What was she doing up there this time of night? That place was private property. She was going to get into trouble up there. She needed him. He could tell from the sound of her voice that she needed him.

"Excuse me, man," he said, stepping past Bill. He went to his motorcycle. He swung on and kicked the engine to life. "I've got to get up there. To her."

Her song turned into a scream as the cycle roared to the top of the hill.

Ireland, A.D. 805

The oak grove was an ancient place, sacred to the people of her tribe long before Patrick brought Christianity to Eire. Her family had always been keepers of sacred places and knowledge. The transition from druids to priests and monks had taken place easily, and both old and newer ways were still followed by Brianna's kindred.

Brianna had been born with the Sight and the singing magic of the old bards. She was naturally closer to her family's druid tradition, so the sacred oak grove inspired her more than the stone church in the center of the village. Here was a place that centered and sheltered her.

There was a light mist falling when she came into the grove. Instead of seeking shelter under the circle of trees she walked to the great gray slab of altar stone set in the very center of the grove. She took a seat on its damp moss-covered surface, closed her eyes, and opened her mind.

Nothing happened.

She didn't understand. Something always happened when the prickling heavy feeling that preceded her visions came upon her.

She could feel the time passing, the mist turned to rain, a salt-scented wind came up from the sea to rattle the leaves of the surrounding oak trees. It caressed her cheeks like the touch of a lover. A shudder went through her that turned into a prickle of anticipation. The silence of the grove, usually so comforting, brought on a melancholy loneliness. A restlessness for a nameless something began to grow in her.

She began to sing.

As the words of her song formed, she could see as well as feel a man there with her, someone amazingly tall, sun-bronzed, hard-muscled. His eyes were dark and laughing, like shaded ocean pools with a sense of humor. Deep in her mind she could hear his laughter.

It was the laugh of a man who loved life, it made her want to laugh with him.

She did laugh, and with her laughter the vision faded. Brianna shook her head in puzzlement. She'd never had a vision like that before. She was used to seeing things that were going to happen. She was not used to having people just appear. She was certainly not used to having visions where handsome men looked at her and touched her and made her happier than she'd been in a long time.

She blinked and wiped wet hair out of her eyes as a shiver raced through her. It had stopped raining. A ground fog had risen among the trees while she was singing, making the familiar grove eerie and almost unrecognizable. Overhead the sky hung with heavy, black clouds. The wind still rattled the leaves and the surf crashed against the shore not so far away, yet the day had gone silent to her.

Brianna slowly turned around, hugging herself beneath her bright red cloak. Her inner senses prickled with a warning of danger in this safe, sacred place. Fog obscured sight, and her Sight obscured her normal senses.

When the men rushed toward her out of the woods she didn't know if they were real or imagined. The terror they brought her was devastatingly real. She screamed for help at the top of her lungs.

The line between the dry, clear night and the wet fog was so sharp it could have been cut with a laser. Intent on helping the screaming woman, Sammy barely noticed crossing the line. One moment his motorcycle was roaring up a concrete drive, the next he was fighting for control as it bucked over a rough, muddy track. He was still going uphill, and the woman was still screaming.

He ignored the terrain and followed the sound to the top of the hill where the trees spread out into an open area. The woman had her back to a stone bench, holding a small knife even as she cried for help. The three men who surrounded her were laughing. They looked like cats playing with a mouse; what was on their minds was obvious.

The craziest thing about the men's appearance was that they were all holding swords. Swords? And the girl had a knife. She was wearing a long skirt and a cape.

Brianna heard the monster roaring toward her, but she didn't dare take her eyes off the jeering swordsmen. She couldn't understand their harsh language, but she knew by their laughter and lewd gestures that they intended to rape her.

She'd screamed for help while she prayed and swore silently. Then the rumbling thunder of the monster's cry filled her head, and it was all she could do to concentrate on the men who'd backed her against the ancient stone altar. She wanted to run screaming from the monster when it appeared, more than she did from the swordsmen.

She didn't know if her attackers were deaf or merely mad, for not one of them noticed the monster until it was in their midst. It came bellowing up, a great beast of flesh and metal with a man's face and black, spinning wheels. Brianna screamed even louder as the monster ran down one of the swordsmen. The man's cry of pain joined her sound of terror. The other two swordsmen spun to face the monster. Brianna jumped up on the altar.

* * *

Sammy ran into one of the attackers, rolling over his arm as he hit the ground. "Sorry," he called with a nasty laugh as he heard the crunch of bones. People who intended rape deserved a lot of pain.

He saw that the woman had sensibly gotten out of the way while the other two men turned on him, swords swinging. One of them screamed at the sight of him, dropped his weapon, and ran for the woods.

Sammy switched off the cycle and left it lying on the uneven ground while the last man ran toward him, dirty blond hair flying around his angry red face. Being faced by a maniac with a sword wasn't exactly an everyday martial artist's problem, it was more of a martial arts movie problem.

"I sure as hell hope Bill's called the cops," Sammy said as he dodged the swordsman. An LAPD patrol helicopter would be welcome just about now. The man lunged at him again. Sammy dodged again, trying to remember why he'd gotten off the motorcycle. The smart thing would have been to ride this man down as he had the first one.

The first one. Sammy remembered he had a sword, too.

"Awright!" Sammy cried as he dived for the moaning man on the ground and grabbed up the weapon. He had studied the Japanese sword art of *kendo*. The swords in *kendo* were wooden, but the techniques worked with the real thing just the same. He brought the heavy weapon up and blocked a swing from his attacker.

When Brianna saw the monster come apart she wanted to faint. She swayed with dizziness and fear, but the giant who stepped away from the wheel and metal part of the monster drew her attention away from the brink of darkness. He was beautiful, a creature of gold and bronze, tall as a tree, broad as a wall, with the face of an avenging angel or Finn McCool, the great legendary warrior.

She watched the giant take up the sword and turn toward the last of her attackers. If she had thought him beautiful before she had been mistaken. He didn't become truly beautiful until he moved with purpose and grace, smiling as he circled and slashed, feinted and blocked. Metal rang on metal, sweat formed and flowed, but no one died. The attacker couldn't strike and the giant wouldn't. Again and again the giant could have killed the other swordsman, but he didn't. He never did more than block the other's blows.

Eventually the swordsman, panting with fear and exhaustion, cried, "Thor!" He quickly backed away from the giant, who didn't try to follow as the man turned and ran.

"Silver Surfer!" the giant called after him as the man ran off into the woods. "Wolverine!"

Brianna had no idea what either word meant, yet they seemed familiar. Curses, perhaps? Calls to pagan gods?

Sammy laughed as the man took off. The one with the broken arm had long ago struggled to his feet and gotten the hell out of the clearing. The cops still hadn't arrived. Sammy wiped the sweat out of his eyes and turned to the woman.

She was still kneeling on the stone bench. Her black hair was like a wild mane surrounding her small, pale face. She stared at him with her gold-flecked blue eyes. He smiled at her, trying to look reassuring. He took a step toward her, then stopped as a wave of dizziness hit him. So he just kept smiling at her while he waited for the dizziness to go away.

It didn't, it got worse. The world started spinning, but the girl on the bench didn't spin with it. He felt as if they were in the eye of a hurricane together. Fog and trees and his Harley, the grass and the sky, it all whirled around them. The whirling made him sick, and the dizziness got worse.

Her eyes were the only thing in the world that had any steadiness at all. He kept looking into them until the ground seemed to come up and hit him in the face.

2

Brianna was sitting with the giant's head in her lap when her brother and her foster brother, Ailill, came into the grove. Ailill's two dogs and a dozen sheep came with them. The boy and his beasts spread out and quickly took up much of the available space inside the circle of trees. Donal hurried to her side. His dark robes were spattered with mud, and he was breathless and red-faced from running.

"A longship has been sighted." He pointed toward the cove just beneath the oak grove. "I thought you might be up here. I heard screaming and a great, awful noise. Did they—who's that?"

She stroked the giant's forehead. "Three men attacked me. This one appeared and saved me."

A sheep came up and started cropping grass near the giant's ear while the herd dog came up to sniff the man on the ground. Ailill raced up and settled down on Brianna's other side. He touched the giant's muscular arm. She smiled reassuringly at the boy and was rewarded with a smile in response. Ailill paid very little attention to anyone but her, and the attention she got was sporadic at best.

"What is that thing?" Donal asked, pointing at the silent metal monster.

"Shhh!" Brianna warned. "Would you wake the beast? It has a deep, mighty howl." She brushed her fingers across the giant's smooth brow. "He controls it somehow. He saved me," she repeated. "When the others were attacking me he came from nowhere, and saved me."

She was suddenly so grateful for what he'd done she wanted to kiss the giant, to put her lips on his. His wide, full-lipped mouth looked like the sort that would enjoy being kissed. This was the first man she'd had the urge to kiss.

"Who were those men?" she asked. "There were three of them. With swords."

"Norsemen," Donal said.

"What's a Norseman?" Brianna asked.

"Sea raiders. Father had news from a traveler of these barbarians raiding on the coast," Donal explained. "That's who must have attacked you."

Donal left the grove, heading toward the seashore. He came back a few moments later and said, "The ship is sailing out of the bay. I pray they won't come back, but we should set a guard." He fingered the hilt of his sword, the only sword in the village, and looked pleased at the idea of fighting these Norsemen.

"It would help if you knew how to use that thing," Brianna told him. She studied the face of her rescuer. Was he a barbarian sea raider? Somehow she didn't think so. But who was he? Where was he from?

"Are you unharmed?" Donal asked. He glanced back at the metal beast. "What man rides such a creature? It has wheels like a chariot," he said after studying it a bit.

"It must be under an enchantment. While he rode the beast it was alive," Brianna said. "Then he jumped from it to fight the men."

"I heard its roar," Donal remarked. "I hope it doesn't eat the sheep." He spared a worried glance at Ailill's charges. None of them was near the beast, and the dogs were ignoring it. Ailill was standing by the altar stone, staring wide-eyed at the giant.

"What is that mark?" Donal asked. "The one on his arm."

Brianna had noticed the design, she'd even ventured to trace it with her fingers before the others came into the grove. She'd seen tattoos before, but never anything more elaborate than lines and geometric patterns drawn in black on pale skin. The bronze giant wore a whole painting on his arm.

"It's a white bird," she said.

"It is very beautiful. The symbol of his tribe, perhaps?"

"A white bird," she repeated slowly, her voice full of awe. "Does Ban Ean not mean 'white bird'? Perhaps this man was sent to protect Ban Ean from these northern barbarians."

"Perhaps."

"He saved me from the barbarians," she went on, "but he killed no one to do it." It gladdened her to know that no one had died, even though her attackers surely would have killed her.

A sheep began to nibble on the giant's hair. Brianna shoved its head away. The herd dog yipped and chased the woolly creature into the dispersing fog.

She glanced at her young foster brother. He looked worried and a little frightened. She hated to see him disturbed, so she spoke to him, slowly because he understood her better when she carefully formed the words. "What do you think of the giant?" she asked the silent boy. "It is in my mind that he might be one of the fair folk." Her expression was cheerfully encouraging as she went on. "Do you think he's a fairy come from under the hill to help us?"

Ailill glanced around to see that the black-and-white dog was tending to the sheep. His rough-coated gray wolfhound nudged his hand for a petting. The wolfhound, a grave, gray-furred creature bigger than the boy, was there as protection for Ailill as well as his charges. The boy looked from the giant to her and gave a quick nod.

Donal rubbed his jaw. "A fairy. Perhaps that's true. He has the look of the fair folk about him." Donal ventured to touch the silent black and metal beast. "A fairy warrior might control such a thing."

"He rode it," Brianna said yet again. "It's his steed." She leaned forward and spoke into the still man's ear. "Will you wake up, giant?"

With her fingers curled in his tangled golden curls, she went back to singing a healing song. She noticed that the lashes shadowing his cheeks were long, darker than the hair on his head, but still gold, as were the high-curved arches of his brows.

"Wake up," she said after she'd sang for a while. "For the day is getting on, dear giant, and I've another patient who needs me in the village." He made a small sound, as though he had heard her words. Brianna tugged on his hair. She'd had enough of waiting. "Wake up," she demanded, "or I'll throw your porridge to the pigs."

Donal laughed. "There's a threat that's gotten me out of bed a few times. You better wake up," he said to the giant. "She's wicked in the mornings, is our gentle lass."

"Uh," the giant said, and waved one hand before his face. "In a minute. Promise."

The giant's voice was deep and rough. His accent was so thick she barely understood his words. She wanted to hear it again, even if he was a foreigner. She shook him harder.

"Wake up, Giant! Talk to me."

He grunted, and opened one eye. It took her a moment to realize that the color was not black, but a deep, rich purple. No human being had purple eyes, none she'd ever heard of.

"You *are* a fairy!"

Brianna gasped and jumped to her feet, knocking into her twin. Donal caught and steadied her. The giant opened his other eye and sat up. He was staring at her. Brianna turned to flee but his hard hand reached up to circle her wrist. He tugged her away from Donal and back onto her knees beside him.

"Sorry," he said, and immediately released her. "I didn't mean to scare you."

Sammy realized that the pretty little thing in the ugly plaid dress was as frightened as he was. It occurred to him that she might be afraid of him, though he didn't know why. So he let her go and lay back down slowly as a wave of dizziness hit him. He closed his eyes for a few seconds. He realized that he was lying in wet grass, but he couldn't remember how he'd gotten there.

When he opened his eyes again an angel-faced little boy with long black hair was looking curiously down at him. Sammy lifted his head a little as the woman put her arm around the boy's shoulder. A man in a costume that looked like something from the Middle Ages stood behind them. In fact, he noticed, all three were in costumes.

The girl's skin reminded him of milk and white marble, or Snow White in the Disney cartoon. Her hair was black as night and about as thick. He was surprised he didn't see stars glinting in it. Her eyes were big and blue and flecked with gold.

The boy tugged on his hair, so Sammy returned his attention to him. A big Irish wolfhound was sitting next to the boy, who rested a hand on its head.

"Hi," Sammy said to the boy. "Who are you?"

Ailill looked at Brianna. She spoke to the giant. "His name is Ailill, and he cannot understand you."

She tried to smile reassuringly, though she was more than half-afraid of this tall, strong, dangerous stranger. She'd wanted him to wake up, she reminded herself. She had to deal with him no matter what he was. He'd saved her life; surely he didn't mean to harm her now. The giant said something else to Ailill. He did indeed have a fine deep voice.

"Doesn't he speak English?" The giant asked her.

She shook her head, not knowing what that language was.

"Korean?" Sammy asked. "Japanese?" He tried a phrase in each of these two languages. He wasn't expert in either of them, but he knew enough to get by in a *dojang.* The boy just continued to stare at him, and the girl looked equally blank. Sammy fought dizziness as he sat up all the way.

"Where am I?" he asked. He had no memory of recent events. "This isn't the Mormon temple, is it? Am I still in Westwood?"

"Westwood?" Brianna repeated the word, slowly sounding it out. Where had she heard that word before? "West," she repeated. As she spoke, memories of her visions came to her. West Hollywood. She knew of this place. Was he indeed from the city of her visions? Was it a real place after all?

She looked at the giant, who was smiling at her. It was a concerned smile, but she thought a smile of any kind would look good on his handsome face. He had dimples. She had seen dimples before, but not like these. And the corners of the giant's extraordinary eyes tilted up when he smiled. Such amazing eyes. She sighed.

"This is not Westwood," she told him. "Welcome stranger," she said. "Peace be with you."

Ailill bent forward and daringly stroked a finger across the giant's eyebrow.

It was Donal who asked, "Do all fairies have purple eyes?"

Sammy didn't know what the man said, because he couldn't seem to make out anyone's words except the girl's, but he understood the boy's gesture. "Lots of people have purple eyes," he said defensively. "Okay, not lots," he admitted, recalling some of the fights he'd gotten into as a kid when he was called things like "Pansy" and "Violet." "Both my sisters have violet eyes too, Mom calls it our Liz Taylor gene." He paused and climbed unsteadily to his feet. "Who are you, anyway?"

He noticed another dog, and sheep, a circle of trees, and a worn, muddy path. He could hear the distant roar of waves and smelled salt in the air. Rags of fog twisted around the nearby trees, and clouds rushed by high overhead. He saw seabirds soaring on the wind, but no jet trails. Where was he? How had he gotten here? Who were these people? Why did they have sheep?

Most importantly, did they have a phone? He was definitely going to have to cancel his date with Nora, because he just wasn't feeling up to bungee jumping right now.

"I must get back to Ban Ean," the girl said with an anxious glance over her shoulder.

Ban Ean? That sounded familiar. He scratched his aching head and tried to think where he'd heard the name before. Nothing came to him immediately. When he noticed the girl watching him worriedly he gave her a reassuring smile.

"Can you walk?" she asked.

He ran his fingers through his tangled curls and shook his head to clear it. It didn't help the headache. "I'm fine," he said anyway.

The man who looked so much like the girl that he might be her twin brother glanced in the direction of the sea. He said something to her.

She answered, "I have nothing to fear from the giant, that I'm sure of." After another question that Sammy couldn't understand, she said, "Yes, you'd best set a watch on the shore."

The man nodded, satisfied with her answers, and went off through the trees. The boy and the big gray dog followed, leaving the herd dog with the sheep. The girl shook her head.

"Oh, Ailill." She sighed and looked back to Sammy. "The lad has no skill as a shepherd. Come along, then." She turned and headed down the path. Sammy followed.

Brianna was supremely aware of the man that walked close behind her like a golden shadow. She had told Donal that she had nothing to fear, and she was sure she didn't. Still, knowing his gaze was upon her made her feel distinctly odd. She hurried down the track, telling herself she should worry more about the sick village boy than her obviously healthy savior at present. She could tell that he was confused and lost, but since that state wasn't likely to kill him she would tend to him later.

Uncle Sean, who was the best healer in the kingdom, had taught her to deal with the most serious cases first, after all. Perhaps, if she was lucky, Uncle Sean would return home soon and deal with the problem of the giant's presence himself.

She sighed as she walked, interrupting the song that she hadn't even known she was singing under her breath. She had little hope that luck would relieve her of this new responsibility.

Sammy followed the girl in strange clothes toward what looked like a medieval village off in the distance, away from the patchy fog on the hill. The path was deep, muddy, and spotted with sheep droppings. He found himself more interested in the way her hips swayed as she walked and the way the wind played with her thick black hair, but eventually he got up the courage to really look at his strange surroundings.

It was a very primitive community, Sammy thought, observing the place as they approached through a meadow dotted with sheep and great gray standing stones. The buildings were mostly stone as well, conical gray piles of rocks, or small structures patched with mud and roofed with thatch. Most of the houses were no bigger than a single-car garage. A village square was dominated on one end by a long building that had a beautifully carved cross on the front of its peaked roof.

Sammy scratched his head as his guide stopped in front of one of the thatched huts on the outskirts of the town. "This place looks familiar," he said, meaning the town, not just the tiny dwelling.

She pointed to a stone bench as she knocked on the door. Sammy could hear a crying baby inside. "Wait here, Giant."

"Sammy," he said just before she ducked into the house. She gave him a quick look back. "My name's Sam Bergen."

"Sammy Sam Bergen," she said slowly, as though the words sounded very strange to her. "Ah. I am Bri—" A pained shriek from the crying child cut off the introduction. She disappeared inside.

Sammy didn't settle down on the bench as she'd directed but wandered in behind her. Inside it was dark and so full of smoke he could hardly breathe. The roof was so low he had to bend considerably to fit inside. It took a moment for his eyes to adjust. When they did he saw Bri standing next to the woman who held the crying child. The woman's face was young, and a mask of stoic sorrow.

Sammy came up to them. The mother gave him a wide-eyed look and clutched the baby closer. He disregarded her obvious fear and concentrated on the sick child. "What's wrong with it?"

Bri answered without looking at him. "A fever."

"Babies get them a lot," he agreed as she began singing quietly, her fingers brushing across the baby's forehead. He stood back and listened to her beautiful, oddly familiar voice for a while before he asked, "You giving it aspirin? Aspirin's mostly for pain, but it's good for fever."

She kept singing for a while, frowning in concentration, ignoring him. Finally she spoke to the baby's mother. "I couldn't find any vervain. I'm sorry."

Bri sounded so hopeless, Sammy suddenly wanted to hug her. "You should try aspirin," he said.

Brianna turned a baleful look on the giant. He looked concerned, and sounded helpful. "I've no idea what you're talking about." The baby was growing weaker. Her magic had no effect on the fever. "I know not what medicine or magic you possess, gi—Sammy Sam Bergen, but the child can use whatever you have to offer."

The giant—Sammy—frowned. "You've never heard of aspirin?" When she shook her head he said, "Ibuprofen? Tylenol? Never mind," he said as he opened an odd shaped pouch strapped around his waist. The pouch was made of a shiny black material. It opened with an unnatural rasping sound.

He fingered through the contents for a few moments, then brought out a tiny bottle. "Got some," he said, looking at her with a bright smile that made Brianna think of sunlight pouring over her on the warmest day of the year. He was most definitely a man of fire, this Sammy Sam Bergen.

He opened the bottle with some difficulty and a few most ungodly words, then held his hand out to her. His palm was as big as a king's gold serving dish, and in it were two small white pebbles. "Here you go, Bri."

She looked from the pebbles to his face. "Yes?"

"I wouldn't give an infant more than half of one," he said while she continued to stare at the pills.

She looked from his hand to his face. "And how do I give half a pebble to a baby?"

Sammy's fist closed on the aspirin. "You break it in half," he said. He looked around for a glass. "Then you dissolve it in water. No, something sweet 'cause it tastes terrible. Soda or one of those fruit drinks kids are supposed to like." He looked back at Bri. "Well? You got a glass I can use?"

Brianna took Sammy Sam Bergen's meaning. She

nodded, and snatched a cup off a wall shelf. "You crush the pebble, Giant, for I certainly could not. I'll mix the pebble dust with honey water."

Sammy split the pill in half and ground it into the pottery cup. He chuckled as he worked. "You know, they're only called extra strength on the bottle. Anybody can do this."

She didn't seem to believe him, but she did give him a grateful look as the baby cried louder. The mother spoke anxiously. Bri took the cup as she said to him, "She's frightened of you. Could you please wait outside while I finish this."

Sammy's neck and back were aching from stooping under the low ceiling anyway. "Sure," he said, backing toward the door. "I hope this works."

"So do I," he heard her say as he went outside.

He settled down on the bench and waited. And tried to think, tried to remember. The baby's crying gradually quieted, and Sammy started to get hungry. Eventually, he leaned his head back against the wall, stretched his long legs out before him, and took a nap.

3

A rough, exceedingly wet tongue licking the back of his hand woke Sammy up. When he opened his eyes he saw that the wolfhound was busy giving him a bath, while Ailill stood next to the dog, watching. There was amusement in the boy's eyes, and a shy smile lit his features.

Sammy reached into his fanny pack and pulled out a roll of Life Savers. He popped one into his mouth, then held one out to the boy. Ailill looked suspicious of the bright red candy. The dog looked very interested.

"It's cherry," Sammy said.

As he spoke, the door opened and Bri came outside. She looked up at the sky. "Not yet noon," she said, voice full of amazement. "This is surely the longest day I've ever seen and it's not even midsummer."

The breeze stirred her black hair. Sammy was amazed by the length and thickness of it, and the way its dark color contrasted with her milk-pale skin. Despite his earlier comparison to Snow White, the sensual width of her mouth reminded him more of Julia Roberts's than a Disney cartoon. While Sammy watched her, Ailill took the candy out of his hand.

"How's the baby?" Sammy asked as Bri sat down beside him with a weary sigh.

"Better," she answered. She reached out, as if to touch him, then thought better of it and folded her hands demurely in her lap. "Thank you, Sammy Sam Bergen."

"You're welcome, Bri. And it's just Sammy Bergen," he corrected her. "Everybody calls me Sammy."

"Ah," she said. "My name is Brianna, not Bri. Brianna daughter of Colum the abbot of Ban Ean, granddaughter of Brian, bishop of Nariade." Ailill had come up to lean against her. She ruffled his hair and added, "My tribe is kin to the O'Niall of Tara." She flashed Sammy a sardonic grin. "But just barely."

Sammy took all this information in and tried to make some sense of it. While the dog watched the roll of candy in his hand and thumped its tail hopefully on the ground and Ailill sucked loudly on his cherry Life Saver the girl hummed and Sammy thought. Everything she'd said sent little itches of familiarity through his muzzy memory.

Brianna had many things she wanted to ask the stranger, but she wasn't sure where to start. In truth, she was almost afraid to learn anything about where Sammy came from and why.

Just being near him made her skin prickle with the energy of an impending vision. While magic and the Sight were useful in small doses, an excess of them would strip away her control completely.

Besides, this stranger was so big and full of life, she had no idea how to set about dealing with him. He was an untamed force loose in their little community. Surely, there were wiser people who would know better than she what to do with this helpful giant.

"Ban Ean," he repeated at last. That was the most familiar thing she'd said. He found himself rubbing his thumb over his belt buckle as he tried to remember. The silver eagle design on the buckle almost reminded him of something, but nothing came to him immediately.

He came out of his reverie and offered Brianna a piece of candy. "You look tired." He would have been happy to offer a massage or a shoulder to lean on, but he supposed it was best to start with the Life Saver. "Here. Have a sugar fix."

She eased carefully away from Sammy when he presented a brightly colored little thing to her. It didn't look like an aspirin. She wished that it was, for her head ached and he'd said the white pebbles were good for curing pain.

When she didn't take the thing in Sammy's hand, Ailill darted forward and snatched it for himself. That drew a laugh from Sammy.

The sound was as big and deep as the sea and washed over Brianna like a wave. She wanted to throw herself into his arms and let his laughter and warmth comfort her, to wash all her tiredness and worries away. She didn't know whether to be frightened or angered for this sudden longing to rely on someone else.

"I'm taking you to my father," she told him. "I wish Uncle Sean was home, though. He's wise and Father is, well—holy."

Sammy took this to mean that she thought her father was impractical. Before he could speak she went down on her knees beside Ailill and put her hands on his shoulders.

Speaking slowly and carefully, she said, "I think you had best go back to the sheep, dear heart." After a while he nodded. Once she was sure he'd understood, she added, "Remember to come home for supper." She got another nod, then the boy spun around and took off, with his wolfhound following close on his heels. Brianna looked worriedly after Ailill for a moment, then stood and began walking into the village.

Sammy hurried to catch up. "Is the boy autistic?" he asked. "Or just hearing impaired?"

She didn't know what he was talking about. "He's a good boy," she answered.

"I think he likes me."

She had noticed, and it disturbed her. Ailill was normally shy and cautious. It was safer for him to be so, for even the gentle people of Ban Ean sometimes mocked and mistreated him, thinking their actions no more than small jokes. Sammy seemed kind, but she sensed the force of the storm in him.

Whatever this man touches, she thought, he changes. He'd saved her, helped the babe, and so far everything he had done had been to the good. So far. It was her duty to protect Ban Ean. He might be a demon disguised as one of the Fair Folk, wolf rather than watchdog. She could not afford blind trust in Sammy's benevolence, no matter how much his bright smile encouraged her to.

"You said your dad's an abbot," Sammy said when she didn't answer his questions about Ailill. "And your grandfather's a bishop."

"Yes."

"So, you're what? Anglican? Anglican priests marry, right?"

"Most priests marry," she said. She turned around and pointed.

The village was situated on a wide semicircular bay. A steep-sided little island sat at the head of the bay, about a half mile from the mainland. Sammy wished he could place the familiar landscape. Brianna was pointing at the island.

"The Culdee monks who live out there follow the Roman rule," she went on. "But they enjoy being miserable, with their hair shirts and fasting. My uncle Gerald's a Culdee," she added. "He wants all of Ban Ean to follow the Roman church. Father says the faith we've followed for centuries is good enough for him."

"Oh," Sammy said. Somehow her words made sense to him, as if this was an explanation he'd heard before. Something about how the rules had been different somewhere before some year. He couldn't remember where he'd heard this, but there had been a girl involved. "Mary," he said, rubbing his chin. "I think her name was Mary."

Brianna kept walking rather than ask why Sammy invoked the Holy Mother's name.

Soon they reached the square. She had to clear her throat and look away from Sammy before she could speak. "While it's true we're not so famous as Armagh or Iona, Ban Ean is not a small monastery despite how it looks at the moment. Grandfather took the teachers and the students with him on pilgrimage." She pointed at two large deserted buildings and then a third one off in the distance. "My aunt Ethni dwells there with a score of holy nuns."

When she could think of no more to say about her small world her gaze returned to Sammy's handsome face.

"Iona? Armagh?" Sammy said, as though they were the only words he understood. "I thought those were ruins," he muttered, "but there aren't any ruins here."

His puzzled look made her want to run her fingers along the lines of his lowered brows.

As they walked on, Brianna showed Sammy gardens and animal pens, the bakery and the brewhouse, weavers at their looms, the dairy and the drying of fish. When he said he was hungry she took him to the communal kitchen for a meal of bread and curds.

Finally, when he'd seen all the places and tasks that made up the day in Ban Ean, they made their way back toward the square. They passed the church and came to the shed where Brother Fergus and his apprentices were working. The sound of metal ringing on stone came from inside the shed, along with Fergus's bellowed prayers as he worked.

She explained what was going on as Sammy looked curiously toward the noise. "Grandfather wants a new church up by the time he returns, but I think it would be best if the stonemasons and sculptors make improvements to the one we already have."

"Budget problems?" Sammy asked.

She didn't understand what he meant, so she ignored the question "What need have we for grandeur? Ban Ean has always been here. "Before Patrick came to Eire this was a holy place for my tribe. The standing stones have been here forever, and the church for two hundred years. It was built to last."

"Patrick?" Sammy repeated. "Eire?" He looked around and scratched his head. "This place really looks familiar." He squinted at her. After a very long silence, he asked, "Am I in Ireland?"

"Eire?" She was confused by his terrible accent.

"Yeah, Eire. Ireland." She nodded. His tanned face went pale, his eyes widened in shock. He gasped. "But—how?" He stumbled and sat down on a block of stone just outside the stonemasons' hut.

"Sammy?" His dazed look frightened her. She took his hands and he held on to them tightly.

"How did I get to Ireland? Why? How?" He looked at her pleadingly. "Huh?"

He needed reassurance so badly, she couldn't help but cup his upturned face in her hands. "I know not how you came here."

His big hands settled on her waist, circling its small circumference. Gradually, so slowly she hardly noticed moving, he drew her closer while they continued to gaze into each other's eyes. She wanted to look away but couldn't. After a while she didn't want to.

"I don't know how I got here, either," he said at last.

Neither spoke for several minutes, but his expressions shifted slowly from utter panic back to a faint semblance of cheer. She could tell that he was frightened as well as confused but determined to make some sense of his roiling emotions. She searched for something to say, but her tongue could find no words.

"Excuse me," a familiar voice said from behind her.

Brianna jumped and pushed away Sammy's hands as she whirled to face the speaker. She found Fergus the sculptor smiling knowingly at her.

The man's voice was mild when he spoke. "I've a use for the stone the fairy lord is sitting on."

Two of Fergus's apprentices appeared behind him. When Sammy got to his feet the young men hurried to heft the stone and cart it away.

Sammy watched them go, then looked at the small

round man standing beside Brianna. Like most of the men he'd met in the village he wore a simple brown robe belted at the waist, standard monk gear. And, like the other men, a wide band of hair was shaved across the top of his head, from ear to ear. A sort of reverse Mohawk hairdo. Sammy had been wondering about the haircut just as he'd been wondering about everything else. He supposed that since the men were monks, it must be their version of a tonsure. He tugged on a strand of his unruly long hair. He hoped they weren't going to ask him to shave his head.

"I usually wear a ponytail," he said, but neither Brianna nor the monk answered him.

"This is Fergus," Brianna told him. "The finest sculptor in Eire," she added proudly. The monk looked delighted at her words.

Fergus stared intently at Sammy's waist. Sammy didn't know what the man found so fascinating down there, and hoped he didn't have to ask. Once again the word *Eire* tickled his buried memories. They were closer to the surface this time, trying harder to break through.

Fergus said something to Brianna. The conversation went on for quite a while, with Fergus occasionally pointing at Sammy. Sammy couldn't make out much of what they said. He wondered why he could understand Brianna when she spoke to him, but had trouble understanding her when she talked to someone else. And he couldn't make out a word spoken by anyone else he'd encountered. He might as well be as deaf as Brother Bill.

He'd almost forgotten about Brother Bill. Now, where was it he'd last seen him? They'd been talking and something had interrupted—

"Brother Bill," he said, and remembered the way Brianna spoke to Ailill. Sammy made a swift hand gesture. "There's a thought."

Before he could elaborate on his sudden idea, Brianna said, "Your belt."

"What?"

"Can he have your belt?" Brianna asked.

"Belt?"

Fergus stepped up to Sammy. He pointed at Sammy's waist.

The baggy striped pants Sammy wore were fastened with a drawstring, he was wearing his black leather belt with the Harley belt buckle strictly for decoration. His fanny pack was strapped on over the leather belt, but the silver buckle was clearly visible. It was the buckle Fergus had been eagerly eyeing.

Fergus took off the rope belt cinched at his own waist and held it out toward Sammy with a smile.

"He wants to trade for it?"

"Borrow. He's fascinated by the design," Brianna explained. "He wants to copy it."

"Copy it? It's the Harley-Davidson logo. He wants to copy the Harley eagle?"

Memories surfaced in Sammy's brain—of the conversation about Ireland he'd had with Brother Bill—of his first sight of the twelve-hundred-year-old stone sculpture that so closely resembled the Harley-Davidson eagle. The sculpture had been part of the ruins of an Irish church.

He looked around him. For a moment he saw the place not as it was but as he knew it. In his own time. As an archaeological dig instead of an inhabited settlement. Most of the trees were gone from the place he knew, but the hills held the same gentle contours. The standing stones remained, and the humped island at the head of the bay. The sea was ever the same, and sheep roamed the same meadow, but the people, the place—gone.

For a very long time.

But he was here—now. But now was then—then was now.

Somehow.

"I need to sit down," he said, staggering backward. The stone was gone, so he ended up settled in a dizzy heap on the ground, his head resting on his drawn-up knees.

Just sitting down wasn't good enough. Within moments he'd passed out completely.

"He keeps doing that," Brianna said as she sank down beside the prone man.

She didn't know whether to be worried or frustrated by Sammy's tendency to fall over in a faint. It seemed to her that such a big, strong fellow shouldn't be so sickly. It also worried her that he might be reacting to things she said or did.

She felt his forehead as Fergus and his apprentices gathered around, asking questions. She said, "Well, he's not feverish, at least. Though I suppose his pebbles would help if he was."

"Pebbles?" the sculptor asked.

Before Brianna could explain, the men moved politely aside to make room as the abbot came up to join the group. Brianna was happy to see her father. Finally, here was someone who could deal with the giant, whose head was once more resting in her lap.

"Daughter," her father said, without seeming to notice the man on the ground, "Rory MacMurdo has sent you a gold bracelet this very day. Rejoice."

Brianna could not rejoice, even at her father's command. "Rory," she said. The word came out as a groan. "Will that fool never leave me be?"

Her father reached down to pat her shoulder. "You'll make him a fine wife."

She held her tongue on the sharp answer she was tempted to give. She had no intention of marrying the king, but this was not the time to discuss it. Sammy groaned, and that gave her a reason to avoid speaking about Rory.

"I've a patient to deal with right now," she said.

"Oh," her father said, finally taking notice of Sammy. "Is that the man Donal said saved you from the Norsemen?"

She was surprised her father was aware of that much village news as unworldly as he was. She just nodded and looked around at Fergus and his strapping apprentices. "You men help me get him to Uncle Sean's house," she said. "I'll care for him there."

And the devil with Rory MacMurdo.

4

Uncle Sean's house was a simple, single room, lit by the smoke hole and the fire. Sean's home had the highest ceiling of any building in Ban Ean, except for the church's. Fragrant bunches of dried herbs hung from the angled stones supporting the corbeled, conical roof. Scrolls were tucked into cubbyholes like pigeons in a cote around the walls. Leatherbound books fought for space with earthenware pots on the table and a double row of wall shelves. It was the house of a scholar, like many another house in Ban Ean, but also the home of a druid and a mage-healer.

The druid's house wasn't actually in the village, but on an outcrop of land not far from the outskirts of Ban Ean, overlooking both the sea and the sheep meadow. This was the place where Brianna was the most comfortable in the whole world, so it seemed natural for her to bring Sammy here. Transporting the giant had not been an easy task though, even for such strong men as the stonemasons.

Now he more than filled Uncle Sean's bed, so much so that his feet hung over the end. They were the only part of him that moved, and they kept poking out of the covers no matter now many times she pulled the blanket back down.

Other than his feet, and the slow rise and fall of his chest as he breathed, he lay as if dead. As time passed Brianna found herself watching the movement with rapt fascination she simply didn't understand. He sighed when she sang to him. She found that looking at him brought the tightest, strangest constriction to her chest.

She got a small fire going in a brazier next to the bed to help keep him warm. His hair and bronzed skin shone in the light. After a while Brianna found that she had tangled her fingers in the blond giant's thick, curly hair and wished she had noticed doing it.

She supposed she should be grateful that since she couldn't seem to keep her hands off of him she'd settled for touching his hair. He was so large and masculine, she was afraid it must surely be a sin to let her hands rove across any bit of his hard skin.

Lord, but the man was distracting. Being near him made her feel as if she'd never seen a man before, which in turn made her feel rather foolish. There were many men in Ban Ean and she had helped nurse most of them through fevers and such since she was a little girl. As far as she could tell, Sammy wasn't even ill, but her urge to care for him was the strongest she'd ever known.

It was the voice singing "You Could Be Mine" in his ear that woke Sammy up. He knew the voice; it had haunted him for weeks. But he was used to the beautiful soprano singing haunting Gaelic melodies, not old Guns n' Roses. He was also gradually coming to the realization that his feet were cold. The combination brought him not only awake but very much aware of his surroundings. He knew even before he opened his eyes that those surroundings were going to be very alien indeed.

The first thing he noticed was Brianna seated beside him on a low stool. Her eyes were closed, her body relaxed. Light from a tiny fire in a nearby metal pot cast shadows on her cheekbones. She'd taken off the short red cape, and Sammy could see the rounded outline of her breasts beneath the shapeless plaid dress she wore.

She was singing in her sleep.

As he propped himself up on his elbows to look around she opened her eyes and said, "I was dreaming of a red-haired boy named Bailey. Rather like Rory Mac-Murdo," she added, "but skinny. Ah, well." She rubbed her eyes. "'Twas not an important vision."

Sammy didn't ask what she was talking about but studied his surroundings. They were in one of the primitive stone dwellings, and the air was cool, scented with herbs and smoke. The mattress under him was thin, and it smelled as if it was stuffed with some kind of sweet grass. The blanket covering him was rough wool, scratchy but warm.

Finally, he looked at her and asked, "How come you speak English?"

She repeated the word slowly, drawing it out, "English?" She shook her head. "I know only the language of Eire."

"You were just singing in English," he pointed out.

She blinked. "Oh. Well, I often do strange things in my dreams."

"Like sing songs from the twentieth century?"

"The what?"

"A time over a thousand years in the future."

While she gave him a puzzled look, Sammy swung his legs over the side of the bed. His thighs brushed briefly against hers before she stood. She backed away from the bed.

"I dreamed a song from the future?" Her voice, beautiful whether she was singing or speaking, held an edge of fear. "Are you saying I dreamed of the far future?"

"Dreams?" he asked. *Please,* he thought, *not another psychic!* Not after Karen. He put aside thoughts of the one woman he had almost loved to concentrate on this other woman. "You've got magical powers, right?" He hoped she didn't, but if she did it gave him the beginnings for an explanation of how he'd gotten here. It wasn't a logical explanation, but he wasn't a logical kind of guy.

"I dream true," she answered. "I have the Sight."

Sammy noticed that Brianna didn't sound particularly happy about this statement. He wasn't happy himself. If there was one thing Karen had taught him, it was to stay away from women with psychic abilities. Problem was, he seemed to draw them like a magnet.

"Just what I need," he complained, "to be stuck in the Dark Ages with another one."

"Dark?" Brianna asked. She looked around the smoky interior of the house. "Shall I fetch some more candles from the church?"

"No," he said. He stood up. His head didn't touch the ceiling. Not quite. "What you can do, is get me out of here."

Brianna hurriedly crossed the room and opened the door. Sammy sat back down on the bed. After a few moments hesitation, Brianna closed the door and came back to sit on the stool.

"If leaving the house was not what you meant, what do you want?" she asked.

"To get back to my own time."

She pressed her fingers to her temples. "I do not understand. My Sight tells me you are from a place I didn't think was real."

"Oh, yeah? What place?"

"A dry place, far in the—"

"Future," he supplied when she couldn't seem to say the word she wanted. "I'm from the future. Tell me how I got here." She shook her head. "Of course you know," he said, trying not to be irritated. "It was you I heard singing."

"Singing?"

"Singing."

"Aye," Brianna said, with a slow nod. "I often sing. I was singing in the grove before the Norsemen came."

Sammy tapped himself on the forehead. "You've been singing in here for weeks. You've been driving me crazy."

She looked as if she understood him but didn't believe him. "I have?"

"Yeah," he said.

He felt restless, constricted by his dark surroundings. He wanted to get up and pace, but there was not enough room. He had learned stillness early on in studying martial arts. He kept himself still now with more effort than he was used to, and confronted the psychic young woman.

"You've been singing to me. I've heard you everywhere, no matter what I've been doing. You've been in my head, calling to me. Even when I was making love to other women I'd hear your voice in the night." She blushed bright red when he told her that. "It was weird," he admitted. "Having background music nobody else could hear. I thought I was going crazy, but it turns out it was you."

Brianna listened to Sammy's words, but she did not know what to make of them. "I always sing," she said. "Lessons from my uncle, old songs, spells, hymns. I sing when I'm happy, when I'm tired, when I'm lonely. I always sing, but I did not sing to you. I just sing."

"You sang to me," he insisted. "You called to me. You brought me here."

Sammy's certainty convinced her that it was true, but she did not know how it could be. "I did?" She had a sudden memory of the visions she'd had in the grove before the Norsemen came. All the fear and worry afterward had driven the memory away until now. "I saw a man," she said, looking Sammy over carefully, matching the details of the vision to the man before her. "I saw you. I called to you. Out of my own—" She cleared her throat before going on, unwilling to ask herself why she had called to him. "Perhaps I did bring you here."

"You betcha."

"But how?"

"Some kind of magic."

"I know singing magic, but—"

"You ripped a hole in the space-time continuum with just your voice. You're good!" he added with one of his bright smiles.

His smile helped ease her confusion, but only a little. He had come out of nowhere on his magical beast, but he wasn't a fairy lord despite looking like one. She knew he came from the city of her dreams. It appeared her city was real and was located in the distant future. She knew it was mad, but she believed it to be true.

"How did I sing you up out of the old spells without knowing I was doing it?" she asked. She knotted her fingers together nervously and tried not to think of his talking about making love to women. "How could I sing to you without knowing?"

"You screamed," he said. "I'd heard you for a long time, but I didn't come to you until you needed help. Maybe your panic is what triggered the magic."

She ducked her head. "I am truly grateful for your help, Sammy Bergen."

He seemed embarrassed. "No big deal. You're welcome."

She stood and took a step toward him, standing eye to chest. He put his hands on her shoulders. His hands were hard with calluses but gentle for all their strength. Gentle and warm.

She looked up slowly, into his deep, dark eyes, and for a moment she could neither breathe nor think. For him this was a casual thing, she thought. Touching women came easily to him, but no man had ever touched her like that and she did not know what to do.

She knew she should tell him that touching her was not proper, for he was neither father, brother, uncle, cousin, or husband. She knew she should move away. She wanted to reach up and put her hands on his shoulders, or twine her arms around his waist, to touch him with as easy an intimacy as he touched her. Instead she did nothing, and he eventually removed his hands and looked away as well.

Sammy didn't like being in such close quarters with Brianna. She was soft and warm, her hair smelled of herbs and her mouth looked sweet to taste. She seemed so vulnerable, as if she needed to be held and taken care of. Just looking at her distracted him from the purpose of the conversation.

Putting his hands on her shoulders had been a bad

move. He hadn't meant anything by it, it was just a platonic gesture. She obviously saw it differently, though, and his body reacted as if it was seeing it differently, too.

"I do not have time for this," he told his body firmly. He swept his fingers though his hair, then said, "Listen, Brianna, I can't stay here. I have to get home."

He wanted to believe he was dreaming, that he'd wake up in his bed in West Hollywood and everything would be fine. But he knew what he wanted didn't mean anything. Maybe it was a dream, but if you're in a dream, you live by the dream's rules. The rules told him he was in the early ninth century.

"Send me home," he said. "There's a man's life depending on my getting home."

Whether this was a dream or a hallucination or real didn't matter. Jerry Park's murder trial started in three weeks. That was real. Sammy had to be there to testify.

Her throat tightened around words she didn't want to say. Finally, she cleared it and made the words come out. "I don't know how."

A long, tense silence followed. Brianna almost cried at the helpless feeling that settled over her. Sammy looked frustrated, disappointed, and thoughtful by turns. Visions of him standing in the gold yet somehow dirty sunlight of his own land flickered at the edge of her vision. For half an instant she thought she saw herself with him, her hand in his. She blinked the Sight away to concentrate on how to undo what she'd done. Her mind stayed blank.

After a while, Sammy rubbed his hand across the back of his neck and said, "Oh, boy."

Brianna hung her head. "I'm so sorry."

The pain in her voice cut Sammy to the heart. "Hey, it's not your fault," he reassured her. "I know you didn't do it on purpose. It's all right." It wasn't all right, but he couldn't stand to see her looking so sad and guilty. "You'll think of something."

What he really wanted to do was scream and shout and shake her, but that was just his own fear trying to get out. Still, he thought it would be safer to get out before the fear made his control slip and he did do something stupid.

"I better go get my Harley before it starts to rust." The door to the house didn't have a handle, so it took him a few seconds to figure out that he had to slip his fingers between the door and the frame and tug it open.

He paused outside to get his bearings and quickly spotted the path that led toward the hill where he'd left the motorcycle. A trail of smoke from the fires inside the house followed him as he started toward the hill. It was earthy and fragrant and still made him cough.

"I have definitely got to get out of here," he said as he hurried along, "before the secondary smoke in this place kills me."

Sammy Bergen was not good for her Sight, Brianna decided after he'd left. Or, rather, he was too good for it. Ever since he'd ridden his roaring beast into her life—had it been only a few hours ago?—all her magical senses had been alert to the point of nearly overwhelming her. It was unnerving, it was exhausting, and it was also exhilarating. Just being near him made her feel more alert and alive. And more confused and fragile than she had ever been in her life.

"And it has given me a headache," she said as she rubbed her temples. "I will be glad when he goes back to his own place and time. Though I've no idea how to get him there."

She was going to have to think of something. It was her responsibility. She prayed Uncle Sean would come home soon and help her find the spell to send this disturbing man back to his own world.

"For I do not need him in mine," she added with a weary, confused sigh.

She went out the door he'd left open and was surprised to see it was still daylight. So little time had passed since Sammy had been carried into the house—if one did not count the thousand years separating his world from hers.

She could see Sammy in the distance, striding, sure-footed and purposeful toward the sacred oak grove. His orange-and-white trews and sleeveless tunic and heavy white shoes had not seemed out of place to her before, but now she noticed how foreign his clothing was. As foreign as the beast he went to fetch from its resting place. She determinedly looked away, trying not to worry about how foreign she must also look to him.

Were the women of his time also giants? she wondered. She knew the answer, since she had seen golden women in her dreams of the smoking city. *Does he find me little and ugly? Does it matter what he thinks?* her practical side asserted. *Do you have time for such vanity?*

Twilight would be approaching soon, and she had to start preparing her family's dinner. She vowed she would not think of Sammy for a while, but of the round of mundane things that gave her life some sense instead.

"First," she said to herself, "I will see if Murcha is still sleeping since the fever broke. Then I must return Rory's golden bracelet. Then I should check the boil on Brother Trian's neck and then there's peat and water to bring in. And—"

"Brianna!" Her twin's voice cut off her list of practical matters. Brianna turned around as Donal hurried up to her and demanded, "Where's the fairy lord?"

She did not like the glint of excitement in her brother's eyes, or the hint of slyness in his manner. "What do you want with Sammy?"

Donal stopped in front of her and put his hands boldly on his hips. He gave a short, triumphant laugh and told her, "I've come to ask the fairy lord to help me marry Moira and Bridget."

Brianna did not know whether to groan in frustration or merely to hit her brother very hard over the head. "Oh, Lord," she said, "not that again. You know Father will never let you marry both of Fergus's daughters."

"He will."

"You're to be a priest. A priest can have only one wife."

"I'm going to be a warrior. That's why I need to talk to the fairy lord."

This had been Donal's dream for all their lives. Brianna saw no sense to it, but she'd mostly given up trying to talk him out of the notion. Donal wanted to become a great warrior, with status and treasure and an abundance of wives. While she wanted—well she didn't know what she wanted, but like Donal, her dreams went beyond what their family had planned for them. At least Donal knew what his dreams were while she only knew what she didn't want.

She didn't see how dealing with a man from the future was going to do either her twin or herself any good.

She put her hands on her hips, mirroring her brother's stance. "And how," she demanded, "is Sammy supposed to help you become a warrior?"

5

As the healer Sean Nariade came down the path leading to his house, he saw his niece and nephew standing outside his door, arguing. He was weary, and happy to see the smoke curling up from the hole in his conical stone roof. The sea beyond his house was quiet, a vast gray mirror of the overcast sky. Sheep dotted the meadow above the rocky shore, but Sean saw no sign of Ailill or his wolfhound among his charges, just the black-and-white herd dog keeping order.

He'd left his borrowed horse back at his brother's house in Ban Ean and finished the short journey home on foot. He carried his bag of medicines hung over his shoulder, and used his staff to help him along the muddy track. The twins didn't notice his approach, but his goat did. It came running up to him, loudly demanding attention.

"You were going to be a stew," Sean reminded the nearly grown kid. "How did you turn into a pet?"

As Sean approached Brianna and Donal he overheard their heated conversation.

Brianna tossed a thick braid of hair over her shoulder with an angry flick. "Sammy is no great warrior for you to pledge your service to."

Sean wondered if this Sammy was the fairy lord his brother had mentioned. He'd been told the fairy lord was ill and had been taken to his house. Sean was weary and a bit concerned that his bed might be occupied when he longed to lie down and rest on it himself.

"If he's no warrior, how did he come to save you from the Norsemen?" Donal asked.

Brianna blushed. "He didn't kill anyone."

"Did he drive them off with magic?"

"No. He used a sword."

"Then he is a warrior. A great warrior, or he would not command the great wheeled beast."

"Wheeled beast?" Sean interjected, but his presence was ignored.

"Grandfather wants you to be a priest," Brianna reminded Donal.

Donal just laughed, not pleasantly. "Grandfather wants you to be Rory MacMurdo's second wife. I don't see you meekly trotting off to marry him."

"I don't have time to marry Rory," she countered. "Grandfather told me to watch over Ban Ean as well. Just as he instructed you to do."

"Which is why I must become a warrior," was Donal's triumphant defense. "So I can protect Ban Ean."

"So you can marry both Fergus's daughters," Brianna corrected him.

"Are they not of Ban Ean?" Donal asked with an innocent look. "Will I not be caring for them if I become their brave, warrior husband?"

"Good point," Sean said.

"Don't encourage him," Brianna said, acknowledging Sean for the first time. To Donal she went on, "What is so important about being married?"

Donal laughed. "Keep looking at your fairy lord the way you did in the grove and you'll understand the importance of marriage soon enough."

Brianna blushed again. "I was not looking at him the way you do Fergus's daughters."

"Oh, but you were. I saw how you combed your fingers through his hair. You've never thought to touch Rory MacMurdo that way, have you?"

"I never think of Rory MacMurdo at all."

"Perhaps you should marry the fairy lord," Donal suggested. "I'm sure you'd make him a fine fifth or sixth wife."

"Fifth or—"

"Well, see sense, lass," Donal cut her off, not with teasing but with kindness in his voice. "It's sure his first wife and the ones beneath her must be as tall and fair and immortal as your Sammy himself."

"I don't think he's immortal," Brianna answered rather than comment on this stranger's probable wives. "And I still don't see why he'd take you on to train as his sworn man even if he were the greatest warrior in all of Eire and his own land as well."

"It's obvious, isn't it?" Donal said. "Because he's the true protector of Ban Ean, sent to us from the fairy realm. With the Norsemen raiding the coast will we not need warriors and this great champion to train them? Don't you see the danger, with your eyes if not with your Sight?"

If she did sense danger, she didn't acknowledge it. She put her hands on her hips. Sean thought she looked a ▒▒ jealous that anyone might fill her role as the village's guardian. "How do you come to the conclusion that he is Ban Ean's protector?"

"Because he wears the mark of the white bird, of course."

Donal's words struck a chord in Sean's memory. Holding his staff in one hand he tapped his nephew on the shoulder with the other. "White bird?" he asked. "What mark is this you speak of?" He glanced at Brianna. "Do you remember that spell song I taught you about the summoning of the white bird?"

"Aye," she said. "I've been singing it as a hymn in church most every day."

"You have? Why? It's a song from the days of the old gods."

She frowned. "It is? I thought it was a Christian song, about Christ's dove hovering protectively over His people."

Sean pinched the bridge of his nose. He was tired and wanted to get inside to his fire and a pot of porridge rather than spend time teaching lessons about the symbolism in two different religions. The goat butted its head against his thigh, so he bent over to scratch it between the ears. A musty, dry smell rose from the animal's fur.

When he didn't explain further, Brianna said, "It's a very pretty song. I like singing it. Perhaps I sang it too much." She seemed disturbed. "And it starts to explain how I drew Sammy out of his world into ours."

"He's here to protect us," Donal declared. "Therefore, he will teach me to be a warrior."

Brianna sighed. "Perhaps." Her shoulders drooped as if she held a heavy weight on them. "I'm going home to start supper." Belatedly, she planted a kiss on Sean's bearded cheek. "Welcome home, Uncle."

As she hurried up the path Donal called after her, "Where is your Sammy?"

When she didn't answer Sean took his nephew by the arm. "Come inside and have a drop of poteen," he said. "You can worry about being a warrior after you've told me all about this fairy lord that's come to dwell in our midst. He isn't in my bed, is he?"

"Son of a bitch," Sammy said, almost in awe, as he ran his hands over chrome and steel and leather. He shook his head, then scratched it, then methodically examined every inch of his motorcycle one more time. He stepped back. "Damn."

He sat down on the stone bench in the center of the grove and just stared at his street machine for a while. The Harley was a Heritage Softail, king of the open road. It looked out of place sitting on the damp, emerald Irish grass, but it didn't look any worse for wear. The cycle was not made for off-the-road riding, and he remembered riding it up the bumpy, muddy track to the top of the hill. It wasn't meant to lie on the damp ground for hours; it had probably gotten rained on. Instead of being wet and mud-caked, though, its chrome and black lacquer gleamed in the afternoon light. In fact, it almost seemed to glow, as if it had some sort of force field around it.

"You're beautiful," Sammy said to it as he hopped up off the seat. "You have no business being beautiful." He shrugged and looked around. "I got no business being here, either. None of this makes sense, you know?"

The cycle didn't answer, though Sammy wouldn't have been surprised if it had magically acquired a voice. At this point, he didn't think anything would surprise him.

"She's good," he said, thinking of the beautiful dark-haired woman who was responsible for his presence in the past.

He went over to the cycle once more. "She better be good, cause she's going to have to get us home. Oh, man," he went on, frustrated at being where he was when he was needed back in Los Angeles. "Jerry didn't kill that gang banger and I'm the only one willing to say so. I gotta get out of here."

He was so frustrated he felt as if he was going to explode. He didn't like the feeling; it was too close to being out of control. Between the disciplines of Zen and martial arts he usually managed to keep himself in control of his emotions and in harmony with his surroundings. He didn't like this seething feeling of being just on the edge of anger, on the edge of hysteria. He had to relax. He had to get himself back into focus.

He started the way he usually did, by centering his mind, blanking out his thoughts, and doing the stretching exercises that would prepare his muscles for a fighting workout. After stretching he began practicing forms, moving with grace and precise control.

He'd been studying martial arts since he was six years old; the routine was comfortingly familiar even if he was performing it over a thousand years and many thousand miles from his *dojang*.

He was moving through the form sequence, his left leg extended almost vertically behind him, when Ailill and his wolfhound wandered into the grove. Sammy was used to being observed, so it didn't bother him when the boy sat down with his back to a tree and watched his every move. When Sammy finished the workout he turned to Ailill and gave a slight bow.

Ailill's face lit with pleasure, then he jumped up and

repeated Sammy's gesture before sitting back down. Sammy shook his sweaty hair out of his face and came to squat in front of the boy. On impulse, he leaned forward and whistled loudly in Ailill's ear. The dog growled, but the boy didn't even flinch.

"Deaf," Sammy said. "I thought so. But not since birth," he pronounced as Ailill looked at him intently. He was not scared, Sammy noticed, but concentrating, trying to understand. "See," he went on. "If you'd been deaf since birth you probably wouldn't be able to read Brianna's lips. I've seen her talk to you real slow and careful, so I'm guessing you're reading her lips. Brianna," Sammy repeated, forming the word carefully.

He's used to watching faces Sammy thought, as Ailill nodded his recognition of the word *Brianna*. Sammy didn't think the boy had understood anything else he said, since Brianna did seem to be the only one who communicated with him. Maybe spoken language wouldn't matter if he could teach the boy to sign.

"Well, all I can do is try." Sammy sat back on his heels and concentrated on the moment, and on Ailill. "Okay," he began as he held up his hands. "Just watch, you won't get it for a while. This is the sign for my name."

"It is nothing to me if he has a dozen wives, all fair as the morning," Brianna muttered as she chopped onions for the stewpot.

Cutting the onions made her eyes sting and tear, for she had forgotten to use the simple magic that would keep the onion juice sweet and harmless.

"Donal is an idiot if he thinks I care for Sammy. Of course I care for him," she added as the onions went into the steaming pot. "I care for his welfare." She gave a slight toss of her head. "Just as I care for everyone's welfare. It is my—" She laughed at herself rather than finish the words. "All this whining about welfare and duty makes me sound like a fine martyr, doesn't it? I've a roof over my head, people who need me, and food in my belly. I need nothing else."

The words come out too firmly, too hollow, and she knew it. Then she could hear Sammy's deep laugh booming in her mind, as though it was calling to her. Perhaps it was laughter and joy that had drawn her to him, for she knew she lacked them in her life. Well, that was as good an explanation as any for why her songs had reached his faraway ears.

She picked up the plucked chicken she'd accepted as a gift from Murcha's mother and cut it into pieces with quick, deft strokes. It went into the water with the onions. She waited until the contents of the pot were boiling, then eased it to the side of the fire so it would slowly simmer through the rest of the afternoon.

There, she thought, *supper is done. Father and Donal won't have to drop by the common house to share the unmarried monks' meal tonight.* She felt a certain amount of embarrassment for the times her menfolk were left to fend for themselves because she was nursing the sick. On her way back from Sean's she had gathered fresh loaves from the bakery and a jug of dark brew from the alehouse. She was determined to produce a fine meal to make up for last night's missed cooking.

"Besides," she said as she surveyed her handiwork, "we have a guest. We shall have Uncle Sean and Sammy share the meal." If she could, she would have given Sammy a feast, for hospitality's sake since he was a guest who had come from a very long way away. "For we are a generous people."

"Well, here's a new thing," Donal said as he came in the door.

Brianna whirled around in surprise. "What?"

"You're talking to yourself instead of singing," her brother said. She caught the scent of Uncle Sean's whiskey about him as he came to sniff the pot. He looked up with a teasing glint in his eye. "I think your fairy lord has rattled your mind. I get that way around Moira and Bridget," he added slyly.

Brianna did not intend to put up with any of Donal's teasing. "I have things to do." She reached for her cape.

"Where did your fairy lord get to?" Donal asked as she opened the door.

Where indeed, she wondered, though she left without answering her brother. She knew Sammy had gone to the grove. It occurred to her that perhaps he was lost, or that he had been drawn back to his own time. Which would be for the best, of course, she told herself firmly as a flutter of panic went through her stomach. He belonged in his own time. It would be for the best if he just disappeared as quickly as he'd come.

Still, she hurried for the grove, wanting to find him as quickly as she could. She told herself it was to guide him back to Ban Ean if he was there. "For it would be a pity for the man to miss my fine cooking," she said. Then she started singing to keep from talking to herself anymore.

When she reached the grove, a little breathless from hurrying up the hill, the first thing she saw was the black beast crouching on its silver wheels. It looked to have three eyes, one large and two smaller to either side, all clear as if covered with the finest glass. They were open and staring blindly in her direction.

She would have screamed, but her attention was caught by the sight of Sammy standing in front of Ailill.

Sammy pointed at the hound who was sleeping next to the altar. He snapped his fingers and then he slapped his thigh. After Sammy gestured, Ailill copied it exactly. Sammy repeated his movements, so did Ailill.

Curious, she sidled past the beast, which didn't move, and came closer to man and boy. "What—"

"Hi," Sammy said before she could finish the question. "I'm trying to teach him the word for dog. I don't think he's gotten the meaning yet, but at least he's copying what I do."

"I can see he's copying you," Brianna said as she watched Ailill move his hands. "But what are you doing?"

Sammy turned his attention from Ailill to look at her. "I don't know if it'll work, but I'm trying to teach him to talk."

Brianna's nerves jumped with anxiety for the boy. She wanted to rush over and take him protectively in her arms. "Teach him to talk? He has no voice!"

"He doesn't need one," Sammy said. "He has hands."

Before she could question further the nonsense Sammy was spouting, Ailill came up and tugged on her skirts. She immediately dropped down to his eye level. "Yes, love?" she asked as she ruffled his hair.

Ailill's hound had come stalking up beside him. The boy pointed to the dog, then made the gesture, smiling all the while.

From behind her Sammy said, "Maybe he does have the hang of it."

Brianna looked between Sammy and Ailill. Then she looked at the dog. "Do you know what they're doing?" she asked, thinking she might get more sense from the hound than the giant looming above her. She stood up and Sammy put a hand on her shoulder. She quickly stepped away from the casual but intimate touch.

"Ailill just said dog," Sammy said.

"He didn't say anything."

"Yes, he did."

"He can't speak. He can't hear. Are you mad?"

He seemed faintly exasperated but far from insane. "I have some deaf friends. They talk all the time. Sometimes they talk so fast I can't keep up with them. They use sign language." Sammy moved his hands. As she followed the gesture, he said, "This is the sign for *dog.*" He did it again and pointed at the hound. "Dog. Do you get it?"

Brianna thought for a moment. "That gesture is the same as a word?"

"It is a word. Sign is a language. I'm trying to teach Ailill."

Whatever this man touches, he changes. Brianna had had the thought before, and she was more disturbed by it now. Did he change things for good or ill? She remembered how Sammy had saved her life, and helped break Murcha's fever.

She didn't know what to think of this plan to teach Ailill a language. Was Ailill able to learn? Would it do him good? Would it make him happy or too miserable to live peacefully with the affliction God had given him?

She was going to have to find a way to return Sammy to his own time before he changed everything in sight. The Lord knew she felt changed enough after only a few hours of knowing him.

She didn't know what to do or say, or what was right or wrong. So she said, "Dinner will be ready soon. I thought you might be our guest for the evening meal."

Sammy didn't know what Brianna was so bent out of shape about. He had thought she'd be happy about the possibility of Ailill's learning to communicate. Instead she seemed worried, or maybe a little afraid. He didn't get it, but it still worried him to see her worried. He didn't try to talk about sign language anymore.

"Sure. Fine," he said in response to her dinner invitation. He went over to his motorcycle. "I don't suppose you have a garage where I can put this? Somewhere inside to keep it dry?"

Brianna eyed the beast worriedly. At the moment it didn't even seem to be alive, but she well remembered its roaring power. She did not think it was a good idea to take it into the village, no matter how tame it seemed with Sammy by its side.

"There is a shed in the pasture where Ailill sometimes sleeps," she told Sammy. "Perhaps you could stable it there."

Sammy rubbed his jaw thoughtfully and noticed that he was sticky with sweat. He bet he smelled like a pig. He found himself wanting to look his best at Brianna's, kind of like an insecure teenager who'd just been asked on a date by the prettiest girl he'd ever seen.

"Shed," he said after he found he'd been gazing into Brianna's eyes for a minute. "Yeah. That sounds good." He looked around his primitive, pastoral surroundings and chuckled. "It's not like I have to worry about the bike being stolen. So," he added, "is there anywhere I can get a shower after I stash the bike?" He could hear the ocean crashing not far away, but a cold salt water swim wasn't what he had in mind.

"Shower?"

Sometimes he thought communicating with Brianna was as hard as communicating with Ailill. But how come he could communicate with her at all? He decided he should not analyze that question right now, or he'd never get cleaned and fed. "How about a bath?"

Her lovely face grew lovelier as she smiled. "Oh, you wish to bathe. A stream flows down to the sea through the pasture. There's a pool the monks use to bathe there. Ailill will show you." She turned to the boy.

Sammy toed up the kickstand on the Harley and stood with it braced against his side while Brianna knelt again. He waited while she took some time to get Ailill to understand where she wanted him to take Sammy. Sammy was impressed by her patience and gentleness with the boy.

"Do you remember how to get to my uncle's house?" she asked as she got back to her feet.

"Sure."

"Good. Then I will meet you there. For I need to ask him to dinner as well."

Brianna went back the way she'd come. Ailill pointed the way, then ran out of the grove. Sammy, pushing the Harley, rather than riding it over what in no way resembled a road, followed as quickly as he could after them.

Brianna walked swiftly, singing to keep her thoughts occupied as she went. The words came easily, making her step light. She felt happy for no reason she could name, but the sight that greeted her as Uncle Sean's hut came into view soured her mood.

"Here's trouble," she murmured, and wondered if it was too late to run the other way.

A half-dozen riders on fine, tall mounts waited in Sean's yard, displacing and annoying the goats and chickens that roamed there. One of the riders had dismounted and was holding the reins of his own horse and those of a fat white pony. Brianna recognized the pony.

She recognized the riders as well—a poet, a priest,

two guards, and two serving women. They were just enough companions for a queen to travel in honorable style. From the escort alone she knew who was inside with her uncle.

"Maybe this is a good time to start saying a prayer," she muttered as one of the alert guards noticed her on the path. The greeting he called out was friendly enough, but she wished she could just turn around and hide in the oak grove until Uncle Sean's visitor was gone.

Well, it was too late now. She kept walking up the path, not even bothering to straighten her simple red cape or try to comb her fingers through her tangled hair. Her own pride wouldn't let her try to make herself presentable in front of her enemy's people.

"An enemy I didn't ask for, don't want, and don't deserve," she complained as she stepped into the yard.

No one spoke to her as she wove her way through the horses toward the door. Uncle Sean's favorite goat came up and demanded to have his head rubbed, then followed after. The goat complained loudly when she ignored it. People snickered at the animal's behavior, but Brianna just hummed and pretended they were not there.

She couldn't ignore Lady Deirdre when the door opened and Rory MacMurdo's wife stepped outside to face her.

"You!" Deirdre cried, her eyes going wide and angry.

She sounded more like an angry goose than a queen. Seeing Brianna made her forget the dignity required of her station. Brianna knew Deirdre would be ashamed later for losing face in front of her people, and would blame Brianna for it, no doubt.

"What are you doing here?" the queen demanded.

Deirdre was of the tribe of Raithlenn, a wife from outside Rory MacMurdo's lands. In a year as Rory's wife she had yet to learn the bonds linking his people. "Sean is my uncle," Brianna reminded her now.

Deirdre's already pink complexion darkened. "So he is. I suppose that explains why you follow the evil, pagan ways."

Brianna gave a quick glance at Deirdre's swollen belly. She did not point out that the queen was the one standing in the druid's doorway. "I study to be a healer, lady," she answered. She tried to keep her tone humble, but all her senses were reacting to the hostility Deirdre directed at her. "Healing is how I serve my king."

Deirdre obviously heard a taunt in Brianna's words. "Some say you are beautiful, the most beautiful woman in all the countryside around. Rory does not say so," she added triumphantly.

Rory did say so, much to Brianna's discomfort and annoyance. He had been saying she was beautiful and that he would make her his since she'd grown breasts and a curve to her hips. Before that she'd been no more to him than a skinny girl relation he'd teased when he visited his great-uncle the bishop. When he'd come back from a war with a foreign princess he'd met at a greater king's court, Brianna had nursed hopes he'd forget about her. He had for a while, then he'd started pestering her again when Deirdre grew big with child.

"He does not want you."

"I wish that were true, lady," Brianna replied. Deirdre did not look as though she believed her.

Brianna carefully did not mention the gift the king had sent to her this very day. She didn't want to hurt Deirdre's feelings. Rory was doing a good enough job hurting his wife without Brianna adding to her pain. Brianna had liked the queen on the few occasions they'd met, even though she was a stranger who made little effort to be anything else to her husband's people. Brianna thought Deirdre was gentle and shy, and that it was the pregnancy that was making her quarrelsome, and frightened for her place in Rory's heart.

Deirdre put her hand on her abdomen. "He will forget you when I give him a son."

"I hope so."

"You are nothing," Deirdre added as a farewell, and stepped around Brianna to go to her horse, her hands folded on her round belly.

She might have made it as far as the spot where a guard stood holding her pony without a flicker of emotion and her dignity intact if it hadn't been for the goat. The silly creature bleated loudly behind her, making her jump, then butted her in the behind. She screamed; her guards rushed forward. One grabbed her and hauled her unceremoniously up on her pony. Others rushed toward the goat with their spears at the ready. Her ladies laughed instead of hurrying to her side. Brianna would have run to see to her welfare but knew Deirdre would not want her help.

Then Sammy was there and she was aware of no one else but him, with his strong body and his hair wet and slicked back from his handsome face. She stood very still, almost breathless, all her senses alive at the sight of him. She forgot the crowd as she watched him come toward the hut from the pasture. She would have smiled and waved, but he paid no attention to her. Instead, he waded into the shouting crowd and grabbed up the goat in his arms.

"Hey, cool it!" he called out in his deep, rumbling voice.

Deirdre screamed at the sight of him. The guards surrounded him. Brianna moved protectively in front of him without a thought that the guards were carrying spears. And the man himself just smiled, showing his even white teeth and deep dimples.

Sean came rushing out of the hut, yelling at the top of his lungs. "Do I have to put a curse on the lot of you to have peace in my own yard?" he demanded. "Leave be!" Sean ordered the guards. The white-bearded druid had a deep, commanding voice, hard for anyone to resist. "This man is my guest. I'll curse the member of any man who threatens a guest in my house."

The guards backed away before Deirdre could give an order of her own. The queen snatched at the reins of her pony and turned its head with a sharp tug. Then she vented her anger loudly on her tittering women as the party rode away.

Brianna winced as Deirdre began shouting at her servants, but she was glad to have the pregnant woman's dark mood directed anywhere but at her. She was even happier the men had put up their spears. She pushed Sammy backward. Sean made way and they ducked inside the hut and closed the door on the noisy crowd outside. She turned to the goat as Sammy put it on the floor. It sniffed curiously at the edge of the firepit.

"You've no guilt at all, have you, you troublemaker?" she asked the rough-coated beast. She rubbed its head and the goat bleated happily. "You'll end up in the pot yet."

Sammy was giving her a questioning look. "Deirdre," she explained to Sammy. "The king's wife. She doesn't like me."

"I thought it was the goat she didn't like." He shook a finger at her. "You had no business getting in front of me. You could have been hurt."

"You had no business getting in front of the guards," she countered.

"I was protecting the goat."

"I was protecting you."

Sammy's mouth opened to retort but no words came out. He opened and closed his mouth like a landed fish a few more times, while he looked at her in shocked surprise. Finally, he said, "Nobody ever—I mean, I don't need to be protected."

"Everyone needs to be protected," she replied.

Then she ducked her head and looked elsewhere because Sammy was looking at her in a way she didn't understand. It was as if the light in his eyes was shining just for her. It took her breath away, and her thoughts, and warmed her from the inside out.

Uncle Sean gave her a wry look from under his heavy white brows. It brought her out of her dazed reaction to Sammy's presence. "By St. Brendan and the goddess of wisdom that woman hates you," he told her.

"Aye," Brianna agreed, happy to think of something besides Sammy. "I can't convince anyone I don't want that husband of hers."

"She knows he wants you and that's what hurts her." He motioned for her and Sammy to sit. They took places on a bench by the hearth, while Sean sat on his bed. "It doesn't help that she's not having an easy time carrying this babe."

"Was that why she was here?" Brianna asked.

Sammy tapped her on the shoulder. When she looked at him he asked, "Should a woman that—" Sammy gestured, circling his arms out wide in front of his flat belly, "—should she be riding when she's pregnant?"

She repeated his question to Uncle Sean. "I was wondering about that myself," she added.

"She should not have ridden. She came for me to have a look at her," the healer answered. "Woke me out of a sound sleep, she did. It would have been easier for her to have sent for me," he added. "But I don't think she was thinking very clearly as she nears her time. Her worthless servants should never have let her out of the house."

"Will the babe be all right?" Brianna asked, because she did worry about any woman with child. "Will Lady Deirdre?"

"You tell me," Uncle Sean answered. "You're the one with the Sight." Sean pointed at Sammy. "Or perhaps your fairy lord knows the weave of the future."

He doesn't know the future, Brianna thought as she looked into the fire. *He is from the future.* She made herself stop thinking about Sammy and tried to concentrate on Dierdre. "I don't know," she said after a while.

The Sight didn't come at her bidding, and she never missed the absence of the ability to see the future. She felt like a witless fool when the deepest, truest visions were on her. It wasn't the gift everyone without it thought it to be.

"What do you think?" she asked her uncle.

"It'll be a hard birth," he answered. "I sent her back to her husband with some herbs and some kind words."

"Good."

"As for the king and you—"

"I'm not marrying the king."

Sammy tapped her on the shoulder again. "Excuse me, did you just say you aren't marrying the king?"

He'd been following the conversation as best he could, picking up more from the tension underlying their words than the words themselves since he couldn't understand the white-haired dude at all and Brianna just barely when she was talking to somebody else.

"I thought the pregnant lady was married to Rory."

Brianna had her hands clasped on her lap, and Sammy couldn't help noticing how white they were with tension. She cleared her throat and said, while looking into the glowing fire pit, "Rory wants me to be his second wife, yes."

Sammy's thoughts froze for a moment, while an unfamiliar jolt of emotion shot through him. Jealousy, he realized, with stunned surprise. He looked at the still figure of the girl seated next to him, with the firelight lending color to her pale face and a closed expression on her face.

Jealous? What did he have to be jealous of? She was in his life only until he got back to the future. Then she would be, quite literally, history. Brianna would have been dead for a very long time by the time he got back to Los Angeles.

That thought sent a disquieting shiver through him. He refused to dwell on it. But, looking at Brianna, he knew he wanted her. He didn't like the idea of anyone else wanting her. Which was crazy.

He'd never thought possessively about anyone before, not even Karen. She'd never felt as if she'd been his, not in his heart. She'd taught him that his heart was not the place where love for any one woman was ever going to settle permanently. So many women, he'd often told Brother Bill, who teased him about all the girls in his life, and so little time.

You are not getting involved with this woman, he told himself. *Don't even think about it.*

He told himself he was just curious about her peoples' customs when he said, "So this Rory is married to the pregnant lady, but wants you too."

"He wants me to be a secondary wife," she explained, looking into the fire as she spoke.

"Oh. Polygamy. I see. We do serial monogamy where I come from."

Brianna looked totally lost. "You do what?"

Sean asked Brianna a question. She shook her head, but the older man didn't seem convinced. He looked at Sammy and asked the question again. Sammy shrugged.

"What he say?"

"My uncle wants to know if you are a fairy."

Sammy looked at the older man curiously. Actually, Sammy welcomed the change of subject. "Nah, I'm not a fairy," he said. "I like women."

"So I've gathered," Brianna answered, her tone a bit sharp. "What has being one of the fair folk to do with your women?"

"Fair folk?" Sammy repeated. "Oh, that kind of fairy. Don't you think I'm a little tall to be one of the little people? Tinker Bell I'm not."

"Tinker Bell," Brianna repeated, and Sammy watched her eyes glaze over just the way Karen's used to when she saw something nobody else could.

"Uh oh," Sammy said, and reached out to steady Brianna as she went limp beside him. He darted a quick look at her uncle. He watched Brianna carefully but wasn't surprised by her behavior.

Brianna wasn't out for more than a few seconds. When her gaze cleared, she chuckled.

"Well?" Sammy asked, expecting some sort of weird revelation.

"I saw a little bad-tempered flapping thing with wings." Brianna eased away from him and stood. "Well, now I know why you think fairies are little creatures. Tinker Bell," she said again, and Sammy nodded enthusiastically as she spoke. She mimicked the flight of a butterfly.

"Right," he said. "Tinker Bell's a fairy!"

Brianna gazed at him in wonder. "What an odd land

you come from. Our fairies are tall, fair warriors who ruled the land before man came. They live in the twilight now," she explained. "And can never quite be trusted."

Brianna's beautiful eyes were trained on him; a half smile shaped her wide lips. She was obviously waiting for him to say something, maybe explain twentieth-century fairies. It occurred to him that just because she saw into the future she didn't necessarily understand what she saw. She obviously thought Tinker Bell was real.

Before he could think of anything to say, her uncle asked another question.

Brianna responded with a groan. "I'm sorry," she said. "I'd come to invite you to supper, Uncle Sean. Encountering Deirdre drove everything else out of my mind."

6

Sammy had been liberal in his praise of the food, but the meal had turned out to be a disaster. Brianna tried not to think about it the next morning as she made her way through misting rain to her uncle's home, but she couldn't help it.

Sammy had only been polite when he praised her cooking, for he had eaten nothing but the bread and ale, and she had made neither. He said he was a vegetarian, which he then explained meant that he'd taken a vow never to eat meat.

Upon hearing this, her brother had made too many jokes about what other sort of self-denial the fairy might practice. She had not appreciated Donal's teasing, though at least Sammy had not been able to understand the ribald jokes.

Uncle Sean had, and he'd laughed too loud and

drunk too much ale, which he did sometimes after losing the fight to save a patient's life. He'd told a vivid tale of the destruction the Norsemen brought to the nearby village, speaking with bitterness about having buried more people than he'd saved. His descriptions of the wanton violence had made Brianna feel too sick to finish her meal.

The worst part of the evening had been Father. Sammy's presence made her father as nervous as a frightened rabbit. The stranger's size and looks, his every word, unintelligible to all but her, his refusal to eat the flesh of mortal animals, with each passing moment her father had become more convinced Sammy was indeed from the fairy realm.

She'd tried to convince him otherwise, but to no avail. Father did not know whether Sammy's presence was for good or ill, whether he should try to convert him or drive him from the presence of the godly people of Ban Ean.

Finally, Uncle Sean offered to let Sammy stay with him so his brother wouldn't die from fright, and his niece and nephew could get some sleep. Sammy hadn't liked the idea of leaving Brianna, though it had not been for the reason Donal teased her about. Sammy wanted to go home and thought her magic was the only means he had of getting home. She'd told him they'd work on the spell to return him to his own time, but they all needed to rest first. So Sammy had gone away with Sean, looking worried even though she'd promised to come to Sean's house as soon as she could the next day. Well, it was the next day and she was keeping her promise.

*   *   *

Sammy could hear the roar of the sea, cold and bracing, but what he really wanted was a bath. A nice, hot bath. Yesterday's cold wash had gotten the sweat off, but he didn't feel really clean. The sound of the sea had helped lull him to sleep on the pallet Sean had laid out by the fire. He waited until Sean got out of bed and trudged over to a pot by the door. After the older man was done, Sammy stripped off the underwear he'd slept in and followed his example.

Sean looked politely away as the naked giant relieved himself. "I know you're not a fairy," he said, though he might as well be talking to himself for all the other man could understand him. "For I doubt that fairies snore."

As he spoke Sammy turned toward him, completely unashamed of his unclothed condition, and began to gesture. It took Sean a while, but he finally got the idea that the man wanted hot water to bathe in. Sean found this a reasonable request and got out his biggest pot. He set it on the banked fire and filled it with water from a bucketful he'd brought in the night before.

"Thanks, man," Sammy said and rummaged through his fanny pack while Sean built up the fire. He pulled out a pink plastic razor and a folded travel toothbrush. He couldn't find the small tube of toothpaste he normally carried, though.

"Must have left it at Nora's," he mused as he zipped the pouch back up. "Don't have any clean underwear, either."

He glanced at the pile of dirty clothes he'd stripped off the night before. He was in no hurry to put them back on. He hoped he could do laundry and find something else to wear while he did it. Meanwhile he was happier naked than with his filthy clothes on.

Sean handed him a piece of cloth out of a wooden chest. Sammy dutifully wrapped the material around his waist. Sean spoke as he pointed at the chest. Sammy saw that there were clothes inside. Then Sean pointed at the fire and said a few words. Sammy got the idea that Sean was going for more wood, and that he should see if he could find something that would fit while Sean was gone. Sammy nodded his understanding, and Sean left.

"I was the tallest man in the village until he came along," Sean said as he closed the door behind him. "I hope some of my old clothes will fit him."

He was immediately surrounded by hungry livestock. It was well past dawn, far too late to have lingered in bed, but his head and old bones were aching.

"Too much ale," Sean chided himself as he set about the morning chores. "And poteen before that."

Fortunately for his aching head his niece came into his yard just as he finished feeding his animals. He called to her as she headed for his door. "Come, sweetheart, and sing a spell to put my head right."

Brianna shook her head, knowing full well what had put her uncle's head wrong, but hurried over to him just the same, singing as she went. The spell to cure him was an easy one, just a few simple words. Uncle Sean had taught it to her himself, but he did not have the singing magic, so it never worked when he tried it himself.

His magic was of the earth, a practical knowledge of herbs and roots. He said her magic was of the air, borne on the wind, and he taught her all the song spells that had been passed on to him by his teacher. While she did the best she could as a healer, Uncle Sean was much better at curing the sick than she was.

And his magic seemed to take less out of him.

"There you are, good as new," she said when the spell was done and she was left feeling drained, and a little hungry. "I hope you have porridge for me to pay for your cure," she added with a teasing smile.

"Not until I replenish the peat box," he told her.

"And Sammy," she went on. "How is he this morning?"

Sean combed his fingers through his thick, white beard. "Well, he didn't go up in a puff of smoke in the middle of the night."

"You seem to wish he had."

"The man sounded as if he was sawing down a forest," Sean answered his niece's reproving words as he walked with her toward the door.

Sammy grinned when he heard voices outside. Sean must be back with the peat for the fire, and bringing Brianna with him. Sammy reached to open the door for the old man, and as he did, the cloth around his hips slipped. Before he could bend over to retrieve his makeshift covering the door was opened from the outside. Sammy ended up facing Brianna, whose shocked gaze took in everything he wasn't wearing.

Sammy froze.

Brianna's mouth fell open.

Sean chuckled at the sight of the pair of them. "Wasn't it our warriors that used to go into battle naked?" he asked as he glanced at the fair young man over his niece's shoulder. He put a hand on Brianna's arm, and found her muscles stiff with tension under his fingers. "Perhaps this is the great Finn come back to life after all," he commented after a further scrutiny of the naked man.

The young man snatched up the fallen cloth and

tied it around his waist. He was blushing from head to foot, Sean noticed. And his manly member had begun to go rigid from the girl's intense regard. Sean was glad to see Sammy was embarrassed about his arousal.

Sammy was about the finest long-limbed figure of a male the healer had ever seen, his tanned skin well muscled and unscarred, and the fur that pelted his chest and tapered down to his member was as gold as the thick curls that fell to his wide shoulders. And his eyes, full of shock and embarrassment and hunger as they looked straight into his niece's, well, Sean had never seen anything like the stranger's eyes before. Yes, he nodded, this was a fine figure of man or god or fairy. It was obvious Brianna thought so as well.

With a low chuckle Sean bent forward to whisper in the immobile girl's ear. "What king can compete with this giant?" he teased. She jumped at the sound of his voice and managed to drag her gaze away from Sammy.

"What?" she asked, voice low and husky, spots of color bright on her pale cheeks.

An aching had been awakened inside her, forceful enough to set her quivering inside and out. Brianna struggled hard to keep her feelings from showing to the people around her. Sammy had turned away, looking everywhere but at her. She bunched her hands into fists at her side to keep from giving in to the urge to snatch his covering away once more.

Sean drew the girl back from the doorway. He pointed her toward his garden. "I think you should gather a basket of greens for the supper pot."

Brianna blinked and repeated, "A basket of greens?"

She may never recover from this, Sean thought, realizing how puny every other man in Eire was going to seem to her after a long look at the magnificent creature on the other side of the door. There was a king who wanted to marry Brianna. There hadn't been much hope of her accepting him, but Sean was certain the marriage to the king would be out of the question after Brianna's reaction to this Sammy.

Sean passed his hand in front of her face. "Brianna."

She let out her breath in a long sigh. "The greens," she said. She looked toward the garden. "I heard you, Uncle. I'll fetch them right away." She turned away, but he heard her mutter dreamily, "Sammy. Oh, my," as she crossed the yard and back toward Ban Ean without any thought to gathering anything but the shreds of her self-control.

"Hey! Wait a minute!" Sammy called when Sean sent Brianna away. "I need to talk to you!" he shouted through the closed door and over the old man who stood in front of it. Swearing, he hurried to dress, then moved past Sean to go looking for Brianna. By the time he raced outside, she was nowhere in sight.

Rory MacMurdo sat sprawled in his high-backed chair while Cormac, captain of his guard, told him about a stranger in Ban Ean. He stroked his fingers through his rich, red beard while an entertaining tale of a gold giant unfolded. A brace of hounds snored at his feet as though they were still tired from yesterday's good hunting.

He'd slept out on the heath last night with those hounds and only a few companions, coming back to the hall just before dawn. It had been a fine night, with a bright moon, but he'd missed his bed and his wife. At least his hunting had brought back plenty of meat for this morning's meal.

His jester was juggling in the middle of the room; the priest and the poet were playing chess at a low table near Rory's chair. The men pledged to him out of kinship and his hired soldiers sat at laden tables around the four walls of Rory's great hall, while some of the finest-looking slave women in all of Eire served their morning meal.

Rory proudly noted that at least three of the women were ripe with child. While he'd planted none of the babes himself and had no intention of siring children on any but his wives, he was happy to be raising up a crop of warriors and servants to serve the children his queen would bear him.

At the thought of Deirdre he forgot to listen to the wild tale Cormac was spinning, and glanced fondly up to the gallery at the other end of the hall where his lady was taking her meal. Her women surrounded her, full of talk and laughter, but Deirdre's gaze met his as soon as he sought her out. Her gown was the color of wood roses, the silk veil covering her deep auburn hair was pale pink. Over her gown she wore a white cape trimmed with seal fur, fastened with a heavy gold brooch. Rory touched the twin of her brooch, which he wore on his own short woolen cape. A smile lit her features at his gesture, crinkling her tiny nose in a way that made him want to stride up to the gallery and make a quick, kissing count of the dozen freckles that decorated her cheeks and nose.

He could not, of course, just now. It would lessen his honor as a king to do just anything he pleased whenever he pleased. The days and nights went by in official, ceremonious, symbolic rounds. It was ill luck and worse politics to deviate a hairsbreadth from all that was right and proper to a king's honor. His dignity was the most important possession a king could wield, more powerful than his sword in influencing the people. Or so he was forever being reminded by those whose duty it was to know.

He did, however, send the fosterling who hovered at his side to serve him up to the ladies gallery to ask his wife to join him when she was done with her meal. She came as soon as the message was delivered, moving slowly through the hall. Her waiting women trailed after her, one with her footstool and one with her embroidery. A musician also came down from the gallery and began to play a soothing song on the harp as soon as the queen was seated next to the king. Deirdre rested one hand on her swollen belly, Rory took her other between his two big hands.

They gazed silently into each others' eyes until Cormac cleared his throat and said, "About the giant, my lord?"

Rory turned his attention to the guard commander with reluctance. Cormac was his older half-brother by a slave woman, and they looked much alike. He was a good man but given to flights of imagination. Imagination was a good thing in a poet but not necessarily an asset in a soldier. Rory had heard his story, now he supposed it was time to weed the truth from the embellishment.

"Giant?" he questioned skeptically. "And how high was this giant?"

"Very tall." It was Deirdre who answered. "Near as high as a house."

Rory stared as his wife. "And was he a gold-pelted barbarian as Cormac says?"

She looked thoughtful, her head tilted to one side. "I could not say if he is a barbarian, my lord," she replied. "He spoke in a foreign tongue, but he seemed friendly enough. He rescued the goat."

"Goat." The king looked back at his guard commander. "Goat? I don't recall any mention of a goat. You told of encountering this naked giant coming out of the sea—"

"He wasn't naked," Deirdre interrupted. She blushed as he glanced back at her. "I would have noticed," she added, with her gaze downcast.

"Then what was he wearing, since you're so observant," Rory inquired, piqued at her noticing any man but himself.

She gave him a conciliatory smile. "He was dressed oddly, it is true," she answered. "His tunic was sleeveless, and clinging to his muscular—I mean, he wore rags and tatters. Tight, short, open rags and tatters that showed his— I did not see if he came up from the sea," she concluded, her face flaming. She made a helpless gesture with her free hand. "Though I think his hair was wet."

The harpist had stopped playing and was leaning forward, along with the serving women, to listen. The priest and the poet were ignoring their chess match. Rory gave them all a dark look and everyone moved away. The music began again as Rory turned his frown on his wife. He was holding her hand too tightly, he knew, and eased his grip. He knew he had no reason to be jealous where Deirdre was concerned. She must have been very disconcerted by the sight of this giant in Ban Ean.

"And what sea path was this, my love?" he asked gently.

It was Cormac who answered. "Near the druid's house."

Cormac's answer settled all Rory's questions for

him. No doubt this giant was some new student of Sean's, come from a far land to learn the old wisdom. Rory had more to worry about, with the Norsemen raiding his coastal villages, than some overgrown would-be druid at Sean Dal Nariade's. The only student of Sean's Rory had any interest in was the lovely and illusive Brianna.

"Sean called him a guest," Cormac admitted as an idea occurred to Rory.

"I am going to Ban Ean," Rory declared to his household as he stood. "To see this giant with my own eyes."

Cormac bowed. Then he hastened to gather up the men required to make up the king's escort and hurried out with them to prepare for the short journey. The priest, the poet, the jester, and the lawyer were among the party. A king never traveled without advisers and entertainers. He was never alone.

Deirdre rose to her feet, kicking aside her stool. "You're going to see Brianna with your own eyes," she whispered fiercely in his ear. "Not this giant of Sean's."

He quickly touched his wife's silk-soft cheek, but he didn't look her in the eye. "Ah, no, my star of the morning," he soothed. "I go only for the safety of my people."

"Liar."

Deirdre simply refused to understand that he only wanted Brianna to insure the safety of his people, of his kindred. Of her children. It was duty. It would hurt his honor to argue with his wife in public. True, Brianna was a great beauty, and her presence in his household would add greatly to his status. But he wanted her because she could see the future, not because she was— Very well, he wanted to possess her as much for her beauty as for her talent, and her connection to a great ecclesiastical family, but it had nothing to do with love. He could not explain to his gentle wife just how potent a combination were pride and lust.

He took his lady in his arms and whispered, "You are the only one I will ever love."

She put her hands on his shoulders and dug her painted nails in hard, a painful loving gesture. Her voice was as low as his had been, keeping the staring crowd from overhearing their words. "You need my permission to take another wife," she reminded him.

"I do not. The Brehon Laws state—"

"I refuse to allow—"

"I'm going to Ban Ean now," he said. "To see the giant for myself."

"I'm going with you."

He put his hands on her thick waist and pushed her gently from him. "No. You are too close to your time to leave the house."

Her eyes snapped angrily, but Rory gestured for Dillon, who was both bodyguard and his stand-in in battle. As the two men left the hall, the hounds stirred from their favored spot by the fire and hurried after their master.

"Off to see the giant, indeed. Forbidden to leave my house, am I?" she called after him. "Too near my time, am I? We'll see about that, Rory MacMurdo!"

It had been well over an hour since she'd come back to Ban Ean, but Brianna still couldn't get over the heated feelings that coursed through her, though she knelt in the church and prayed very hard to forget what she'd seen. What she felt was far more than embarrassment, but she didn't want to think of it as lust. Lust was wicked. How could she go to her confessor and admit to lust? Especially when her confessor was her father?

She didn't want to think about what she was feeling, and prayer didn't help, so she decided to find something for her hands to do. She left the church and headed for the well. Perhaps if she gave the stone floor of the church a good scrubbing it would be some penance for her wicked feelings.

"You'd think I'd never seen a naked man before," Brianna berated herself as she hauled a brimming water jug out of the well in the village square a few minutes later.

"Yeah," Sammy said from behind her. "You'd think you'd never seen a naked man before."

He'd come up behind her so quietly she hadn't known he was there. When she whirled at the sound of his voice she would have dropped the jug, but he caught it and set it on the ground.

"Hi," he said, quelling the urge to tease her. He hadn't come looking for her to talk about this morning's incident, no matter how cute she looked when she blushed. "We need to talk."

Brianna took in the sight of him, dressed in a pair of short trews that were definitely too tight across his muscular thighs and a tunic that had been slit from the neck nearly to the waist to accommodate his wide chest. She supposed he must have borrowed his clothing from Uncle Sean. He was barefoot, with spatters of mud on his bare legs. He looked like a great king despite his dress. His posture was utterly relaxed, casual, like a gold wolf at rest. Brianna's breath caught at the sight of him. How foolish she was to react so.

"Aye," she agreed, trying to control her reeling senses. She'd worry about the church floor later. Sammy was more important. "You need to go away."

"That's what I came to talk about. I don't have much time," he went on. "A man's life de—"

"Tell the fairy we need to talk," Donal said.

Brianna hadn't heard her twin approach from behind her, either. Now, not only was her brother here, but Fergus's eldest daughter, Bridget, with him. Donal was carrying her water bucket for her.

Brianna sighed, and Bridget took the time to look Sammy over with an interest that brought a resentful glance from Donal.

Donal handed Bridget the bucket. "Tend to your chores," he said gruffly.

Then his pale cheeks colored brightly when the girl made a face at him before she busied herself at the well. He watched her go with longing in his eyes as she left with her full bucket. Brianna noticed Bridget's hips swaying in a most immodest way as she passed Sammy to go into the common house. Identical growls escaped from each twin's throat once more. They looked at each other and made a silent agreement not to laugh at each other's jealous reaction.

"I think I said the wrong thing to her," Donal admitted. "They're not easy girls to court. Not with what I have to offer."

Brianna swallowed her own disapproval of Donal's choices for wives, put her hand on her brother's arm, and said loyally, "They will love you when you are a warrior with a thousand head of cattle."

Donal brightened. "That's what I want to talk to the fairy about."

Brianna didn't want to bring the subject up to

Sammy, but she supposed Donal would pester her until she did. "My brother wants you to train him to be a warrior."

"I thought we were going to talk about getting me back to Los Angeles," Sammy said.

"My brother would follow you into battle," she went on, ignoring what he'd just said. "He would be your sworn man. He would freely bind himself to you to be trained."

Donal was grinning at him like a hopeful puppy. Sammy tried not to pay any attention to him. "Los Angeles," he insisted. "E.T. go home, okay?"

Brianna remembered Sammy facing the warriors in the oak grove. She remembered her own fear, but it was a small part of the emotions the images conjured. She looked at Sammy now and in her mind she saw him as he'd first appeared to her, a creature of grace and speed. No living thing had ever been so beautiful as this great, gold man wielding a sword.

"If anyone can teach a man to be a warrior," she said, "it is you."

"Of course I can teach him, but what's that got to do with my going—"

"He says he will teach you," Brianna told her brother.

"No, I didn't!"

"Yes, you did," she said, while Donal whooped with joy and danced around them.

"No, I—let's not argue about this, okay? Let's just concentrate on your getting me home."

"I will get you home," she said. "As soon as I can."

He crossed his arms. "How soon is that?"

"I don't know." She pointed back toward her uncle's house. "I have to talk to Sean."

"He's not there," Sammy told her. "Some nun came

looking for him after you left. He grabbed some stuff and left."

Brianna looked annoyed. "The abbess of Canaire must think she's dying again. He might not be back for days."

"Forget about Sean," Sammy insisted. "You're the one with the magic. That's what's important."

She looked uncertain. "I have to find the right spell. Consult the right spell scrolls. The scrolls are all at Uncle Sean's house."

"Fine," Sammy said, putting his arm under her elbow to urge her along. "We'll just head on back to Uncle Sean's, then."

Brianna went with him without protest. Donal, singing with delighted abandon, came hurrying after them.

7

"*You've the look of* magic about you," Donal told her as they accompanied Sammy on the narrow path.

She eased her arm out of the big man's gentle grasp and took a step back to walk beside her brother. "Do I, now?"

He nodded, then jerked a thumb toward Sammy. "Did you sing a love song to bring him to you?"

She frowned, felt herself blush, but didn't try lying to her twin. He ever knew her mind, as she did his. "Perhaps."

She still wasn't quite ready to explain to anyone but her wise uncle where she'd brought the man from. She didn't like thinking about it herself. It was easier to think that he was a magical being from under a fairy hill than something so inexplicable as a man from the future.

"You'll have to sing a love spell for me sometime," Donal said. "A pity I can't sing it myself," he added, with only a trace of bitterness.

Someone in each generation of their family inherited the mage power. It was usually a male child who was born with some kind of magical gift. She and Donal had shared the same womb, but the power—the strongest dose of it in generations, Uncle Sean had said—had passed to her, the girl child, instead of this generation's only son.

Donal said he didn't mind, but Grandfather had certainly complained about it all their lives. He'd planned on passing his Sight to an heir holy in Christ and wise in the old ways of the druids. Having a granddaughter with the power had been a sore trial to the bishop of Nariade.

"Grandfather's going to be very annoyed if you aren't a priest by the time he gets home," Brianna said, assuming her twin would know where her thoughts had skipped to.

"I don't care. Sammy will have taught me what I need to know to be a great warrior by the time Grandfather returns. But Grandfather will be very annoyed if you aren't wed to Rory MacMurdo by that time."

Brianna gave her brother a wry smile and glanced at Sammy's broad back. "Perhaps—"

Ailill and his hound came racing up out of the pasture, leaving the herd dog to do the work once again. Brianna started to frown and wave Ailill back to his duty, but the boy grinned at her, pointed at the wolfhound, and made the sign Sammy had taught him the day before. She could tell by the shining light in his eyes that this was no mimicry.

"What's he doing?" Donal asked as Sammy turned around to look at them.

"He's talking," Brianna said, with her gaze not on the boy but on the man who'd taught him. The joy she felt at saying the words went all the way to her heart. She repeated the gesture, and both Sammy and Ailill nodded. "So, I've said it too, then."

Donal put his hand on her shoulder. "Waving your hands around doesn't make words."

What Donal said had sounded true to her the day before, but today his attitude was pure nonsense. "And why not?" she demanded. "Why shouldn't a gesture be a word? What makes it any less a word than a scratch made on a piece of parchment, or a sound coming out of a mouth? What is language, but a way to understand one another?"

"Yeah!" Sammy agreed, in his loud, enthusiastic way while Donal gaped at her. "You tell him, babe."

"I have told him," she said, and walked on. The others followed her, and after a moment she said thoughtfully, "Sammy, if you teach Ailill this hand language you must teach it to me, also." *Then Ailill will have someone to talk to when you are gone,* she thought but did not say out loud. While the man's presence did nothing but disrupt her life and her thoughts, she was already finding it difficult to imagine what it would be like without his large, enthusiastic presence.

"Sure," he said, moving to walk beside her. "No problem."

"And Donal to fight," she added.

Sammy picked up a stick and tried throwing it for the hound. The dog ignored it and continued loping by the boy's side. Sammy chuckled, a faint, low sound. "You trying to make some kind of deal, here?" he asked Brianna. "Your help in return for mine?"

He watched her face while she puzzled out his words. He noticed that her eyes, which were a sort of bluish hazel, shifted color a bit with her thoughts and emotions. He wondered just how long it would take him to figure out what was going on in her head by watching her eyes change. Not that he had time to hang around and get to know her that well.

"Am I trying to strike a bargain?" she questioned as they started up a slight hill that hid Sean's house from the village. "No, I would not try to coerce you into helping my family. I brought you here and it is my responsibility to send you back."

He appreciated her sense of responsibility. It was a quality that was becoming rare in his own time.

She went on. "I know not how long it will take me to find the correct spell. I think teaching my brothers is a way for you to pass the time while you are here."

"Well," he said, his initial reluctance ebbing under her reasonable words. As anxious as he was to get home, he had no control over how long it was going to take. If he kept busy, maybe he wouldn't hover over Brianna constantly while she worked. "I am a teacher," he went on. "I have my own *dojang,* that's a fighting school, back home. I need to keep in shape anyway, so I guess I can teach Donal."

"He has his own sword," Brianna said. She didn't look happy about it.

Sammy didn't explain that sword fighting wasn't what he taught. Which was a pity, considering the era he was in. "Maybe I can teach him some *kendo.* I'm not great at it, but I'll see what I can do. But first we're going to go through the magical stuff at your uncle's."

"Aye," Brianna agreed.

She gave Sammy a reassuring smile, though she had no idea whether there was anything helpful to be found among Sean's writings. It was Uncle Sean's own wisdom she needed, for she felt she had little of her own.

She knew talking Sammy into teaching Ailill and Donal was not wise, but it was what one needed and the other wanted. She had to take care of her brother and foster brother, even if it meant losing them to new ways. Besides, perhaps keeping Sammy busy with Donal and Ailill would keep him from turning her whole world upside down.

When the beehive-shaped stone house came into view it became obvious that they weren't going to be going through Sean's spells any time soon. The house was surrounded by a band of colorfully dressed horsemen.

Standing in the riders' midst in his boxy chariot, his red hair as bright as an upturned copper kettle, was the ruler of them all, the last man she wanted to see: Rory MacMurdo himself.

Brianna swore to several old gods as well as to the newer one she prayed to constantly. "What's he doing here? And why can't the abbess ever send for *me* when she's on her deathbed?"

The dog backed up against Ailill and began to growl. "Who's that?" Sammy asked.

Donal gave her a teasing look. Brianna swore again. "The king," she replied.

Then she stepped to the front of the group and led the way to Uncle Sean's house before the impulse to flee reached from her brain to her feet. "Very well," she said with false bravado. "Let's see what he wants before we send him on his way."

Brianna's hair shone like a raven's wing in the sunlight. She moved toward Rory with all the grace of a swan, her fine high breasts moving sensually beneath the cloth of her dress as she negotiated the rocky path.

He watched her with covetous interest, letting his gaze roam freely over the object of his longing while he left his men to keep watch on those with her. He got down from his chariot to meet her at the edge of her uncle's yard. He put his hands out to take hers, but she bowed and quickly sidled away before he could touch her.

That she fled from him only added edge to his desire. "You are as beautiful as the star-filled night," he said.

"My uncle isn't home," was her short response to his compliment.

Rory frowned at her rudeness. She was going to make a most difficult wife, but he had to smile at the knowledge that her spirit would prove a delightful contrast to Deirdre's gentleness. After the stimulation of the scratching and biting of this night angel, he could count on his morning love to soothe and cozen him.

"Why are you looking at me like that?" Brianna's fierce whisper brought him out of his reverie.

"I was thinking of our future, dear nightingale," he answered, low and seductive. "About how well you'll fit into my household. Into my bed."

"That's what I thought. For shame! Surely, it's a sin to look at a woman so in the daylight."

"'Tis no sin for a man to look at his wife."

"Which I am not."

"You will be."

Rory would have reached for her again, but her brother stepped in front and bowed to him. There was nothing he could do but acknowledge Donal's presence. Then he looked over his head to the yellow-haired man standing behind Brianna.

He was tall indeed, this stranger he'd come to meet, taller than himself by half a head. Broad, too, and fair of face with eyes the color of a king's royal cloak. A giant the stranger had been named, and he almost was.

"Are you truly a fairy, then?" Rory found himself asking as his first words to the outsider.

An odd light of amusement lit the stranger's face. He said something in a foreign tongue. "*Sidhe* means 'fairy,' right?"

Brianna laughed. "Aye. That is the word for fairy."

"Thought so. My reputation is being ruined around here. Maybe this'll prove I'm no fairy."

The next thing Rory knew, the big man had grasped Brianna around the waist and lifted her into a passionate kiss. As her arms went around the stranger's neck, Rory forgot that it was a stain on his honor to confront a man without prior challenge. He drew his sword.

Brianna heard the gasps, and the rasp of iron against leather behind her. She knew what the sound meant, but she was busy experiencing her first kiss and found it impossible to let imminent violence distract her from the sensations rushing from head to toe and deep inside her. There was an instant of shock when Sammy lifted her like a feather, then his mouth covered hers and she felt too wonderful to be outraged.

She didn't know how kissing her would prove that he wasn't one of the fair folk, but he'd said it would and she was happy to help him settle the matter once his lips touched hers. Oh, but they were warm and supple, soft and commanding all at once. His tongue probed and teased her into opening her mouth. When she did, the kissing only got better.

Her mother had told her that kissing was not a very interesting thing. Grandfather had told her it was wicked. Uncle Sean had told her not to ask so many questions. Father said Donal liked doing it too much. Well, she was Donal's twin, and if this aching, melting, delicious sensation was what kissing was all about, perhaps she was going to like it too much as well. She knew it was not right to be kissing this stranger, but it was wonderful. She didn't want it ever to stop.

Sammy's tongue was doing swirling, heated things inside her mouth when Rory MacMurdo shouted, "Enough!"

She wouldn't have moved away, but Sammy did. He broke the kiss and set her down, very sedately, as though he'd done no more when he lifted her than help her to the other side of a high fence. She looked up at him in wonder, flushed and breathless and aching. He looked down at her for a moment, and she saw hunger in his eyes until he turned her to face the angry king. Once she was no longer looking into his eyes she remembered all the women he'd spoken of. She did not like knowing that this had not been a first kiss for Sammy one little bit.

Rory's men had moved closer, swords and spears and long daggers drawn; his bodyguard loomed menacingly at the king's left side, ready to strike at his master's command. Rory stood before her, face red with outrage, blue eyes full of hate. He glared at Sammy.

Looking up, Brianna saw that Sammy recognized the danger but was unconcerned. She noticed that Donal stood tensely beside Sammy on one side, Ailill on the other. Sammy had no weapon at all, she realized, and yet he seemed completely relaxed.

"Are you brave or just stupid?" she asked, feeling stupid herself but ignoring her emotions to concentrate on the situation she should never have let happen.

"Both," he answered. "That is the guy you don't want to marry, right?"

She nodded, though why Sammy should care about

that she did not know. He put his hands on her shoulders and spoke to Rory. "Ask him if he's got a problem. It's not like I was kissing his wife, or anything."

Brianna felt a stab of pleasure at Sammy's teasing Rory. She translated.

Rory's color deepened. "Not my wife! What's that got to do with—"

"I'm not!" Brianna shouted him down. "I'll kiss whomever I please. It pleases me greatly to kiss Sammy," she added before she could stop the words from coming out. Against her back, she felt Sammy's chest rumble with a self-satisfied chuckle. The sensation sent a shiver through her. The cause of it annoyed her.

"You'll kiss whom I allow you to," Rory told her.

"She will not!" an outraged Donal declared.

"I'm the king here and she'll not be kissing foreigners in my presence."

"In truth, my lord," one of Rory's men spoke up as he stepped in front of the king, "according to the nine judgments of Padriac given at the Council of O'Curry when the Brehon of the Ard Righ proclaimed . . ."

The man went on for a long while, counseling the king and boring the rest of them near to tears. Weapons were returned slowly to sheaths. The king's bodyguard stepped into the background. Rory's high color gradually faded to something closer to normal. Ailill wandered off with his dog.

After a few minutes Sammy said to Brianna, "The dude doing all the talking is a lawyer, right?"

"Indeed," she replied.

He chuckled again. "Looks like some things just don't ever change."

It had really been a dumb move to kiss her, he told himself. Dumb and thoughtless and delicious. Brianna had a mouth that needed kissing, wide and soft and sensual, but it could have gotten her and the kids in trouble.

There had been no use provoking a situation in the first place, especially when innocent civilians had been in the line of fire. *Bad move,* he castigated himself. *But the girl's got great lips.*

"I shouldn't have kissed you," he told her, tugging a loose strand of her hair off her cheek. "Not just like that. But I'm just tired of being called a fairy, you know?"

The faint hint of amusement that had been there left her expression. "No," she agreed, "you should never kiss anyone as a joke. They might not be as understanding as I am."

She sounded as if knowing it was a joke had somehow offended her. Women were like that, sometimes. It was hard to tell if they were serious or just out to have a good time, and they always made you guess which was which. Most of the time you guessed wrong.

"It was a nice kiss," he went on. "A very nice kiss, but I didn't mean anything by it."

"Oh?"

He hated to hear that dangerously cool tone from a woman. It was a clear indication that whatever he said next was going to be taken the wrong way.

Sammy cleared his throat. "I mean, I don't want to interfere, with your life and all and I . . . " He trailed off as Brianna stepped away, her expression cloudy with anger. "I mean," he went on as she backed a few steps away, "I'm not only in Ireland but hundreds, thousands of years in the past. I don't think I'm quite in my right mind to begin with, and then he said that, and I thought, oh, what the hell, and you're so pretty and all. . . . " It was no good, she wasn't listening and he wasn't making sense anyway.

"Pretty?" she asked, some of the clouds clearing from her expression. "You think I'm pretty?"

It was Donal who laughed. "Every man in Eire has called you a beauty. Why are you casting nets for one more compliment?"

Brianna whirled on her brother. Sammy took one look at the fire in her eyes and backed quickly away from this confrontation. Yelling at her twin was a safe way to vent the anger she felt at him, and the king. Sammy didn't feel quite brave enough to get in the way of what looked to be a major explosion.

"Are you calling me vain? When do I have time to be vain? Do I spend my days combing my hair with a silver comb and counting my silk gowns? Have I even a silver comb or a silk gown to my name? No, I've got to deal with sick villagers, and a strutting king, and the magic that controls me more often than I control it. Does attracting things I don't want make me vain? You're the one who is confident in satisfying every woman you see, and you're calling me vain?"

"Aye," her brother countered quickly. "Vain and proud, or you would not keep waiting to choose a man to be your husband."

"Am I the one with the notion I can keep two lively girls happy at once?"

Donal smirked. "It's not a notion."

"Men!" she snarled as Rory left his lawyer to approach her. "Men are the vainest creatures God ever made."

Instead of answering her, instead of defending their miserable existence as they should, the three men looked not at her but at one another, all in perfect accord, communicating their smugness without need for words. And it was obvious they were in complete agreement on how they felt about her opinions.

Instead of screaming in outrage, Brianna turned to stomp away from the lot of them and was the first to see Rory's queen riding up to join the gathering.

"Here's trouble," she grumbled. Then she took note of the gray look of Deirdre's face and concern replaced anger as Deirdre rode up to the gathering. Deirdre did not look at her but at Rory.

"So," she said, "have you looked your fill of the giant, then? For I'm sure there's no one else you came to look at," she added bitterly.

Brianna could see that it hurt Deirdre to see Rory with her. The woman should be at home resting, with her feet up and her harper playing a soothing song. Instead, she had come chasing after Rory, jealous and worried. Brianna was more annoyed with Rory than with his wife. It would be his own fault if his heir was born right here in a muddy rut!

Brianna almost felt the pain that tore through Deirdre as she was helped off her pony, it showed that clearly on the queen's face. Brianna saw that the babe was indeed going to come early. She forgot all her confusion and annoyance at the men as her attention centered completely on the woman who was going into labor.

Deirdre made a small sound as her feet touched the ground, and her women hurried to her side.

Rory was there before the servants, his hands holding her by the elbows. "Foolish woman," he said. "I told you not to come."

She turned her face tiredly away from his anger and retreated into excuses. "I came to see Sean." She put her hands on her husband's chest, letting him support her weight. "I've need of a physician."

"I've a physician of my—"

Rory stopped suddenly, as he recalled that his own physician had died a few weeks before. He had not replaced him, thinking to have Brianna serve double duty as wife and doctor.

"A queen should not be left standing out in the road," she complained petulantly.

Rory touched his fingers to her brow and wiped away sweat. "No, you should not be left standing here."

So saying, he swung her up into his arms and turned toward Sean's house. Her women followed, squawking like hens. "Damn!" Rory shouted as moisture soaked through the layers of her clothes. He kicked open Sean's door. "Where's the druid!"

Brianna hurried into the house behind Rory and the women. It was time she took the situation in hand. "Set her on the bed, then get yourself out of this house right now, Rory MacMurdo. It's a midwife she needs, not a bellowing ox."

"But—"

"And take her hens with you," Brianna ordered, pointing at the servants who had gathered by the hearth. "I don't need any help just yet."

"But—"

"Don't leave me alone! Not with her!" Deirdre cried out but was ignored.

"Go," Brianna said, as commanding as she could manage. "Go to Ban Ean," she told the king who looked at her with frightened eyes. "Share a cask of my father's poteen. I'll send word when the babe arrives."

Rory went without a backward glance, sweeping the servants out before him. Brianna set to work, then went to stand over the bed to watch Deirdre carefully while her body tightened with pain.

"You're going to kill me, aren't you?" Deirdre asked

her as the contraction eased.

"No," Brianna said, stroking a cooling damp cloth across her forehead. "I'm going to deliver your baby. We're alone," she added, squatting down beside her, taking her hand. She gave Deirdre an encouraging smile. "Alone with your midwife, even a queen can scream when the pain comes, lady."

"The babe is early," Deirdre said.

Brianna nodded. "But not so early as to be dangerous."

She didn't tell the terrified woman that Uncle Sean had said it would be a difficult birth. She kept that knowledge to herself, and the knowledge that this was only the third babe she'd ever delivered. The first had been an easy delivery that needed no real help from her. And the second had been Uncle Sean's goat.

8

"*So, if your wife's* in labor, how come you're leaving?"

The king stopped to look at him, obviously not understanding Sammy's question. Rory seemed worried, Sammy noted, but if he was so worried, why wasn't he in there?

"Okay, I can't think of anything scarier than a woman in pain, either," Sammy went on. "You want to make it stop but there's nothing you can do."

Sammy wished there was someone to translate for him while the king stood and stared at him as his posse gathered around him. The women who'd come with the queen stood over by their horses, wringing their hands and glancing worriedly at the house. A priest was on his knees praying, with the goat nudging him in the back and the chickens pecking at the ground. Sammy wondered how Brianna was doing but supposed he'd get kicked out too if he stuck his head in to ask.

"Besides, it's not my job," he said with a stern, challenging look for Rory, who gave him a stern look back.

Sammy pointed at the house. "What are you going to do about your wife?"

The only answer he got was one more glare, then Rory walked to the painted cart in the middle of the yard and climbed into the back. All but one of his men mounted their horses, as did the women, and then they all rode away. Sammy was left in the yard, bemused, surrounded by livestock, his would-be students, the guard, the crashing of waves onto the nearby shore, and a lot of horse manure.

He turned to Donal. "Come on, let's go down to the shore and get started."

Brianna was right, Sammy thought, it was something to do to keep his mind off whatever was going on in this crazy place. After some hesitation, Donal hurried to catch up to him, then Ailill followed them both. The boy sat on a rock and watched. Sammy stripped off his ill-fitting tunic and began to stretch. It took Donal a while to get the idea that Sammy meant to teach him exercises. Eventually Brianna's twin stripped off his outer garments and followed Sammy's lead.

After a half hour of warm-up exercises Donal stopped and pointed to the sword that lay abandoned on the ground with his clothes. Sammy knew what Brianna's brother wanted, but he was reluctant to teach anything but the basics just yet.

He remembered the archaeological dig of this place and its evidence of fire and sword. It had been destroyed by Vikings sometime in the early ninth century. Ban Ean was in a world of trouble, and maybe he'd been sent back here to do something about it. Maybe there was some meaning to what Brianna had done. He couldn't stay here long—the need to get back to help Jerry Park ate at the back of his mind all the time—but he'd do what he could to help while he was here.

He rubbed a hand worriedly across his jaw. "I don't kill people," he said to himself before he addressed Brianna's brother. He made his voice and expression stern as he spoke, hoping to convey his meaning that way. "We're not too formal at my *dojang.* But, if you want to be my student you do what I tell you." He went on to explain although he knew the other man couldn't understand his words. He pointed at himself, then back toward the village. "In martial arts it's always the student's choice to come or to go. But if you come to a teacher, you obey him."

Donal looked thoughtful. Sammy had given this lecture more times than he could count to cocky young men looking to learn how to kick ass, who thought it was going to be instant and easy. Donal continued to look puzzled and a bit annoyed, but he finally nodded.

Sammy started the exercises again. The wind coming off the North Sea wasn't exactly cold, not freezing cold anyway. Brisk was probably the best thing that could be said for it. It was summer, it just wasn't Southern California. It felt good, though, invigorating as it dried the sweat off his bare chest.

He noticed that the man Rory had left at Sean's house had wandered down to perch on a gray boulder. He watched them with confused concentration while he occasionally petted the wolfhound that had trotted over to check him out.

After another ten minutes or so, Sammy called a halt. When Donal pointed to the sword again, Sammy shook his head and said, "Tomorrow."

Donal stared for a while, looking disgusted. Finally,

he picked up the tunic he'd shed to exercise, used it to wipe the sweat off his face, and then headed up the rocky beach. Sammy followed him as far as where Ailill was lingering on a boulder. The guard got up and went back toward Sean's house.

Sammy sat down a few feet from the boy. "Okay," he said as he picked up a water-polished stone, "let's see if we can learn *rock* today."

Although he kept himself occupied, he couldn't help but worry about what was going on inside the little dwelling up the hill.

Brianna didn't know how Sammy's black beast had gotten into Uncle Sean's house, but she draped a blanket over it before Deirdre had a chance to see it hulking in the shadows and become even more frightened than she already was. She wished she'd had the courage to throw the thing out of the small house the same way she'd thrown out Rory and the women. The blasted thing was in the way. She grew to resent it more and more as the day wore slowly down to night.

"I should have gotten rid of you and kept one of the serving women," she complained, moving past where the beast slept between her and the fire one more time. "You're more a pest than a beast," she went on, daringly poking at the metal horns she'd seen Sammy grasp so confidently.

She carried a cup of a strengthening potion to Deirdre. "Here," she said, holding Deirdre's head up to help her drink. "This will do you good." Between panting breaths Deirdre obediently took a few small sips.

"Tastes good, doesn't it?" Brianna asked in a cheerful tone she would have hated to hear if she'd been the one writhing in agony on the bed. "Not that you care how anything tastes just now," she added. *And if you can't say anything that isn't foolish,* she chastised herself, *just keep quiet and do your job.* Brianna went to the end of the bed to check the progress of Deirdre's labor.

The sharp aroma of herbs from the brew steaming over the fire temporarily overlaid the scents of peat smoke and blood. Brianna breathed deeply of the smell, glad she'd taken the time to gulp down a cup of the potion.

"This is going too slowly," she whispered to herself.

Deirdre arched and cried out as a fresh contraction took hold of her body. In the same instant the labor pain began, someone started knocking loudly on the door. Brianna grabbed Deirdre's hands and held on tight, ignoring the continuous banging until Deirdre quieted. Then she marched angrily to the door, flexing hands that ached from the other woman's fierce grip.

"What?" she demanded when she opened the door to find herself facing Rory's guard captain. "What is it Cormac?"

The daylight was nearly gone, but she could see that Cormac's color was about the same gray-white as a gull's wing. She also saw Sammy lingering nearby, worry creasing his mouth.

Cormac gulped. "How is my lady?" he asked without looking past Brianna into the house.

Sammy, on the other hand, walked up and peered over the soldier's shoulder. "The wait is driving me crazy. Anything I can do?" he offered.

It was the strangest request Brianna had ever heard, unless he was a healer as well as a warrior. "What can you do?" she asked.

When Sammy spoke, Cormac turned, his hand going

to his sword hilt. "Peace, Cormac," she said, putting her hand on his shoulder. "There's nothing you can do for Deirdre," she told the soldier. To Sammy she said, "You could take the beast away."

Behind her, Deirdre gave an anguished cry. Cormac flinched at the sound, and Sammy shouldered him aside. Brianna stepped back as the big man entered the already crowded room. He slammed the door, pushed the beast in front of it as Cormac began pounding on it again, and followed Brianna to Deirdre's bedside.

"How can you guys do natural childbirth without a coach? Sorry about bringing the bike in here," he added. "But it seemed too far away in that shed. I was going to check it again and—"

"Natural childbirth?" she interrupted. "Is there an unnatural kind?" The man was dear to her, but he rarely made sense. And when, she wondered, had he become dear to her?

"Never mind." His words echoed her answer to herself. "Just let me help. I've done this before. There was this girl. I was birthing coach for my pregnant girlfriend a few months ago. It wasn't my kid. She eventually married the father, and I gave the bride away."

While Brianna wondered why he had given one of his brides away instead of killing the man who had fathered the child, Sammy went on talking. "Anyway, I know about breathing. And there's this Zen technique for blocking pain I can maybe—"

"If you can do something, do it," Brianna interrupted, her voice harsh with strain. "Get over here!"

"Okay," he said, and moved to the head of the bed.

"Will your pebbles help her pain?"

Sammy's gaze flashed up to her. "Aspirin? No, I don't think so." He knelt and gently began to massage

Deirdre's temples. "It's going to be fine," he whispered, voice sure and gentle.

New terror flashed across Deirdre's face at this masculine intrusion. "You've brought him to kill me!" she accused Brianna wildly, trying to pull away from Sammy's touch. He didn't let her go, he just kept talking, insistent, reassuring, lulling, whether the words were understandable to her or not.

Brianna leaned close, catching the suffering woman's gaze with her own. "He has magic for you," she said, matching Sammy's tone, shaping the sounds into song, into a kind of hypnotic magic she hadn't had the energy to try before Sammy brought his confident strength to lend to her. "Trust him, my sweet. He comes from the fairy realm. He's come to help at the birth of a prince. Listen and all will be well."

Deirdre's gaze could not leave hers. Sammy spoke and Brianna translated. "Concentrate on breathing, take your mind away from the pain. Think of something else. Picture a flower in your mind. Think of nothing but the flower. There's no pain, just the flower. See it? Watch it grow. A bud. A blossom. A bloom. Count the petals one by one. Breathe. Yes. That's it, just concentrate on that flower. Listen to the voice. Go away from the pain."

Sammy's voice went on and on. Brianna slipped away to the other end of the bed, coaxing but caring for Deirdre's body while Sammy soothed her spirit. She and Sammy were separated by a short distance but connected by compassion, and determination to save both mother and child. The hours rolled on endlessly, and through the trying time Brianna found that she had never felt so close to anyone as she did to the man who was helping her deliver Deirdre's baby.

*　*　*

"It's going to be a breach birth," Brianna said hours later, unable to keep the news to herself any longer. She knew what she had to do, now that she was certain the babe was twisted in the birth canal.

She exchanged a worried glance with Sammy. Dark marks of exhaustion stained the skin beneath his eyes. She supposed she looked no better, and poor Deirdre was growing weak. There wasn't much time to save both mother and child. Lord, but it seemed like it had taken years to reach this moment of crisis.

A storm had blown in from the sea the night before, but the three of them had remained snug and secure in their own private little hell. With the coming of the day, Brianna was certain Deirdre's travail was near an end. There were no windows in the hut, but she could tell it was after dawn from the sound of men and horses out in the yard. Rory had come to see to his wife and child. She was confident he wouldn't try to come in to the hut, and that the beast would hold him out if he did. Brianna had no intention of leaving Deirdre's bedside for even a moment to bring Rory news.

Sammy had ventured several unflattering opinions during the long night about Rory's absence. Brianna found herself agreeing that perhaps a father ought to take some responsibility at the birth of his child. It was an interesting idea—Sammy seemed to have lots of ideas about how men and women should deal with one another. She thought she might have some questions for him about those ideas, if ever this child got itself born.

"It will be over soon," Brianna promised the woman on the bed.

Thanks to Sammy's aid, Deirdre was doing much

better. She was weak, but she'd gone through the pain-filled night with grim determination instead of the fearful panic that had consumed her before he offered her his strength. Brianna blessed the man for his help. She trusted him now to keep the woman calm while she explained what must be done.

"The babe's turned wrong. I have to reach in and turn him the right way. It'll be over soon. Just push as hard as you can when the next pain comes. Get her to push. Push," she repeated the word to Sammy in her language. He repeated it slowly, so Deirdre would be sure to understand.

With complete faith in his ability to aid Deirdre, Brianna concentrated on what she had to do. She eased a hand inside the birth canal, ignoring Deirdre's scream. She found the babe's tiny shoulder as Deirdre's next contraction began. She tugged the little body, helping it move as the mother's inner muscles worked to expel it. Brianna felt the soft bone of its shoulder give as she turned it, positioned the head correctly, and prayed.

"It's coming!"

The hopeful relief in Brianna's voice permeated deep into Sammy's being, into muscle and bone and strung-out nerves. The whole room seemed to light up with just the sound of those two words. He kept talking gently to poor Deirdre, but his gaze was on the woman who was delivering the baby.

She looked up at him from between Deirdre's widespread legs and they shared a brief, triumphant smile, sparing only a second for each other. He gave her a quick thumbs up sign, then she busied herself with finishing the delivery.

Deirdre gave one last groan, and pushed. Within a

few seconds a feeble cry filled the room. Almost immediately, that tiny, tentative sound swelled into a fierce complaint.

Deirdre exhaled a tired, delighted sigh. She whispered something, voice rough and barely audible. Brianna held the baby up, tiny, greasy, and bloody, and very unhappy with this new state of affairs. Deirdre held her arms out for her child.

Sammy threw back his head and gave a whoop as Brianna lay the baby across Deirdre's abdomen. The mother reached down to stroke her child's wet hair, while Brianna dealt with the afterbirth. Sammy left Deirdre's side to bring the bowl of warm water and pile of cloth Brianna had left by the hearth. Once she had the umbilical cord severed Sammy gingerly picked up the baby.

"He is beautiful," he acknowledged as he and Brianna cleaned up the wriggling little form. "And so tiny." Sammy surprised himself by adding, "Someday I wouldn't mind one of these."

"I, also," she agreed.

"Boys or girls?" Sammy questioned. He was amazed at the eager speculation he was aiming at her. It was ridiculous. He was a loner. Loners didn't take on the responsibilities of fatherhood. He was just reacting to the intensity of having helped to bring a new life into the world, that was all.

The look she gave him from under her long black lashes was both amused and assessing. "Men want sons. Is it a hundred sons you're wanting?"

"Boys are nice," he hedged. Then he grinned. "But I'm completely helpless around little girls. I'm going to spoil my daughters rotten."

"I'm happy to hear it," she answered, with a smile

that left him thinking about kissing her. Then her expression and tone hardened somewhat. "It's lucky your wives are, since they don't have to fear about presenting you with daughters."

"Wives?" he asked. Deirdre groaned before Brianna could answer. He flashed a quick look at the bed. "How's she doing?"

Brianna was horrified that for a few moments she'd actually wondered what it would be like to be one of Sammy Bergen's wives. The idea was not only ridiculous, it was completely impossible.

She made herself think only of her duty. "The afterbirth came easily. She's weak, though. I'll let her women in to tend her in a few minutes. First we have to see that the child is whole."

"Whole?" He studied the infant in his arms.

"You're a fine midwife," Brianna said, feeling suddenly awkward in the presence of a man. "Thank you for your help. "

"No problem. What's wrong with the baby?"

"This." She touched the baby's right collarbone.

"Looks odd," Sammy said.

"Broken," she said, voice tinged with regret. "Shh." She kept two fingers pressed to the baby's skin. "Just hold him still for me."

He nodded as she closed her eyes and began to sing quietly. Her voice spread out, filling the space around them.

And he felt the magic.

He knew, somewhere deep in his nerve endings and in the dark, primitive section of his mind that she was making magic. She was taking energy from herself, from the earth under their feet, the sky above, the smoky fire in the hearth and the ocean waves boiling to shore in the windy aftermath of the storm. She sang up all that energy, and she gave it to the crying child.

Sammy felt it, felt himself mixed in with her music, and knew exactly what Brianna did. She was committing a miracle, and it felt wonderful.

When the singing stopped and the baby was whole, Brianna collapsed. Sammy grabbed her around the waist, keeping the baby balanced on his other arm. "Great job," he whispered, and kissed her on her sweaty forehead.

She clung to him, her weight warm and limp against his side. "It worked," she said in wonder. "It really worked." She gave a tired little laugh. "How about that?"

"I bet Rory's insurance didn't cover what you just did. The king's gonna have kittens when he gets the bill for this delivery."

He eased Brianna down onto the bench in front of the fire. It was very nice to hold her, but it was time to take care of Deirdre. Time for him and Brianna to get some rest, too.

"I don't think it would have worked but for you," she added. He saw worship in her eyes and went hot all over with both pleasure and embarrassment. She went on before he could think of any disclaimers. "You gave me the strength. You've a talent for magic, Sammy."

"Nah," he said, forcing a shrug. "It's just my training. I understand energy flow, *ki,* we call it."

"Ah. You are a druid, then."

Sammy just laughed as he went to push the Harley out of the way. He opened the door and stepped quickly aside, allowing entrance to daylight, a pair of women who rushed to Deirdre's side, and, after a dignified moment, Rory MacMurdo.

Sammy flashed one more look at Brianna, who now

stood in the center of the hut. He saw her hand the baby to Rory, then he stepped out to get some fresh air. It hit him like a drug and nearly knocked him out.

"Oh, man," he said, rubbing his hands over his stubbled face. "I have got to get some sleep."

"A son," Rory repeated Brianna's words. "I have a son." He took one long look at the babe she held out to him, then moved quickly to Deirdre's side. Her women were fussing over her, cooing and petting her still form. He tried not to see bloody bedclothes and concentrated on her face instead.

"She sleeps," one of the women said. "Poor dear lamb."

He wasn't interested in the servants' opinions. "Is she all right?" he asked Brianna. He tentatively reached out to stroke his wife's tangled hair.

"She needs to rest," Brianna told him. "But with plenty of prayer and Uncle Sean's herbs I think she'll be fine."

He gave a relieved nod and whispered a prayer to gods both old and new. "I'll look at my son now," he said, turning from his sleeping wife. Brianna followed him out of the dark hut. Outside she offered the babe to Rory once more. From the determined look on her face he knew he dared not refuse to hold the child again.

"Like this," she said and showed him. Once he was cradling the babe on his arm she flipped back the cloth covering its head and said, "Look until you're content. I'm going home to bed."

He thought of calling her back but didn't think she'd obey. Her step was tired but firm as she headed up the track toward Ban Ean. "Cormac," he ordered instead, "take Brianna up on your horse and see her to her father's house."

Cormac hurried to obey and Rory was left to contemplate the wonder of his first child. His people gathered around him. The priest prayed, and the poet recited the verse he'd prepared for the occasion. A cart containing more of his wife's servants and the wetnurse she'd chosen came rattling into the yard. While the world bustled around him, Rory looked into the tiny, ugly, wrinkled, red face of his heir and marveled at the wonder of it all.

"There's so much I must do for you, son of my heart," he told his baby.

Rory looked off into the misty distance where ground fog swirled around the hooves of the horse heading up the track. He watched the girl perched behind his brother, her arms clasped tightly around his waist. Jealousy tightened his gut at the sight, not liking to have anyone touching the woman he coveted.

"It's not just that she's beautiful," he explained to his son, cuddling the little warm bundle close to his chest. He began walking toward the waiting wetnurse. "I want Brianna for your sake," he went on. "Her visions will protect us, bring us power. With Brianna's help I'll leave you king of more than three tribes. Now more than ever," he added with one more glance toward the riders disappearing over the crest of the hill, "she must be mine."

9

All Sammy wanted was to find a dry, private place to sleep. He had never been so exhausted in his life. His eyes were burning, begging for a few dozen hours of being firmly closed. His muscles were too tired to ache, and his brain was functioning only on the autonomic level. He wandered off into the sheep field, only to have the black-and-white herd dog run up to him barking and circling menacingly.

Sammy eventually let the dog nudge him toward the sorry excuse for a shed he hadn't thought was good enough for the Harley. He was so tired it looked like the most luxurious bedroom on the planet now. There was a pile of straw or something piled up in the back, and a blanket.

"Thanks, babe," Sammy mumbled to the dog, and was asleep even before he got the blanket pulled up.

The next thing he knew, he was dreaming. He knew he was dreaming because it made a lot more sense than reality did when he was awake. In the dream he was back in Los Angeles. On the balcony. Of his bedroom. Brianna was with him.

"Beautiful skin," he said as he kept on stripping off the heavy layers of clothing covering Brianna's soft, perfect body. She was dressed in layers, like an onion. As he undressed her he licked cool raindrops off her exposed flesh, one slow droplet at a time.

"Sammy?"

"You like that, sweetheart?"

"Indeed I do," her rich, lilting voice whispered huskily in his ear. A breathy sigh blew across his temple, followed by a kiss of soft, warm lips. Her fingers combed through his hair, catching on his curls.

"Ouch!" Sammy complained.

"Hush, love, I'll do you no harm." Her lips found his, her tongue coaxed its way inside his mouth. Her fingers teased at his nipples, his navel, slowly, slowly down to his erection.

Brianna was smiling at him. The raindrops on her bare white breasts sparkled like diamonds. His tongue followed the slow stream of water down to the hard pink tip of her nipple.

He looked up as she touched his cheek with the back of her hand. Her expression was tender and loving and trusting. Sammy felt himself melting inside with a sensation that wasn't lust. He mirrored her gesture, running his rough hand down her silky cheek. She was so soft and delicate and female.

I'm not going to fall in love, he thought. *That's not my style. No commitments. Not me. But—*

Maybe in a dream it was all right to fall in love.

"It's only a dream," he said, and covered her mouth with his, losing thought in sensation.

Then someone kicked him hard in the butt and his reaction was instantaneous and extreme: He pinned the offender beneath him on the ground before he even woke up.

He opened his eyes to find himself looking directly into Brianna's. She seemed both furious and frightened. Her body was warm and soft, just as she had been in the dream, maybe better. And he felt his erection, hard as a rock, pressing against her thigh.

"Uh—" he said stupidly, but he didn't move. His backside ached. "You kicked me."

"Aye, I kicked you. And would have done more!"

He was holding both her wrists in one hand. She struggled, but he didn't let her go. He didn't know why, other than it felt really good to cover her body with his. He could feel her breasts pressed against his chest. Her nipples were hard, as they'd been in the dream.

The dream. Sammy blinked and looked around. Yep, it had been a dream. He wasn't in Los Angeles, but in a shepherd's storage hut somewhere in ancient Ireland. But the girl was the same, and the position was similar, and he still wanted her really badly.

He gave her a slow smile. "I was having the best dream about you."

Her eyes flashed with fury. "Twas a shameful dream, a wicked dream—"

"A damned erotic dream," he couldn't help but interject. "You liked it at the time," he added, then realized what he'd said. He lowered his face close to hers, until their noses were almost touching. "Wait a minute . . . how do you know what I was dreaming?"

"Do you think I don't know when a dream isn't mine?" was her improbable answer.

She squirmed beneath him. Her movements sent

sensual shockwaves through him. He liked the sensations a lot, but he supposed he needed to think with
his head more than with his dick, so he released her
hands and sat up. She scurried to stand while he stayed
seated on the bunched up blanket.

He had a strong impulse to draw her back to him.
She was flushed and breathing hard and he was sure it
wasn't all from anger.

"Brianna, how did you know what I was dreaming?"
he asked, trying to sound calm and reasonable.

"Well, it wasn't a vision," she answered, her expression clearing as she began to explain. "I know what a
vision feels like; it's like watching a moving picture. It
fills the world, but it is something I watch. Dreams are
different; they can come true but they aren't the same
as visions. Not exactly. I know the difference," she
added, though she looked just a little bit confused.
"And I know when they are my own."

"O-kay," Sammy said slowly. He leaned forward,
looking up at her intently. "How did you get into my
dream?"

He remembered that she'd been in his dreams before,
his dreams and his daydreams, calling to him from
across time. "That was invasion of privacy, you know."

"How dare you dream about me!" she demanded
instead of answering his question.

"I can't help what I dream!"

"I was sitting on the back of Cormac's horse," she
went on. "Perhaps I was dozing, for I am so very tired.
Then I felt your hands on me and a soft warm rain and
your lips tasted the rain on my skin. It was—wonderful."

Her cheeks grew flushed again as the last word
came out as a husky whisper. She'd been glaring at
him, but the expression in her eyes turned soft, her lips

parted on a long sigh. It took more restraint than Sammy thought he had to keep from jumping up and taking her in his arms.

Brianna went on. "When I realized that we shared the dream I knew I had to stop it." She glared at him again, and shook her finger. "It was wicked."

He grinned. "It was great."

"It was wrong."

"It was just a dream."

She put her hands on her hips. "You have no business touching me so, even in your dreams. What would your wives think? It's them you should be dreaming of, and pining for."

"Wives?" Sammy tilted his head and repeated, "Wives? I don't have any wives. I don't even have a wife."

Brianna's legs seem to fall out from under her. She was seated on the ground in front of him with an abruptness that made Sammy jump. She looked at him in wide-eyed shock. "You don't?"

"No," he answered, and added a fervent, "thank Buddha. And I don't want any either."

Brianna gave a very slow nod, her eyes never leaving his. There were bright dots of color on her exceedingly pale cheeks. "Well. Then. Good." She cleared her throat. "Good. It's good if you don't want to marry. No one should marry if they don't want to. I certainly don't want to marry."

"Good," he said. "I'm glad. Marriage is—confining. It's better to stay independent."

"Yes, much better."

Sammy suspected that neither of them sounded very convincing, and he didn't know whom they were trying to convince anyway. He gave a big yawn and said, "Listen, babe, I don't think either of us is making much sense. You sleepy?" He could see how the fine skin beneath her eyes was stained with dark rings.

She nodded and rubbed her temples with long, slender fingers. "I have never been so tired in my life," she admitted. "I feel giddy with it."

"Me too," he agreed.

It had begun to rain while they talked. The shed was dry despite the windy downpour going on outside. Brianna glanced outside, but before she could suggest going home, Sammy hauled the blanket from under him and handed it to her. He pointed toward the opposite side of the shed. It was only a few feet away, but that should be enough for propriety's sake.

"Stay here," he said. "The straw in here's kind of comfortable."

She looked from him to the corner to the blanket in her hand, sighed tiredly and said, "A Culdee's rock perch would be comfortable right now."

Without another word she lay down with her back to him, wrapped snugly in the blanket. Sammy watched her affectionately for only a moment before he plopped back down and instantly fell asleep.

Brianna woke to the smell of wet dog, the sense of being watched, and the thought, *He has no wives!*

The thought, she immediately dismissed. The smell was explained by the sight of the herd dog lying in the middle of the floor, exactly halfway between her and Sammy. The sense of being watched came from finding Donal standing with his arms crossed in the doorway.

Brianna sat up as she watched Donal measuring the distance between where she had slept and where Sammy was still curled up, faintly snoring. He must have been satisfied that nothing improper had happened between them because the look he turned on her held no more than ordinary irritation.

"I've eaten in the common house for two days now," he complained. "I'm going to have to get some wives soon, just so I can stay fed."

Brianna did not know what time it was, or even what day, but she felt more rested than she had in a long time. She stood up and stretched, feeling the need to be clean, and in fresh clothes, and fed.

She gazed down at the sleeping giant curled up on his side. She didn't know how long it was since he'd eaten, but a big man like him had to need lots of food, and often. She wondered if she should wake him and take him back to Uncle Sean's, or just fetch him a basket of food from home.

"Lady Deirdre sent me to look for you," Donal said. "She's still at Uncle Sean's. She wants to know when she can go home."

Brianna decided that taking Sammy back to her uncle's wasn't feasible just yet. "I'll go see Deirdre." *After I've had a bath,* she added to herself, *the woman's in no danger.* "How long have I slept?"

She couldn't tell by the dim light outside whether it was dawn or dusk or the middle of the day. It was still raining, but in a soft, misting way.

"I was told you left Sean's just after dawn, it's midday now."

So, she hadn't slept long at all. Well, at least she hadn't dreamed. She nodded and pointed to Sammy. "Don't pester him about lessons. Let him rest."

Donal didn't look pleased, but he gave a grudging nod. Sammy rolled onto his back, then slowly sat up.

"Hey!" he called out as Brianna left. "Where you going?"

He would have followed her, but Donal moved to block the doorway as though he was protecting his sister. Sammy looked up at Brianna's twin and grunted. Then he scratched the gold stubble on his jaw. "I wish I hadn't given up caffeine," he grumbled. "Not that I could get a cup of coffee around here. How's Deirdre and the baby?" he added.

Nobody but Brianna could understand him, and it was starting to get to him. A lot of things about Brianna were starting to get to him. Like how she looked, how she walked and talked, and the things she did. The way she took care of people—he liked that about her. A lot. Except that he figured she was off now to take care of somebody when he needed her to be concentrating on getting him back to the future.

He rubbed his hand across his eyes and wished he hadn't woken up from the earlier dream. It would have been nice to make love to Brianna without any consequences. They could be sleeping peacefully in each other's arms right now if—yeah, if. Why couldn't they just become lovers for a while?

'Cause you're trying to avoid getting tangled up with another psychic who'll just go off and leave you like Karen did, a voice in his head reminded him. *Right. That. Even if she didn't leave you, you'd have to leave her. Yeah, that too. And, judging by how pissed she was about the dream, maybe she doesn't want you.* "Nah," he mumbled, with a slight smile, "she wants me."

Sammy noticed that Donal was eagerly watching his every move. He could tell what Donal wanted. Sammy groaned and stretched. "Oh, God," he said. "Save me from eager students." He got to his feet, though he had to bend over to stand under the low roof. He scratched his stomach while it rumbled hungrily. "I think I'm getting fleas."

He wondered if he should go off looking for Brianna and breakfast, but decided to wait and let her return to him. He wanted to get her in one place, away from all her other obligations, and keep her there while she worked on the spell to get him home.

"Don't worry, Jerry," he said to his friend who waited in jail over a thousand years in the future. "I'll be back soon, man. Everything's going to be okay."

Outside it was warm enough, and not raining anymore. The world Sammy saw around him was green and lush, ragged fog rode the shoulders of nearby hills and the sea stretched out gray and flat in the distance. Tiny fishing boats bobbed on the water of the bay while sheep grazed around the monumental standing stones. Bells—calls to prayer, Sammy guessed—rang out from the village, and the Culdee monastery on the mountainous island just offshore. It was such a peaceful place, Sammy found it hard to remember it was the threat of violence that had brought him here.

"I like it here," he said as Donal followed him outside, where Ailill had been waiting. One couldn't hear him and the other couldn't understand him, but Sammy went on speaking anyway. "I've always liked this place. And I know what's going to happen to it—in a few days or weeks." He sighed. "Shit." He looked at Donal's eager face. "I don't know if I can do any good." He grabbed a long, thick stick up off a pile of firewood just inside the shed's doorway. He held it up and pointed to Donal's sword. "Just draw the damn thing and I'll see if there's anything I can teach you."

*   *   *

At first Brianna thought Sammy was helping her brother chop wood with his sword. From quite a distance, she could see the sword swinging and hear the dull sound of it hitting the branch Sammy held. She realized only as she came close that there was a sword fight of sorts going on. Ailill was sitting on the ground out of the way, leaning against his sleeping hound's broad back. She went to sit next to her foster brother in the damp grass.

The day had turned sunny since she left the pasture, and several hours had passed. She was clean, wearing a fresh white linen dress, her unruly hair was braided into a pair of thick plaits. She carried a basket with bread, cheese, honeycakes, and a stoppered jar of new ale on her arm.

She wore white because it was the druid's color. Wearing white helped remind her of her place, her power and her training. It helped her feel in control, of herself, of the situation, of her raging, confused feelings for Sammy.

Sammy saw her and stopped the exercise to come greet her. "Hi," he said, looming over where she sat. He dropped to his knees in front of her as she busied her hands with the contents of the basket. She passed him a chunk of bread in silence.

He'd taken several hardy bites before he spoke again. "I'm really sorry about the Vikings," he told her.

By this time Donal and Ailill were rooting through the basket. The hound had been pushed aside but was lingering as close as possible to the food, looking beseeching. Sammy tossed the dog some of his bread. It was Sammy's way, Brianna thought, to take care of everything that crossed his path. She admired him greatly for his caring ways.

"Why are you sorry about the Vikings?" she asked him.

She watched Sammy rub his jaw and give an ironic twist of a smile. "'Cause I'm Danish on my dad's side," he said in his beautiful deep voice. "So I apologize on behalf of my ancestors for any inconvenience you might be experiencing."

His chest was bare and she almost didn't pay attention to what he'd said as she studied the flat gold circles of his nipples. Odd, how looking at his made her own go all tight and hard. She smiled at his humor, but he turned back to Donal before she could speak. Which was just as well, since she knew her voice would have been rough with a need she shouldn't be feeling.

Sammy settled beside her cross-legged; Ailill and Donal joined them on the ground.

Sammy spoke to her while he watched Ailill. "I've been wondering about something. Why haven't you used magic to cure Ailill's deafness?"

Brianna's breath caught on an old and unhealed pain; a failure. Her words held no inflection when she spoke. "Do you think I haven't tried?"

"Oh," Sammy said after a long pause. The simple sound held a great deal of sympathy.

Since he asked for no more explanation, she found herself giving it. "I think it is because he cannot hear my singing. I've tried the spell many times, but it never does any good."

"Oh," he said again, and let the subject drop.

"Teach us some more words," she urged. "You have a gift for teaching."

"Thanks," he said, and blushed a little with a modesty she found charming. Every man she knew who was not a monk was given to boasting about his deeds and accomplishments. Sammy did not need to boast, he simply was. Wonderful.

"Anne Bancroft will play you in the movie." She spoke the errant thought aloud as it drifted through her head. "For your miracle working."

Sammy passed a hand in front of her face. "Reality-check time, hon," he said. "This isn't a movie." He shook his head. "I don't know if you're psychic or just hooked up to cable."

"What?"

"Never mind." He patted her on the head. "Why don't I just get back to Ailill?" She nodded and he set to work with his hands to teach her foster brother a new word.

"What word is this?" she asked Sammy after a long silence spent watching them. She tapped her right cheek as Ailill had just done.

"That's the word for 'home,'" he answered. "Watch." Sammy tilted his head forward and raised his eyebrows while he tapped his cheek. "See what I did with my face? I just turned the word into a question. Sign isn't just hand gestures, but a combination of gestures and facial expressions."

Brianna nodded. "I think I see." She repeated what Sammy had done. "Home?" she asked.

"Yeah." His open, friendly expression darkened. "As in, am I ever going to get home?"

Brianna looked away, her fingers curling tensely together in her lap. "I hope so."

"Soon?" He touched her shoulder.

The heat of his touch soaked through the fine material of her dress, deep into her skin. "Uncle Sean's scrolls are—"

"Never mind the scrolls. You weren't consulting any

scrolls when the Vikings were attacking you. Or when you healed the baby's shoulder." He gave her another one of his sunny smiles; the warmth of it flooded her with confidence. "You can do anything." He sprang to his feet. "Do it, right now. Send me home right now."

She didn't think it would be so easy to come up with a spell at a moment's notice, but it was time she started to hunt for the right combination of music and words to send Sammy Bergen back to his own place and time. She felt oddly bereaved at the thought. Perhaps it was just knowing that it was possible to help this big, strong man when she could do nothing for the deaf boy who was so dear to her.

Brianna gave a slow nod, which was rewarded by Sammy's brilliant white smile. "I will try," she agreed.

"All right!" He punched the air with his fist.

Brianna tried to ignore him while he did some odd little dance around her. He was impossible to ignore, so she closed her eyes. While she searched her knowledge to find a clue as to where to begin, Donal stood up and urged Sammy back to fighting practice. Sammy hesitated, but he went, leaving Brianna to concentrate on her work.

The trouble was, she couldn't get her mind off the conversation they'd had about Ailill. It occurred to her that perhaps Sammy was the miracle the boy needed as he was teaching him a language when all her spells had done him no good. Then she recalled how much stronger her magic was in Sammy's presence, how his strength flowed into her when she sang. Perhaps the spell she'd sung so often to bring understanding to Ailill would work if she tried in Sammy's presence. She would try it first, she decided. All it could do was fail again. She would sing for the child, then she would concentrate on Sammy's.

Brianna blocked out her awareness of the world, took a deep breath, and began to sing. Within a few moments, something began to happen.

"Whoa!" Sammy said as the earth moved under his feet. He was from L.A., he was used to it, but this tremor shot down from his head to ground itself in the soil. While the world shook his head rang, his tongue swelled, and everything spun before his eyes.

This is it, he thought, *she's done it. I'm going home!* He became too dizzy to keep his eyes open and watch the world go by. So he closed them and hoped he'd see West Hollywood when he opened them again. The hope was bittersweet, but he tried not to let that bother him.

He would have backed away from Donal if he knew where the other man was. All he knew was that his senses were whirling. He could only hope no one else got caught in the energy field Brianna was generating.

When she stopped singing the dizziness dissipated, and he was sitting on the ground. The grass was damp, the air smelled fresh, of sheep and the sea, and he knew he wasn't back in West Hollywood. He hadn't gone anywhere, but energy tingled through him. Energy and excitement, and he knew *something* had happened. He lifted his head slowly, opened his eyes, and saw Donal sitting next to him, looking stunned.

"Looks like we're both still here. So," Sammy said to the would-be warrior, "what the hell was that all about?"

"I don't know," Donal answered. In English. "But it was a hell of a rush." Donal's eyes narrowed. He looked in confusion at Sammy. "A what?"

10

Apparently, he and Donal could now talk to each other.

"Uh," Sammy said, momentarily inarticulate despite this new development. "Uh. I think—" Sammy saw Brianna lying in a crumpled heap on the ground and rushed to her side.

"Brianna!" Donal called as he sprang to his feet. "What have you done?"

She opened her eyes, found herself in Sammy's strong embrace, and paid no mind to her brother's carping question. "Did it work?" she asked, wondering if she should make some move to detach herself from Sammy. After all, she felt perfectly all right, just tired. She rested her forehead against his bare chest, breathing in his scent, attuning herself to the rhythm of his heartbeats. She put her hands against his chest as he drew breath to speak, and felt the slight shudder that went through him at her touch.

"I'm still here," was his answer as he took her by the shoulders and pushed her gently away.

"Of course you are." She looked around and found Ailill perched nearby on the smallest of the standing stones. "Hello," she said, hoping he would answer her.

He didn't. He just smiled.

"I'm still here," Sammy repeated.

Though she didn't need the assistance she let him help her to her feet. "Of course you are," she repeated. "I was working on the spell for Ailill." She glanced back at the boy. "I don't think it worked."

It was Donal who responded. "Well, something happened. Didn't it?" He addressed the question to Sammy.

"Donal understands what I'm saying," Sammy told her. "And I understand him."

"Ah," she said, somewhat pleased. She rubbed her eyes sleepily. She wanted to take a nap. "The spell does work, then. It just doesn't work on Ailill." The look she turned on Sammy was almost accusatory. "I had hopes."

"What about me?" Sammy demanded. He pointed to his wide bronze-colored chest. Brianna found herself studying the sculpted muscles of his stomach. "You were supposed to be working on getting me home."

"I'll get to that," she told him. She put her hands on her hips and looked from him to Donal. "At least some progress has been made, now hasn't it?"

Sammy looked glum for a few moments, but she didn't think it was possible for him to be despondent for long. Soon his expression cleared and he gave a firm nod. "Yeah, I was getting tired of not being able to communicate with anybody, not that I don't enjoy talking to you, but—"

"I understand," she said.

"Here's some useful magic out of the girl at last," Donal said as he clapped Sammy on the back.

Brianna bristled at her brother's words, but it was Sammy who rounded angrily on him. "Don't you appreciate what you've got in Brianna? Don't you know how special she is? She's got this fantastic power, but does she use it for herself? No. All I've seen her do since I got here is take care of everybody else."

Special? Sammy thought she was special?

Donal backed quickly away from Sammy as the big man went angrily on, "Who the hell are you to make fun of her talent?"

"He's my brother," Brianna answered for her twin. "He is ever the first to defend me when he isn't teasing me himself."

"Brother," Sammy repeated with a derisive snort. "Yeah, brothers are like that," he added, his anger gone as quickly as it was sparked.

That he had leaped to defend her left a glow deep within Brianna. He dreamed of her, he knew the true meaning of her dreams, and he was kind to her and protective. "Sammy Bergen," she said fervently, "I have got to get you home."

Soon. Before he broke her heart with his going.

Donal approached Sammy once more, holding his hand. "I'm almost sorry I can understand your speech," he said as Sammy took Donal's hand in the clasp of friendship, then for some reason, shook it. When Sammy released him, Donal's fingers were white from the pressure the other man had exerted. "The teaching will go faster now," Donal said as he flexed fingers that had to be aching. "And now you can speak to our father about what has to be done."

Brianna knelt down and began to repack the basket of food while Sammy gave Donal a puzzled look. "Rory has fetched his wife home," she said. "I think I should straighten up Uncle Sean's house and have a meal waiting for him when he gets home from Canaire."

"Wait a minute," Sammy said, putting a hand out to stop her as she got up to leave. "What about the spell?" He glanced at Donal. "What am I supposed to talk to your father about?"

"About defending Ban Ean," Donal said.

At the same time she answered, "I can sing the spell while I sweep the floor."

"But," Sammy faltered. "Don't I have to be there, with you, while you work the magic?"

A part of her hoped that he just liked being with her. She dismissed the foolish notion as she said, "I've no idea." And, to keep him from being with her for a while so she could get her thoughts off him, she went on, "Go with Donal. Talk to Father."

"The Norsemen are coming to kill us," Donal added. "The king has many villages to protect. He may not be able to come to us at need. You are here. You can show us what to do to protect ourselves. You must convince Father that we have to defend ourselves."

Sammy didn't know why anyone would need to be convinced of something so obvious. Donal seemed desperately worried, and Brianna was already on her way to Sean's, gone before he could make a decision. Sammy watched her go, appreciating the way she moved, slender, graceful, and unconsciously sensual. The sun was lost in the night darkness of her hair, though it gleamed off the pure white dress she wore loosely belted at her narrow waist.

"Aye, she's a beauty," Donal told him as Brianna walked out of earshot. Donal planted himself in front of Sammy, taking his attention off the view of his sister. "With beauty like that," Donal went on, "some Norseman will take her for a slave soon. I won't have that happen to my sister, or to the women I would marry. Ban Ean needs your help, Sammy."

Cold anger tightened in Sammy's gut as Donal's words conjured up the specter of raped and abused women. Sammy had seen the effects of that kind of treatment in his own supposedly more civilized time. It wasn't going to happen here. Not to Brianna or anyone else. He wasn't going to let it.

"Okay," he said, nodding to Donal in agreement. "Let's do it. We're going to get Ban Ean's act together before those bastards show up."

A fierce grin spread across Donal's face. "I knew you were sent to protect us when I saw the white bird on your arm."

Sammy didn't know if he agreed with that, but he did say, "Let's go talk to your dad."

"Why won't they listen to me?" Sammy asked.

He stopped in front of Brianna and Donal, who were seated on the broad top step of the church. In the hours that had passed since he'd come to Ban Ean with Donal he'd been growing more and more frustrated. He knew he should try one of his usual techniques— meditation or practicing forms—to work off the growing agitation but all he could seem to do was pace.

"Why?" he demanded again.

"They're monks," Donal reminded him. "Men of peace."

"Tell me about it," Sammy grumbled.

With Donal's help, he'd spent a long time talking to the abbot about organizing the villagers against attack. Brianna had come in at some point in the afternoon. and sat down beside him at the table in the common house. She helped Donal interpret, but she hadn't added any enthusiastic endorsement to the plan. It had been good to have her seated beside him since she was the only thing that made any concrete sense in this place. Sammy had had to use a great deal of restraint to keep from putting his arm around her waist, thinking her parent might misinterpret the casual gesture. Her father didn't like him, Sammy could tell.

He liked having Brianna with him, but while she was translating for him she wasn't off working on the spell to take him back to the future. He hadn't said anything to her about the spell, but at one point she did whisper, "Never fear, Sammy, I'm singing to myself."

While she sang to herself the abbot had looked at him as if Sammy might go up in a puff of magic smoke at any minute. Sammy decided the abbot was the most unworldly man he'd ever met. The discussion had been long but not very useful. In the end, late in the afternoon, the abbot finally said he'd talk over Sammy's suggestions with the rest of the monks. They were in the common house talking right now.

"I wish I'd never thought about talking to your father," Sammy complained.

"Grandfather would probably agree with you," Brianna told him. "Of course, he isn't here."

"He took everyone with a bit of sense to Rome with him," her brother added.

Brianna chuckled. "What does that say about us, Donal?"

Donal stood, his gaze on Bridget and Moira, who were walking toward the well. He was smiling broadly at the girls when he answered, "It says we're the luckiest pair of twins in all of Eire." He pointed to Sammy. "Would we have found the loves of our lives if Grandfather had taken us with him?"

He didn't wait for Sammy or Brianna to answer, but hurried off toward his girlfriends.

Brianna looked away from Sammy, embarrassed over her brother's statement. "Pay him no mind," she said quietly. "He is a fool."

Sammy stared at her in shock. He cleared his throat. "Yeah, uh—"

She stood up. "It's all right. People are bound to think foolish, false things if we kiss and such in public."

"Uh," he said. He put his hands on her waist. He didn't know why he did that, but she didn't move away when he did. He did feel a slight shudder go through her, but he knew it wasn't from fear. Such a small, delicate waist. He really could circle it with his big hands. So he did. "Yeah." Such a beautiful, wide mouth. Her tongue darted out to moisten her lips. He couldn't resist the sensuality of the gesture.

"Are you thinking of kissing me?" she asked conversationally, as he began to tilt his head toward hers. "Because it will have to wait if you are."

"Huh?"

She stepped away from him. She was looking past his shoulder. "The meeting in the common house is over," she told him.

He turned to see the abbot and a trio of older monks coming toward them. He and Brianna went to meet them. Face to face he saw that the men looked grave, but he couldn't detect any immediate concern for their safety.

When the abbot gave him a rather blithe, reassuring smile, Sammy said, "Uh-oh." He considered pulling on his hair in frustration even before the abbot spoke.

Brianna translated. "He says that we thank you for your concern, but this is a house of God."

So he wasn't going to get official permission to train the monks. He guessed there had to be some other way to get them interested in helping themselves.

"It was worth a shot, I guess," he said to Brianna.

She ached for the disappointed worry she saw in Sammy's face. The man meant well by her people.

"Father," Brianna began, trying once more to convince her father, "Sammy only wants to—"

"It is Rory MacMurdo's duty to God and man to defend us from the Norsemen," one of the other monks cut her off.

"Rory." Brianna gave a snort. "Rory is miles away, and Sammy is right here."

Before she could go on, her father leveled a stern look at her. "Our king will defend us, daughter," he said. "It is a king's duty to defend the abbeys in his kingdom. We are men of peace. We do not go into battle like our druid ancestors." He shook a finger at her. "You forget that while you are permitted to learn the old ways you have no allegiance to the old gods."

"Yes, Father, but—"

"I am not finished." Her father darted a sideways, accusing glance at Sammy before he continued to lecture her. "You have a duty to the king as well, do you not?"

For some reason her father, her mild and gentle father, had a sly, devious look about him. His attitude worried her.

"No," she answered despite her sudden concern.

She kept her tone mild but gave her father a warning look. "I have no duty to marry him."

"I think you will be marrying Rory MacMurdo soon," he told her. "I think you will have no choice."

"I think you are wrong," she replied. She'd had this discussion too many times; she didn't want to have it today. Usually she just evaded all suggestions, orders, and pleas to wed the king. Now she was just angry and tired of the whole thing, but she hated arguing with her father. "Uncle Sean needs me," she said to get away, though Uncle Sean had sent her home hours ago when he returned from Canaire.

"Go then," her father said. He sounded as frustrated as she did. He glanced uneasily at Sammy, who gave him a friendly smile. "And take your fairy lord with you to the druid. We'll have none of his violent ways in Ban Ean."

Brianna gave Sammy an apologetic look. "I didn't think they'd listen," she said. "But at least you tried."

Sammy could feel the abbot's disapproving gaze on his back until they were out of sight of Ban Ean. "Well, that didn't seem to go well," he said as they took the path across the sheep meadow.

"You've a gift for understatement. My father's not usually so stubborn about anything. In fact, he can usually be talked into anything that doesn't concern Grandfather's marriage plans for me and Donal."

It was a beautiful late afternoon, the world around them was green and bright, with sunlight sparkling off the ocean in gold glints. The standing stones in the meadow threw off sharp, clean shadows, looking more decorative than mysterious reminders of ancient times and gods.

"This is the most beautiful place I've ever seen," Sammy told Brianna.

"Aye," she agreed. "It is."

And you're the most beautiful woman I've ever seen, he thought. *And you're funny and smart and caring and brave, and you dragged me here where I can't do any good, and you are all going to die.* He couldn't stay angry at her; he couldn't blame her. He tried, though, thinking it might be safer to be angry instead of letting himself be attracted to Brianna. That it might be better to be angry than to let the knowledge of Ban Ean's future break his heart.

As they walked along the path to Sean's house he took her hand in his. She didn't pull away, and her touch was unaccountably calming. She was vibrantly alive right now. It gave him hope that something could be done. Gradually the silence they walked in grew more agreeable than tense. After a while she began to sing, and Sammy let himself get lost in the beauty of her voice. The brief peace made their walk seem far too short.

Much to his annoyance, he found the Harley parked out front instead of safely stored inside. He dropped her hand and began to inspect the machine.

"What's it doing out here?"

"Uncle Sean said he didn't like the beast staring at him out of the shadows," Brianna said as Sammy went over the motorcycle, caressing it with the tenderness he reserved for lovers and Harley-Davidsons. "He made me help him push it outside when he couldn't wake it up." She didn't sound at all happy about having to touch the Harley.

It finally occurred to him that these people thought the motorcycle was actually a living creature. He wondered if he should try to explain about internal combustion engines to someone from the Dark Ages, and decided it wasn't worth it. "It's not going to hurt you, you know," he told her, and gave her a reassuring smile. "I wouldn't let it."

Sammy decided the Harley had come to no harm from being hauled outside. He went to the door, but Brianna shook her head. She pointed to the bench by the wall, and Sammy sat, looking at her for an explanation.

"Uncle Sean's asleep," she told him as she sat down beside him. "Poor man," she added. "He never gets enough rest."

Sammy didn't stop himself from putting his arm around her this time. She stiffened, then let herself relax against him as he asked, "And you do?"

Brianna knew she had no business being cradled at the big man's side, but the breeze off the sea was growing cool as the sun began to go down, and Sammy's warmth was a welcome comfort. There was nothing soft about this man, except perhaps his heart. He felt as if he was made of iron, yet she reveled in the feel of his hard muscled body. It was wrong, but it felt very right.

She sighed. "I should be working on the time-travel spell."

"Yeah, you should," he agreed. He touched a finger to her cheek. "Rest for a while. Magic takes a lot out of you. You have to take care of yourself."

No one, not even Uncle Sean, had ever said such a thing to her before. She'd grown up believing that to have the Gift meant spending her life giving. Sammy seemed to think her needs were important. His concern warmed her heart as much as the heat from his flesh warmed her body. She closed her eyes and found herself remembering his dream. Would he ever touch her that way in reality? Did she want him to?

She almost laughed aloud at such childish questions. Of course she wanted him to. She was a flesh-and-blood woman, wasn't she? And he was everything a woman could wish a man to be. Hadn't it been her needs, unknown even to herself, that had dragged him all unwilling from his people and place to her side?

"I should be ashamed," she muttered, then sighed. She turned her head to look at him and saw the concern in his eyes. It burned her. "What if I cannot get you back to the smoking city?"

Sammy saw Brianna's guilt and fear, and it twisted his heart painfully. He wanted to take her face between his hands and kiss all her worries away. To tell her that he was there for her and everything was going to be okay. But that was the point, wasn't it? He was there.

"You'll get me back," he told her. "You have to." Then he explained, trying to keep his words as simple and clear as possible. "I run a school where I come from, teaching fighting. The school is in a town called Venice Beach, which is not the safest place in the world. Still, I like it there. People know better than to bother me, but the local kids do get into fights with my students sometimes. Somebody was killed in one of these fights a few weeks back and one of my students was accused of causing the death. He didn't do it. I was there, I saw what happened. We were in a place where people go to drink, it was loud and noisy and dark, but I saw what happened. Other witnesses say Jerry Park killed the other man. I'm the only one who says he didn't. When he goes to trial in three weeks, I have to be there to tell the judge what I saw."

"To save him," she said, slowly nodding. "To keep him from being executed."

To keep him from going to prison, which in this case

would be the same as a death sentence, since there were members of the same gang as the man who'd been killed already doing time, Sammy knew. But he didn't try to explain modern hatreds and loyalties to an innocent young woman from the ninth century.

"That's right," he told her. "I have to go back to save his life."

Looking into her tear-filled eyes he couldn't help but think, *If it weren't for Jerry I almost wouldn't mind staying.* He was well aware of the irony of the thought, since he was the loner, the man who always moved on. Now, here he was, vaguely considering staying in the one place that was impossible to stay in. Typical.

Brianna looked bereft. "If he's beheaded, it will be my fault."

"I didn't say—"

"It's true."

The pain in her voice caused him to flinch. He wished he'd kept his mouth shut. "Don't worry, babe, I've got faith in you. You can do anything."

After a few moments of looking into his eyes, she blinked back tears. "I can?" She sounded as if she wanted desperately to believe him.

He stood up and took her hands to draw her to her feet. "Sure," he said. He looked around, hunting for a way to distract her from her sadness and worry. He spotted the Harley and tugged her toward it. "Come on, let's go for a ride."

She dug in her heels in and shouted, "What?"

He ignored her resistance and kept pulling her forward. "Sure," he said cheerfully. "It'll get our minds off our troubles."

She stared from him to the motorcycle and back, wild-eyed. "But—the beast—"

"Is mine," he cut her off firmly. "I won't let it harm you." He picked her up and plunked her down on the seat on the back of the bike. She looked at him in open-mouthed horror while he casually swung on in front of her. "Tuck your skirts in."

She shrieked as the engine roared to vibrating life beneath them. Then she grabbed for his waist as the cycle began to roll forward.

He laughed and yelled back, "Hold on tight!" as he gunned the engine and they sped away.

11

The solid warmth of Brianna pressing herself tightly against his back held more reality for Sammy than the countryside around them. It was beautiful, a place of green woods and fields. The sky overhead was going from purple to orange in the west as the sun began to disappear below the horizon. Sammy rode away from the sunset, away from the sea and the village. Away from worries about either his or Brianna's future, away from threats from Vikings and concerns over Jerry's trial.

He went slowly, because the road was almost nonexistent and Brianna was trembling. The last thing he wanted to do was scare her. In fact, he didn't ride for long at all but stopped the cycle about half a mile from the village on the top of a wooded hill.

Brianna was plastered to him, her fingers digging into his ribcage. Her cheek was soft against the back of his neck, her breath tickled through his wind-tangled hair.

He tried not to think about why she was pressed so close to him. *She's just scared,* he thought. *Or cold.* He planted his feet solidly on the ground, balancing the heavy weight of the machine as he turned it off. Brianna stayed where she was as the roar of the engine died. He liked the feeling of her all over him. That was one of the great things about riding motorcycles: there was an element of intimacy and trust that had to exist between two people on the back of a cycle. He let the intimacy continue for a few moments as he looked up at the sky.

Stars were beginning to come out overhead. There were more than he was used to seeing in the night, with no light pollution from any nearby towns spreading up to obscure the darkness.

"You know," Sammy said, "I don't miss jet trails. And it's so quiet here."

His deep, rumbling voice penetrated through the terror that had locked on to Brianna's mind when the beast leaped to life. Just hearing Sammy's voice was calming. The solidness of his big body was comforting. His calm attitude as he straddled the still beast reassured her. Her fear of it drained away, but still she was reluctant to move. Being so near him felt—right. Though perhaps it would feel even better if he were to turn around so she could find out what the front of him felt like.

She lifted her head in shock at her own wanton curiosity. The dark intimacy of dreams was one thing. Out here in the open, beneath the stars of heaven, she knew wanting him could not be right. Or if it was right, it wasn't proper.

Then it occurred to her as she jumped off the beast that she was alone with a strange man as the night drew down. What would her father say? And why had she not considered his censure when she agreed to this wild ride?

Her legs were shaky. Sammy climbed off the resting beast and put a hand out to steady her. "Easy." His voice was soothing. Then he grinned and asked, "How'd you like your first ride?"

She thought that if she told him the truth he wouldn't take her up behind him once more, and she wanted very much to stretch herself out against him again. She'd very much liked that part; she was still tingling all over from it. She simply must accept that she had wanton thoughts and needs whether they were proper or not. Having them didn't mean she had to act on them, though she suspected she would if very much time passed alone with this man. At this moment, she was eager to be alone with this man. Eager for a taste of the forbidden.

"It was—" She couldn't find the words, so she just threw back her head and laughed with pleasure, her worries forgotten.

"Awright!" Sammy crowed. "I knew you'd like it." He took a step closer to her. "Were you frightened?"

Brianna thought that if she admitted that she had indeed been frightened he might feel compelled to comfort her. He might put his arms around her and hold her close again, to make sure she was all right, of course. It would feel very good to be wrapped by the big man's solid warmth.

"Yes," she admitted with a tremulous nod. "I was frightened."

He moved closer. His fingers brushed through her hair, then across her throat, leaving a most delightful trail of sensation. His hands splayed across her shoulders. He drew her closer. "Are you frightened now?" he asked, a teasing light in his eyes.

He moved closer still, and so did she, but before

their bodies could touch a great explosion of light burst into Brianna's mind, beginning to cut off all awareness of the present. She knew she fell down, only because she always fell down when this happened. She closed her eyes and gave herself up to the vision of the future with a melancholy sigh.

The warriors scaled the cliff just before dawn. They'd crossed the whale road on a summer's viking. They came for treasure, to plunder gold and silver and jewels and slaves. They came to drink blood with their swords and battle-axes. Monks were like sheep perched up on their high rocks, easy to slaughter. Taking their lives was no challenge, only a pleasant game.

It was matins. The monks were kneeling in their little windowless chapel, their emaciated forms bent over in fervent worship. Gerald, the youngest of the bishop's sons, was kneeling just before the altar, his eyes fixed on the plain cross hanging on the wall above. When the Norsemen burst into the chapel, they skewered him with a sword through his back, and he died.

There was fire then, mixed with blood and smoke. Screams, pleas, laughter, howling frustration when no treasure was found. Bodies were flung from the cliff, some burning, some screaming. No one lived. Not one single monk survived the invasion of their austere mountain perch.

"Uncle Gerald!" she cried out as her eyes flew open.

Grief tore at her heart. She had not seen her uncle since he'd taken himself off to live in a mendicant's cell three years before. In a few days he'd be dead. He, and all those who followed him.

Brianna whimpered, became aware of tears on her cheeks, a voice speaking anxiously in her ear, and the vision faded. The world came back.

Sammy was in it, solid, large, real, even though the moon had come up and its silvery light on his hair made him seem almost insubstantial. He was seated on the dew-damp grass and she was cradled on his lap. He stroked her cheeks, wiping off the tears, then held her close again while she mourned the future she could see but couldn't change.

Sammy had grabbed Brianna as soon as she went stiff and started to fall. Her eyes rolled back in her head as he eased her to the ground. Then she began to mumble about future events. Watching her awakened painful memories for him. While he comforted the upset girl he tried not to think about other times like this, with Karen.

He'd known people with psychic powers before. "Maybe too many," he said unhappily while he'd held the girl, waiting for her to come out of it. He listened carefully, gradually realizing that she was seeing an attack on the monastery out on the island.

Visions don't always make sense, he reminded himself. There's personal symbolism to take into account.

He didn't know if he had the strength to get involved with another girl with strange gifts again. And to think he'd been regretting having to leave Brianna not very long ago. Now he knew that leaving her would be best for both of them.

"What do you think's going to happen to your uncle Gerald?" he asked once he had her attention.

She wiped the back of her hand across her cheeks.

"He's going to die," she said. "They all are. The Norse-men are coming to kill them."

Sammy brushed damp hair off her face. "Not neces-sarily." Just because you saw it doesn't mean it's going to really happen."

She heard the reassurance in his voice, but she didn't understand what he meant. "Of course it does. I See true."

"You've got a lot of power, but that doesn't mean you've got a lock on the truth. Nobody is one hundred percent accurate. Just because you saw your uncle die doesn't mean he will."

"I saw it. It will happen."

"Maybe. Maybe not."

Why was he questioning her vision? "I saw it. I know what will happen."

"No. You just think you do."

Brianna stiffly removed herself from his embrace. She stood, and looking proudly down on him, she said coldly, "I see. You think I am a liar."

Sammy sprang to his feet and moved with a speed and agility that made her flinch unsteadily back a step. He put a hand out to catch her before she could fall. "I didn't say you're a liar," he said, as he stood with his hands on her shoulders. "What I'm saying is that the future can be changed. 'Always in motion is the future,' like Master Yoda once said."

Brianna had a fleeting image of a wise-eyed creature with amazingly expressive ears. "Warring stars," she said. *"The Empire Kicks Ass."*

"Strikes Back. The Empire Strikes Back. Yoda's—"

"Spoken by the Wizard of Oz."

"Frank Oz. That's who did Yoda's voice." He shook her shoulders just a little. "We aren't talking about Yoda. Yoda isn't real."

"But you said—"

"Oh, boy. I definitely pushed the wrong button in your head, here. Other people have a subconscious, you have a remote control."

"What?"

"Never mind. I'm babbling. I always end up babbling around psychic women. I don't even remember what we were talking about." He paused for a moment to calm his breathing. "I'm sorry," he said when he looked at her again. "I'm mad at somebody else and taking it out on you. It's not your fault you remind me of Karen."

He turned around and did things to the beast while Brianna stared at the bunched muscles of his back.

Why was he questioning her Sight? What did he mean that the future could be changed? Why was he putting new thoughts into her head? Most importantly, who was Karen? And why did she care?

Questions. Too many questions. Too many changes. What had she unleashed on Ban Ean, and herself, when she brought this man into her world?

"I want you to go away," she said. "I need you to go away."

Sammy spun back to face her. He was surprised by the fierceness of her words. Surprised and a little hurt. "Why?"

"You change things," she told him. After a tense hesitation she pointed to herself. "You change me."

Change is good, he thought. He found himself taking a step closer. "Oh?" he asked, voice low. "How?" An inner voice warned that he shouldn't be asking, that he ought to run for his freedom, but he wanted to know. "How do I change you?"

"You make me think new things." After a long thoughtful moment, she added, almost guiltily, "You make me want to see what's beyond the next hill."

He moved closer. "So? What's wrong with that?"

She shook her head, fiercely trying to deny what she was feeling. "Because then I'll want to see what's beyond the next hill, then the next, and then I won't know how to get back to Ban Ean." She scrunched her fists up tightly at her sides. A tear rolled down her cheek. "I won't belong in my own world anymore."

She looked so hurt and lost Sammy couldn't help but take her into his arms. He held her close, trying to give comfort, painfully aware she was a woman. Even trying to give comfort, he wanted her. Even as they'd been fighting, his need for her had been growing.

"I won't belong here," she whispered tearfully against his chest. She looked up at him. "I already don't."

There was anguish in her eyes, and hope. Sammy couldn't stand it anymore. He kissed her. It wasn't the answer to either of their dilemmas, but it seemed like the only thing to do.

The strength of the arms holding her both overwhelmed and comforted. The masculine smell and taste of him heated her senses. This was nothing like their first kiss. There was shared desperation in this kiss, and a little anger. She wanted this kiss, even though she tasted her own tears as much as she tasted Sammy as her lips eagerly opened beneath his questing tongue.

Her body grew taut with desire, her skin heated and sensitive. Trembling, her head fell back against the strong support of his arm. Sammy's mouth moved lower, and then the intimate thrill of having him taste the hollow of her throat amazed and delighted her. His hand touched her breast. She ached inside, and arched against him.

Then she hauled her mind back from all this heady

pleasure, refusing to let it overwhelm her. She put her hand on his chest, and pushed.

"Stop," she said. "Enough."

For now, a wanton whisper went through her. *Forever,* she adamantly answered the demon of longing Sammy had awoken in her. Longing. Passion. Desire. Aye, and pain and suffering too. These were words for the poets and singers, the harpers' stock in trade. She knew all the old songs of lovers forever parted, by fate and war and fairy spells.

Sammy stepped away from her, disappointing a part of her with his instant reaction to her words. "I'm sorry," he said.

"I will not live my life as a song to make the women weep as they ply their needles. Besides," she added, with a proud lift of her head, "I am not Karen."

Sammy wasn't sure he understood exactly what Brianna was talking about, but he did know one thing. "You're not Karen," he agreed.

He'd never felt this way about Karen. Not that he wanted to examine what he felt, because he suspected the *L* word, and maybe even the *C* word were lurking around, waiting to pop out and mess up his mind. Horny, he told himself. He was just horny. He could deal with the *H* word. No problem. Though pulling back when she'd asked him to stop had been very hard to do.

"I better take you home," he told her.

"Aye," she agreed. "It's past time."

Brianna followed him back to the beast. She didn't protest when he lifted her on, just stiffened a little. "You've had a rough time," he said. "I'm sorry."

"It is the vision. They always leave me confused." Though not as confused as Sammy's words and actions had, she added to herself.

She was weary enough to relax against him the moment he settled himself in front of her. She told herself it couldn't be helped, to ride the beast safely she must hang on to him or risk a deadly fall.

The beast came to life, and this time she found the way its deep growl vibrated through her body more pleasant than alarming. She found that she'd eased closer to Sammy's back by the time they began to move.

If it hadn't been for the memory of the future lurking at the back of her mind, and the knowledge both man and monster would soon be out of her life, she might actually have enjoyed this second ride on Sammy's black beast.

Brianna was suffering from a tremendous headache when she crawled out of her pallet the next morning. The thought of eating was impossible, though she fixed a quick meal for her family. Her pain did not fade as the sun came up and the day went on.

She was occasionally ill after a particularly detailed vision of the future came to her. People no longer asked her how she felt when she was pale and drawn-looking, they asked her what she had seen.

She was oddly grateful for the pain pounding through her skull. She accepted it as penance for her wanton behavior and her immoral longings. It also helped keep her from thinking too hard about anything. Especially Sammy.

While silence reigned during mass, she saw the looks sent her way and was prepared for the interrogation that would come as soon as the prayers ended. The vision remained vivid in her mind, but she was reluctant to recount it in words. There was blood and death coming to the monks on the island. She hated to be the one to bring Ban Ean that grim news. For, though the Culdees had shut themselves off from the community to live their anchorite existence, the ascetic men on the island were still the beloved blood kin of the villagers.

Her father stopped her just as she was leaving the church to drag herself about her duties. He took her aside, out of the rain, beneath the carved eaves of the church entrance.

She was prepared to get on with telling him about the coming attack. She wished she'd said something last night, but everyone had made such a silly fuss over her riding alone with Sammy on his beast that she'd pressed her lips tightly together and stubbornly gone off to her bed. Besides, she had been full of the doubts Sammy had planted and feared that she had not seen true. She felt no doubts now, just a weariness of spirit.

But instead of asking her what news her Sight had brought to her, her father said, "It's in my mind that I should speak to you about the matter of your marriage day."

Taken by surprise, all Brianna could do was blurt out, "What? Again?"

"A message arrived from Rory yesterday. He sent a fine silk dress for your wedding, and ten black cows."

"He promised fifty," she said. She was not going to discuss wedding finery, but the cows were important.

Her father was smiling in his kindly, absent way, though Brianna thought she detected a bit of unfamiliar slyness in his expression. "The cows were but a token of honor," he told her. "A present to me, so I might give them back to him as part of your dowry."

"I don't want a dowry." Inwardly, she bristled at the idea she was worth only ten cows, even as a secondary wife. She put such proud feelings out of her head, to concentrate on the more practical matter. "He promised fifty cows to the church if his *wife* gave birth to a healthy son." Brianna had plans for those cows, some for milk cows and some for trade and some for salt beef for the winter. "The man should not make promises he does not intend to keep. You must send word to him that the church must have what it is owed."

Her father shook his head. "You sound like your grandfather."

Brianna sighed but held her tongue on the retort that someone had to. The discussion helped dispel not only her headache but the heavy feeling she realized now was nothing more than self-pity. It put her thoughts firmly back where they belonged, concerned with her care of Ban Ean. It was time, she decided, to settle this marrying Rory nonsense once and for all.

She put the matter of the cows out of her mind for now. "I will not leave Ban Ean to marry Rory MacMurdo. My duty to—"

"It is time you recalled your duty to the family, child," her father said in his mild but insistent way. "Rory's messenger reminded me most strongly about where the king thinks your duty lies."

Rory thinks my duty lies in lying under him, she thought, shocking herself with her own crudeness. She blamed Sammy for putting thoughts of the deeds men and woman did in the dark into her head.

"You're a woman grown, and should have been married long ago," her father reminded her. "Your studies are done. Sean tells me there's little more he can teach you. He told me so just the other day."

"Did he?" Brianna asked, and heard the dangerous edge in her voice.

Everyone, even dearly loved Uncle Sean, thought marriage to Rory MacMurdo would be good for the family. She knew she should feel guilty for jeopardizing any advantage that could be gained for them, but she didn't. Rory was the one thing she could not be obedient about. What was she going to have to do to rid herself of the king's unwanted attentions? Enter her aunt Ethni's convent and take Roman vows? Marry another man?

Marry another man? Now here was a logical solution she'd never considered before. Marry another man. Whom? Everyone knew Rory wanted her. No one in Ban Ean would dare to offer for her. And there wasn't anyone among the dear, gentle souls in Ban Ean she wanted either.

Her father shook his finger at her, a harsh gesture indeed from the gentle man. "Will Rory want you if he finds out you've spent time alone with the fairy lord? Oh, I doubt not your virtue, girl."

She was glad her father didn't doubt it, because she certainly did. She hoped his faith in her would keep her strong if temptation presented itself again. "Thank you, Father."

As she spoke the answer to her dilemma with the king struck her so hard it sent her senses reeling. She almost laughed, though why the answer should fill her with delight she did not know. Of course, she should marry the fairy lord. Of course it would be no marriage, for Sammy would be going away as soon as she could find the correct spell. In fact, he need not even know that they planned to marry. Sammy knew nothing of their language and customs. He could help her without her doing any harm to him.

All she had to do was lie to her father.

It was not easy, but she would do it. And, though the responsibility for her action was her own, she blamed Sammy for giving her this weapon she was going to use. It was Sammy who put new ideas in her head, told her the Sight might not always be the truth, taught her that she could, perhaps, manipulate her own future.

She looked her father in the eye and said, "I have seen the man whom I will wed. I have conjured him up with a spell Uncle Sean taught me." She knew she should say more, but her courage failed her. Her cheeks hot with shame, she rushed away from the church door.

Her father followed her out into the village square. "Come back here, girl!" he called. "What do you mean your uncle taught you a love spell?" She ignored him and walked on. "What devilment have you been up to? Who is this love you've used magic to conjure?"

"Hi," said Sammy, giving her a welcoming smile as he came around the corner of a house and stepped into the square in front of her. Ailill and his wolfhound trotted after.

"Who?" her father repeated, coming up behind her.

Brianna very nearly laughed despite the knowledge that she was sinning against her dear father, despite the knowledge of doom to befall the Culdees weighing her down. Her own problems with the king were at the front of her mind just now and she had to do something quickly.

"Who?" her father asked again, tugging on her cloak.

Brianna turned and gestured toward Sammy. "Him," she said, her voice sure and strong despite her inner trembling. "The lord of the fairies."

12

"Your dad okay?"

Brianna watched as her father disappeared into the church, shutting the door behind him, then looked back at Sammy. "He's fine."

Sammy rubbed his fresh-shaved jaw. "I don't know, he looked like he'd just seen a ghost before he took off. What was he in such a hurry for?"

Brianna did not want to tell the man that her lies about him had sent her father off in a panic. "He has to pray," she said.

He scratched his jaw again. "Oh. You people do that a lot." He laughed softly, self-deprecatingly.

"Aye."

She would have walked past him, but he put out a hand to stop her. He didn't touch her, he just blocked her way. The man confused her, tempted her, and, now that she'd proclaimed her bethrothal to him to her father the sight of him was more than embarrassing. She stood still and looked at his feet—his very big feet in their complicated-looking white shoes—and wished he would go away. Eventually she noticed that his shadow was covering her, and even that much contact sent a shiver of desire through her.

Desire. Oh, Lord help her!

"You okay?" he asked her.

"You're blocking the sun," she answered, and went to step around him.

He moved with her, sidestepping as though they were partnered in some sort of dance. "You know, your uncle makes a mean bowl of oatmeal." It sounded to her as if Sammy was searching for innocuous things to say.

"Aye." She stepped away.

He followed her. "How come he's a druid? How come you are? Ireland's been Christian for hundreds of years, hasn't it?"

"Aye." Step.

Step. "Well, how come?"

Brianna sighed. She noticed her foster brother standing to one side and silently laughing. She stopped trying to escape and looked up at Sammy. There was a light of genuine curiosity in his eyes, and a teasing smile on his lips. It told her he had enjoyed their silly little dance. Oddly enough, so had she. She returned his smile.

"My family has always been druids," she explained. "We were priests in Ban Ean long before Patrick came. One in each generation keeps the old knowledge alive. It was Uncle Sean who had the idea to finally write some of the spells and chants down."

"You don't seem to approve."

Did she? It was odd how the man could read her emotions so easily. "It's not traditional," she said. "The knowledge has always been passed on from memory to memory. It's important to be able to remember all there is to know. I need to take my washing down to the stream," she added as it seemed they were doomed to stay planted in front of the church while the morning wore relentlessly away.

Sammy let her pass at last but followed close on her heels. "How can you remember all there is to know?"

She did not look over her shoulder to answer him. "By memorizing it, of course. There are few druids left, but the bards keep some of the old ways alive in their poems and songs."

She heard his deep-throated chuckle. "We use computers to remember everything for us."

"Computers," she repeated. "So that is what bards are called in your time." Somehow it seemed important that she remember that word, that she know more about what it meant. "Tell me about computers," she said as they came to her door.

His chuckle turned into a laugh as he shook his head. "I wouldn't know where to start."

"You are not a computer, then. Are there any computers in your tribe?"

"Uh, no—but I own a computer."

"They are slaves, then." She drew herself up with pride. "Here we honor our computers. The best wear silk and gold and sing in the households of kings."

Sammy didn't laugh at Brianna's assumption that computers were the equivalent of Irish poets. It did bother him a little that she took it for granted that he owned slaves. It reminded him that Brianna's worldview was completely alien from his.

"This is too complicated to try to explain," he said.

"I see." She sounded skeptical. Sammy answered her tone with a smile and a shrug.

She went inside her house. Sammy stood outside and debated whether to follow her in or go look for Donal. He'd seen Brianna's twin go into the long, low building next to the church where monks copied manuscripts while he and Brianna had been talking in the village square. "Which sort of makes Donal a ninth-century data entry operator," Sammy mused while he tried to decide what to do with his day. He figured he could train Donal, teach Ailill, or try to get Brianna busy on the time-travel spell.

Ailill came and tugged on the bottom of the linen tunic Sammy was wearing, so Sammy dropped down to speak to the boy. "You know, she never has enough time for me. It's starting to drive me crazy." The wolfhound sat down next to him and began licking Sammy's ear.

"Hey, that tickles!" Sammy sprang to his feet to escape the dog's very wet tongue. "Now, if I could only get Brianna to do that," he said as he wiped the spot where the dog had licked.

"Do what?" Brianna asked as she came out of the house, a big basket full of soiled linens in her arms.

When Sammy looked at her and blushed, she decided she didn't want to know what he was thinking.

She looked at her foster brother as she asked Sammy, "Have you taught him the word for sheep?"

"Yeah. Wanna see?"

She watched Sammy's hands, memorizing the gesture. "Good. Then please tell Ailill that we all have work to do, and minding the sheep is his." The clothes were heavy, and she was in a hurry, so she walked toward the stream without waiting for an answer.

Apparently the boy responded to Sammy's sign language, because the next thing she knew Sammy was walking beside her and the basket had been whisked into his grasp. When she looked around, Ailill was nowhere in sight. She gave Sammy a pleased nod. He carried the basket as though it weighed no more than a swan feather. She didn't know how to act now that they were alone, so to avoid conversation, she sang all the way down to the pool at the top of the meadow.

"You aren't really going to do laundry are you?" he asked as they reached the water.

She pried the basket from his hands. "I said I was, didn't I? I have brought it to the stream, have I not? This is the day I set aside each month to do laundry, is it not?" She sighed as she knelt on the grass beside the water. "Be gone with you," she added, not knowing why she felt so irritable.

Perhaps it was guilt at proclaiming him the husband fate had shown her. Perhaps she was just not used to having a man hover over her as she went about her chores. Whatever it was, she was uncomfortable with his presence. Uncomfortable at being alone with this big, handsome, all too vigorous man. Even out here in the wide meadow, with the sea and the sky stretching away to forever around her, his presence filled her senses. He made her world bigger just by being in it. She had no idea how she would breathe in the tiny, cramped place that would be left to her when he was gone from her side forever.

"Ah, well," she said, setting about her work, "I'll think about that tomorrow."

Sammy was on his knees next to her in an instant. He put his hand on her shoulder and asked, "You're not channel surfing on me again, are you, babe?"

Brianna looked into his concerned eyes. "What?"

"You just said—You're not about to say I'll think about that at Tara are you?"

"I've never been to Tara. I've never been past Canaire. What are you talking about?"

"Never mind, I was just remembering lines from an old movie."

She tilted her head to one side and asked, "What's an old movie?"

"You don't want to know."

She did. There was something familiar about the word *movie*. Something she knew from her dreams about the smoking city. "And why," she asked him, "have I spent more nights than I can count dreaming about a place that makes no sense and means nothing to my life? Once you get back I want you to make it stop."

"Me?" His eyes went wide with surprise. "Me? What have I got to do with it?" he asked indignantly.

"Well, you must have something to do with it or I wouldn't have ended up with you getting in my way every second of the day."

"If you'd send me home I wouldn't get in your way, would I?"

Brianna didn't know why it hurt her so to see how anxious he was to leave her, but she turned her head quickly to keep him from seeing the pain that must be in her eyes. She snatched a chemise out of the basket and plunged it into the water.

After she'd spent a vehement few minutes taking her mood out on the blameless linen, Sammy's deep, rumbling chuckle caught her attention. "What?" she asked without glancing up from her work.

"I didn't know people really beat clothes with rocks to get them clean."

She couldn't help but give him a curious look. "You know of a better way? It's either this or boil them, and the day is too fine to spend cooped up in the wash-house." She wiped a splash of cool water from her face as she spoke.

Sammy watched her as she worked, and, while he enjoyed it, he ended up feeling like a lazy oaf. He was used to every possible convenience. He had a dish-washer, a washing machine, a microwave, and more electronic gadgets than he needed. And he lived a pret-ty simple life, really. At home his food came from a grocery store. Here they had to grow it, hunt it, pre-serve it, and cook it over firewood and peat they'd gathered themselves. And that was just the food part of life. They had to do everything else from scratch too. His world had it easy. It was infinitely easier to live in the twentieth century.

There he had everything, and here Brianna's family had—Brianna. All the cooking and cleaning and nur-turing was done by her, without a single modern con-venience. And not much thanks, either, as far as he could see. It seemed as if she didn't take care of just her own family, but also her uncle, and mostly every-body else in town. It was definitely unfair. Here she was, young and pretty and intelligent, and working like a dog.

Sammy leaned his elbows back on the fragrant, springy grass and said, "You know, if you had any sense you'd marry this Rory person."

Brianna shot him a sharp look. "What?"

"Then you'd have servants and courtiers and stuff, right?"

Brianna lifted the tunic she'd been scrubbing out of the stream, balled it up, and tossed it at Sammy's head.

If you
have a passion
for great
historical
romance,
here's an offer
you'll love...

4 FREE NOVELS

Introducing
The Timeless Romance

Passion rising from the ashes of the Civil War...

Love blossoming against the harsh landscape of the primitive Australian outback...

Romance melting the cold walls of an 18th-century English castle —— and the heart of the handsome Earl who lives there...

Since the beginning of time, great love has held the power to change the course of history. And in Harper Monogram historical novels, you can experience that power again and again.

Free introductory offer. To introduce you to this exclusive new service, we'd like to send you the four newest Harper Monogram titles absolutely free. They're yours to keep without obligation, no matter what you decide.

Free 10-day previews. Enjoy automatic free delivery of four new titles each month —— up to four weeks before they appear in bookstores. You're never obligated to keep a book you don't want, and you can return any book, for a full credit.

Save up to 32% off the publisher's price on any shipment you choose to keep.

Don't pass up this opportunity to enjoy great romance as you have never experienced before.

Reader Service.

Yes! I want to join the Timeless Romance Reader Service. Please send me my 4 FREE HarperMonogram historical romances. Then each month send me 4 new historical romances to preview without obligation for 10 days. I'll pay the low subscription price of $4.00 for every book I choose to keep--a total savings of at least $2.00 each month--and home delivery is free! I understand that I may return any title within 10 days and receive a full credit. I may cancel this subscription at any time without obligation by simply writing "Canceled" on any invoice and mailing it to Timeless Romance. There is no minimum number of books to purchase.

NAME

ADDRESS

CITY   STATE   ZIP

TELEPHONE

SIGNATURE

(If under 18, parent or guardian must sign. Program, price, terms, and conditions subject to cancellation and change. Orders subject to acceptance by HarperMonogram.)

He ducked it easily as she demanded, "What would I want servants for?"

"To take care of you," he answered.

Brianna sat back on her heels and gave him a disgusted look. "Oh, aye, you have the right of it. Rory would give me maids and a soft bed and my hands would grow soft and my body fat from the king's good food."

"Yeah," he said. "You could have somebody to take care of you."

Brianna gave a short, very bitter laugh. "And all I would have to do in exchange would be to welcome Rory, in whom I have no interest, to my bed when the mood was on him. And sing to him sometimes, perhaps, and embroider his clothes, too, I suppose. What a dull life that would be."

"I see your point."

Even though Sammy was wincing at the stupidity of his suggestion, she went on to hammer a few more points home. "Oh, another way I'd pay for these servants to care for me would be for Rory to get a child or two from my body. Children may be a woman's joy, but the babes would have wet nurses and servants of their own. A king's wife must keep her body sleek for her lord's pleasure, don't you know. So I'd have little to do with my own babes, and then they'd be fostered out to be raised in other king's houses as soon as they were old enough, not to return until they were grown and trained for war. So I wouldn't even have the task of raising my own children." She gave a vehement shake of her head. Her gaze burned into Sammy's as she went on. "So, I can have a life of ease with Rory, or I can have a real life of my own, hard work and all."

"Yeah, I see—"

"I am not, not—" she sputtered as she hunted for a word, "not a bimbo!" She surged to her feet so she could stomp her foot on the ground. "And I wish people would stop trying to make me into one!" She kicked over the laundry basket for emphasis.

Sammy was on his feet as well by now. He couldn't help but admire her attitude. He couldn't help but be ashamed of his own ignorant assumptions. He couldn't help but look at her in puzzlement and repeat, "Bimbo?"

She gave a decisive nod. "Bimbo."

"Where'd you hear that word?"

"In a dream, I suppose. About the smoking city."

The smoking city. Right. Sammy said, "Calm down, okay, babe?" While she watched, eyes flashing with annoyance, he gathered up her spilled clothes. Once he had his arms full, he said, "You take a rest. I'll finish this for you."

She looked confused. "You'll what?"

"Finish the laundry."

"The laundry?"

"Sure. Have a seat. Get some rest." He knelt by the water and set to work. Brianna stood over him, shocked into silence. After a while he pointed a wet finger at where he'd been lounging. "Rest."

"But—you're doing the laundry."

"So? I know how to wash clothes." At least he knew how to sort light colors from dark, and which settings to use on his washing machine. "This is a cold water wash. You can wash just about anything in cold water on a gentle cycle. An old girlfriend taught me that."

"I'm sure."

Her voice dripped sarcasm, and maybe a hint of jealousy. Which shouldn't have pleased him but did. "I'll be gentle," he assured her. "You rest."

Brianna did not know what to make of this man who offered to do her work for her. This had never happened before. Men did not do women's work. Women's work was, well, just about every task that needed to be done. Men did not do them. Men prayed in the church and worked in the scriptorium and taught in the school. Some fished and some toiled in the fields, but mostly the men of Ban Ean were done for, they didn't do. They were men of God, not men of the world.

At first she wanted to stop Sammy, to tell him that doing women's work was dishonorable. But she didn't think Sammy could do anything that was dishonorable. His honor was not bound up in pride, and he never did anything the way a man of her own time did.

When the notion that he really meant for her to rest finally took root she knew he was concerned for her welfare. It warmed her more than the hottest fire. He was concerned for *her*. His kindness sent such a rush of love through her that words completely deserted her.

So, she sat. And she watched him as he scrubbed and wrung out one piece of clothing after another, tossing them back into the basket with exuberant enthusiasm. He worked with a smile on his handsome, bronzed face, laughing when he splashed water in his face. His tunic grew soaked and clung to his broad chest, outlining the rippling muscles of his arms and stomach.

The morning passed in a kind of charmed silence. Silent but for the bleating of sheep in the meadow, the barking of the herd dog, and the call of birds in the nearby trees. Eventually, as the sun rose toward noon, Brianna began to sing.

And as she sang, her heart ached, for the song form-

ing in her mind was the spell that would take Sammy
away from her forever.

"That sounds pretty," Sammy said as Brianna
showed him how to weigh the clothes down with small
stones as they laid them out on the grass to dry. "What
are you singing?"

Brianna stopped singing. She looked away from
him, out toward the ocean, as she answered. "Your
time-travel spell."

"Oh." Sammy supposed he should be pleased. He
was pleased. He'd be going home soon. He just wasn't
happy about it. "Think it'll work?"

She made a small gesture. "I'm just beginning to
feel the shape of it." She looked back at him, meeting
his eyes. "It feels right. When it is ready, it will work."

"Oh." He gave an abrupt nod. "That's good. That's
real good. But it won't be ready for a while. Right?"
He didn't know why it bothered him that she'd hit on
the right spell. He needed to get back. To help Jerry.
He had to get back.

He just wasn't sure that he wanted to go.

Which was stupid. Really stupid. It was the Vikings,
he told himself, completely refusing to think about the
obvious. He just wanted to help these people fend off
the danger from the Vikings before he left. That was
all. He wanted to do some good before he cut out.

Brianna straightened, then stretched as she looked
up at the clear sky overhead. "I best be getting back,"
she told him. "I have studying to do with Uncle Sean."

"And cooking to do, and firewood to gather and
gardens to weed and chickens to feed and stuff like
that," Sammy added. He flicked a strand of stray hair
off her cheek while she watched him with wide-eyed
curiosity. Her hair felt like silk, so did her skin.

"Why are you angry at my having to work?"

"'Cause it's not fair," he told her.

She shook her head. "I think you are going to drive me mad, Sammy Sam Bergen."

"What? Me? Why?"

"You think that the future can be changed, and that life should be fair and that the deaf can hear and men should share the work. It's insane. You're insane." She glared fiercely at him. "You are driving *me* insane."

He couldn't stop the teasing grin. "Yeah. And you love me for it."

Sammy didn't realize how Brianna might take his casual comment until he watched her face go pale and tears brim out of her eyes.

"Oh, shit. Honey, I didn't mean—"

But before he could do any damage control, Brianna spun away from him and ran. He watched her go, rooted in place by his own sense of futility. Maybe he had meant—something. What? That she loved him? Or that maybe he was starting to love her?

"Shit," he repeated.

Just then Donal sauntered up from the direction of the village and asked, "What was that about?" His eyes narrowed on Sammy. "Have you said something improper to my sister? And what's this my father tells me about your marr—"

"Let's get out of here." Sammy cut Donal off as the idea struck him. "Let's get out of town. Go on patrol, scouting for the Viking positions."

Donal's eyes lit up with enthusiasm. "Patrol? Go scouting? Aye, that's warriors' work. Bridget and Moira will think I'm wonderfully brave."

"Fine," Sammy said, with a decisive nod. "You gather some supplies. I'll meet you at the sheep shed."

He had to get away from Ban Ean. He had to get away from Brianna. Before he went after her and said something stupid involving the *L* and *C* words that they were both going to regret.

Besides, making sure the bad guys were nowhere near Ban Ean would be doing some good for these people. And would disguise the fact that he was a complete coward where one little dark-haired magician was concerned.

"Meet me in thirty minutes," he said gruffly to her twin. "Hurry."

13

Brianna wasn't sure four days had been enough time to get herself under control, especially not with the way her nights had gone. But it was four days later when Sammy came back into Ban Ean.

In that time her nerves had been stretched as she'd worked on the spell while fending off erotic dreams, meaningless visions of herself in the smoking city, and Uncle Sean's increasing requests to get that damned black beast out of his house. It had not been a pleasant few days. Her father's behavior, secretive and furtive, sullen and mysterious, had not been any help, either.

So her mood was anything but pleasant when she stepped out the door of her father's house to the sight of Sammy striding toward her through the early morning fog. Still, her heart leaped so high, she thought for a moment that she was going to die with joy at the sight of him. No, four days had not given her any distance from her emotions at all.

"Oh, Lord," she whispered, throat tight with longing. "What a fool I am."

She couldn't help the smile of delight on her lips. She knew her eyes were shining with everything she felt as he came up to her. The world around them was pewter gray, the familiar buildings of Ban Ean were unrecognizable in the thick morning mist. The sun would burn the air clear soon enough, but for now Sammy, big and grand and handsome in his orange and white clothes, was the most real thing in the whole world. It was all Brianna could do to keep from running into his arms.

"You missed me," he said as he strode up to her and lifted her clear off her feet. He held her up, eye to eye. "I can tell."

She placed her hands on his hard-muscled shoulders. "Missed you?" she protested with a teasing toss of her head. "Not I."

"Did so."

Sammy had told himself he wasn't going to do this. That he wasn't going to make a beeline for Brianna. That he wasn't going to lay a finger on her. That he hadn't missed her. But there he was, and there she was, all soft curves and welcoming smiles. He wanted her so bad it hurt. Being away from her had only made his wanting her more intense—which hadn't been the point of going away at all.

He knew he ought to put her down, but instead he drew her closer. Her hands went from tentatively touching his shoulders to clinging around his neck. It was Brianna who pulled his mouth to hers. Not that he fought the kiss, oh, no.

Their lips met and fire raced between them and he knew he wasn't the only one who'd been dreaming about this for the last few nights. This was stupid, ridiculous, dangerous. He—

Talk is cheap. Shut up and dance.

—didn't know whether the thought was his own or Brianna's, but he took the advice anyway.

He stopped thinking and let the burn of desire take over. Her mouth was soft hot velvet. He tasted it with a hunger he'd never known before. Her body was yielding against him, a perfect fit. He pulled her closer against his hard-muscled thighs. She squirmed, grinding her hips against him. Sammy groaned, while Brianna's tongue darted and teased around the inside of his mouth. It drove him crazy.

At least it drove his body crazy. After a few almost painfully exquisite minutes his brain kicked back in and regained control of his libido. "Hey," he said, almost dropping Brianna in his haste to save both their virtues. His voice trembled when he asked, "Didn't I run away from you a few days ago?"

She looked up at him from where she leaned against the wall of her house. The expression on her face wasn't one of fear but of anger. Anger he was sure she aimed at herself. He knew exactly how she felt, hungry with desire, and foolish for giving in to it.

"Oh, aye," she answered him. "You ran and I was glad of it. You just didn't run far enough to stay out of my dreams."

"Yeah." He couldn't help but smile. "The dreams have been pretty wild, haven't they?"

"Does my brother know what's been going on in that, that—"

"—imaginative?"

"—mind of yours?" A hot blush deepened her already red cheeks.

"You are so beautiful," he said, unable to take his eyes off her. "Even all pink 'cause you're embarrassed."

She touched her mouth. "And with my lips swollen from a kiss I should never have taken?"

He touched his own lips. "Yeah. We're crazy," he added. He made himself take a step back. "I should not have just walked up and grabbed you."

She came away from the wall. "I thought I was the one doing the grabbing."

"No, I grabbed first. You kissed first."

"Oh, right. Well."

She dusted her hands together and looked around. The fog was clearing. It was going to be a fine day. Most everyone in the village was sharing a saint's day celebration in the common house, a fine big breakfast after mass. She was thankful that she had been late in departing for the festivities. Glad no one had seen her behavior just now.

She cleared her throat. "Where's Donal?"

Sammy waved a hand toward the common house. "Went to see his girlfriends."

"Ah. Of course. Have you broken your fast yet?"

"Yeah." He looked as uncomfortable with this mundane conversation as she felt. "How's the spell coming along? Ready to send me home yet?"

She would never be *ready,* but she would do it. "Almost. I've been busy with—everyone. Everything. They need me."

The words came out as an excuse, but she wasn't sure if it was for not having his spell finished or for some other reason. Her most recent visions of the smoking city had been very disturbing. For instead of seeing the place as from a distance the way she usually did, she'd found herself walking the streets, breathing the air. Living there.

The very notion of entering Sammy's foreign world frightened her, and somehow thrilled her with the sheer forbidden enormity of it. She found herself stumbling forward now, looking for support, as even the memory of the visions made her momentarily disoriented.

She leaned into Sammy without thinking about it, wanting his closeness and support. Oh, it was wicked, but he was the most real thing to her in either of the worlds she knew. She took strength from the hard-muscled feel of his broad chest, savored the warmth and the sea and sweat-tinged smell of his skin.

When she looked up at him she found his violet eyes smiling into hers. There were banked fires deep in those eyes, a fire that burned for her. The temptation to stir them into a blaze was very strong. What was between them now was almost more important than any possible future, together or apart. She was breathless and aching, nearly ready to throw away good sense, her good name, and her future, for the promise of a few hours of sensual pleasure.

"I'm going mad," she whispered.

"We definitely shouldn't be doing this," he said. But he didn't move away.

"I think we've already agreed to that. Sammy?" she said, trying to work up to kissing him again right there in front of her father's house. She put her hand up, pressing her palm just over his swiftly beating heart.

He caught his breath in a ragged gasp. But before he could answer or move to push her away, Donal stomped out of the common house and demanded, "Do you know what Father's done while I was away?"

Brianna felt as if her brother had just saved her from drowning. She turned away from Sammy and answered angrily, not really grateful for the rescue, "Of course I know. I haven't been away from my duties for days and days."

"I've been hunting Norsemen," Donal defended his absence.

"But we didn't find any," Sammy said. "Did catch some nice fish, though. Hey, I'm not a complete vegetarian," he added defensively as she glared at him. From his easy tone he sounded as if he'd already forgotten what had been going on between them.

"You're a worthless hound."

He shrugged. "Hey, so I'll eat fish when there's nothing else available."

That had not been what she'd been talking about. She didn't want to hear about Sammy going fishing. She didn't want to think about Sammy's dreams after he settled down with a full belly to sleep around nightly campfires away from Ban Ean. Away from her. *He's going back to the future,* she forced herself to remember. *Donal's problems will still be part of my life when Sammy is long gone.*

"Father's discussion with Fergus has been the talk of the village for days." She turned from Sammy to look at her twin. She kept leaning on Sammy, though, who kept his hands on her shoulders. It was so natural she almost didn't notice doing it.

"Father's named a dowry at last," Donal stated angrily. "For both Moira and Bridget."

She tried to give Donal an encouraging smile. "Then you should be pleased."

"Pleased! Forty cows. Father asked forty cows for the girls!"

"Twenty apiece," Brianna agreed. "Not unreasonable considering their beauty."

"Where's Fergus going to come up with forty cows,

I ask you? The sculptor owns no more than he needs."

"This is a monastery," Brianna reminded her brother. "That is the rule of our life."

"Then why doesn't Father ask for a dowry Fergus can give?" Donal wanted to know. "Father doesn't need any more cows."

With her hands on her hips Brianna stepped away from Sammy. She was reluctant to leave the closeness, but as much as she wanted it to be so, her whole world could not be bound up in her need for the man. Her twin, the other half of her life, had needs as well.

The church bell was ringing, calling the village away from celebration and back to daily routine. The fog had been chased completely away by a wind that brought a light, misting rain. Ban Ean looked like itself again. People passed them, giving them curious looks, but duty kept them from lingering to listen. Brianna ignored the bells, as did Donal.

Nose to chin with her taller twin, she said, "Father's asked such a high dowry because he knows Fergus can't afford to marry his daughters to you this way. As long as father asks such a high dowry Fergus can honorably refuse to pay it, and other suitors can put in lower bids. Father's not a clever man, so I imagine the idea was someone else's."

"But—"

"The point is," she swept her hand around the village, "all this is to be yours. Whether you want it or not, you're going to be a bishop. Unless you think of something quickly, you'll marry whomever grandfather wants you to," she added. "If you don't find a way soon, you won't be marrying the daughters of a simple monk but making an alliance for the family's sake with a king or a bishop's daughter."

Donal pointed at Sammy. "And never mind your visions of romance with him."

"I beg your pardon?"

They ignored Sammy's question as Donal went on. "You'll be married to Rory MacMurdo. We'll both be miserable because Grandfather wishes it."

"Aye," she agreed. With a wicked grin she added, "What are we going to do about it?"

Donal returned her grin. Then he gave a thoughtful glance back toward Fergus's hut. "I have an idea. If I could be certain they'd both take me. They've been teasing and promising for months. Wait here," he said, and marched purposefully away.

Brianna turned back to Sammy. He was leaning against the wall. A fine mist was falling; the water droplets were gathered on his gold curls like a coif of jewels. Her breath caught at the sight of him. She was drawn to him, seeking his warmth and shelter once more.

"By St. Bridget you're beautiful," she said, just before she kissed him.

It no longer mattered to her if they were in front of her father's house. The pain from Donal's words clawed too deeply inside of her for any rational thought. She only knew she had to do something for herself, and that the man she wanted was here in front of her.

"I will not have Rory," she declared when he pulled his mouth from hers. "I won't. Even if I must ruin myself with you."

"Whoa," he said, and held her out at arm's length. "Let's not get our reasons for sex confused here."

"Do you want me or not?" she demanded.

His fingers tightened spasmodically, then dropped

to his sides as if he'd been burned. "Of course I want you!"

She could still feel the marks of his fingers on her. The look in his eyes was as bruising as his touch had been. He was making himself think, when all she wanted him to do was react. "Well, let's do it, then. We want each other badly enough right now. What difference does it make to you once you're gone?"

"It makes a lot of difference to me. You're the one who'll have to live with the consequences if we make love. I'm not going to let you 'ruin' yourself on a whim. This isn't the twentieth century, you know. Once I'm gone, you'll have to pay, won't you? They'd make you enter a convent or something, wouldn't they?"

"Aye." It was a possibility she hated almost as much as being wedded to Rory. Still, she made herself lift her head proudly and say, "Aunt Ethni's convent would not be so bad."

"Bullshit. I'm not worth doing a lifetime's worth of penance for, babe. No man is."

"Why are you being so reasonable?"

"Because somebody has to be."

"Men think with their members. Uncle Sean said so."

He shook his head. "Not me. Not most of the time. Not this time, anyway. You're really gorgeous when you're angry," he added.

"If I'm so gorgeous why won't you let me seduce you?"

"I'd love for you to seduce me. I might let you seduce me, sometime. I hope I won't give in, 'cause neither of us really needs the aggravation."

"Aye," she agreed reluctantly. "We don't."

"You're mad at me about those dreams, aren't you?"

Brianna hadn't considered this before, but once he

said it she knew it was true. It made her want to cry, but she would not do that in front of him. She would not show her loneliness so openly. "I'm afraid no one will ever touch me the way you do in your—our—dreams."

He brushed his fingers gently across her cheeks. "Somebody will. Someday."

But I want it to be you! her heart cried. She said, "It feels so wonderful. In our dreams."

"Yeah," he agreed. "Wonderful and frustrating. You're the only woman who's ever shared my dreams."

As Sammy said the words he wasn't exactly sure what he meant by them. Fortunately he heard Donal's determined stride coming toward them before he had to think about it.

He ran his fingertips around the outline of Brianna's slightly swollen lips. "I think we better talk to your brother," he told her. *I think I better not do that again,* he told himself.

Brianna swung around to face Donal. "Well?" she demanded as she saw how pleased he looked with himself.

He glanced from her to Sammy and then back again, but didn't make any comment. He gave his news instead. "Bridget and Moira and I had a little talk."

Brianna noted that her brother's mouth looked like hers felt, only more so. If Donal kissed at all like Sammy—and she blushed to think of her brother behaving in such a way now that she had some idea of what men and women did together—then Moira and Bridget were presently in a very pliable state.

"Well?" she asked impatiently.

"I've convinced them they want me and no other for

a husband," Donal went on proudly. "We'll be wed as soon as I provide the cows."

"Wait a minute," Sammy said, stepping up beside her.

She wished he'd put his arms around her, but he did no such thing.

"Maybe I'm not hearing this right," Sammy went on. "I thought Fergus had to hand over the cows so you could marry the girls."

"He does," Donal replied.

"But you just said—" Brianna began.

Donal smirked. "I have a plan."

"Oh, Lord," she said, feeling an anxious knot twist in her stomach. She knew what Donal was going to say, and she didn't need the Sight to know it. "Not MacMurdo's cattle." She shook a finger at him. "I'll not have you stealing the king's cattle."

Donal drew himself up proudly. "It will not be stealing. Did Rory not promise the church fifty fine black cows if his lady was delivered of a son? Did you not deliver that son? Does a king not have debts? His herdsmen have not delivered the black cows. I checked."

"Rory MacMurdo has more important things on his mind," Brianna said. "You were not the only ones patrolling the countryside. Rory MacMurdo has taken his men to hunt for the Norsemen who raided yet another village while you were gone. It seems the invaders went many miles north of Ban Ean before striking again."

"Really?" Donal looked even more pleased at this information than he had at having Bridget's and Moira's marriage pledge. He rubbed his jaw thoughtfully. "Took all his men, did he?"

"Uh oh," Sammy said quietly. He put his hand on Brianna's shoulder. "Strategically speaking, you just blew it, babe," he told her.

She knew exactly what he meant. Donal had not needed to hear that Rory MacMurdo and his men were elsewhere. The king's absence could only make what Donal had in mind easier.

"No," Brianna said. "I forbid it! I'll tell father."

Donal looked supremely unconcerned at her words. "Will you?" He spoke far too casually. "Then I can tell him you've been kissing Sammy when Father wants you married to another."

"But—!"

"Hey!" Sammy said.

Donal pointed to the house where the holy sisters lived, then back at Brianna. "Do you want to spend a month fasting and praying all alone in there?"

Sammy looked from one twin to the other. He could see that Donal was serious about turning his sister in for fraternization if she didn't back off. Brianna didn't look as if she was going to. He didn't like the idea of them quarreling. He didn't want either of them in trouble, either. Especially Brianna. This was exactly what he'd been worried about when she'd tried to seduce him.

"I need you to get me home with your reputation intact," he said to her. To Donal he said, "This guy really owes you the cows?"

"Aye," the twins answered together.

"Well," Sammy said, rubbing his hands together. "We can go ask for them."

The pair looked at him anxiously. "Impossible," Donal said.

"I thought you'd say that." Especially since Donal

wanted these cows for his own plans. Sammy thought asking for a dowry was a dumb idea, but he didn't like the way Donal's father was using it to keep his son from marrying both girls. He'd heard a lot about Bridget and Moira in the last few days. Donal was determined to have them both no matter what.

He smiled at Brianna and her brother. "Looks like we go with Donal's original idea, and rustle the herd." "Just what I need," he said to himself as Donal whooped and Brianna frowned. "I'm about to commit grand theft cow."

14

Sammy had told her the black-and-white shepherd was about the only one of them with the skill to pull off the robbery, so they'd left Ailill and the wolfhound with the sheep and borrowed the herd dog. Sammy figured it was the brains of the operation. Brianna agreed with his assessment.

Then Sean intercepted them, coming around one of the tall standing stones as they left the sheep meadow. "A cattle raid," he'd said cheerfully, having obviously overheard the plan Sammy discussed with his niece and nephew. He rubbed his hands together eagerly. "We haven't had a proper cattle raid in this part of Eire for generations. What sport!"

He'd insisted on coming along as well. Brianna explained this to Sammy, who said, "The more the merrier, I guess."

So Donal borrowed four horses from the monastery

stable and they set off in a roundabout way, through
the cover of woods, to the edge of Rory MacMurdo's
property. Along the way, Sean recited the tale of the
Cow of Cooley, which she translated for Sammy.
Donal discussed the charms of his two fiancées, and
they all teased him. The dog trotted along purposefully
beside the horses.

Sammy tried not to think about anything but the
upcoming action, but every time he glanced at Brianna he
remembered kissing her. He kept wanting to do it again.

Though he wasn't any too happy with riding a horse
bareback, he was glad he could concentrate on keeping
his seat rather than just thinking about Brianna. Everyone
else was securely guiding their horses with reins and
knees while he had to struggle just to stay on. It was far
more complicated than riding a motorcycle.

"So, when are stirrups going to be invented?" he
asked at one point, just after he'd nearly fallen off while
fording a stream.

"What?"

"Never mind."

Brianna was too busy hoarding a bit of happiness
inside herself to bother being puzzled by Sammy's
questions. She rode along, basking in his acceptance of
her as his equal. He hadn't said so in words but in
deeds since they'd first met. She'd just realized it, and
loved him for it.

It hadn't occurred to her at first, but gradually the
knowledge that Sammy had not challenged her coming
along on the raid had seeped into Brianna's awareness.
Oh, there were old tales of warrior women, of course,
but no one she knew acted as if they believed they were
true. Of course Donal hadn't complained about her
coming, they were of one mind and blood. But Sammy

was a warrior from a far-off future land. A warrior who had never treated her as less than his equal. Perhaps that was just the way of his people.

She gave him an assessing look as they brought the horses to a halt at the edge of a wood. "I think," she admitted reluctantly, and very softly, as she jumped down, "that I might enjoy living in your time."

Sammy didn't hear her, as he was intent on getting to the ground without falling. It amazed her that a man who could easily master a roaring black metal beast had trouble dealing with the most docile horse in the monastery stable, but it also reassured her to know that Sammy wasn't quite perfect.

She was left holding the horses while her brother and Sammy crept forward to check the pasture beyond the woods. Uncle Sean began to whisper while he gestured with his staff, working a spell to bring a heavy sleep upon any herdsman that might be in the field. The dog went with Sammy and Donal.

Brianna ignored the people, the horses, the dog, and the lowing of cattle in the distance. She looked toward the west as the sun clawed through a heavy bank of clouds, and all of a sudden she was surrounded by light. Images of the future formed in the light and reached out to invade her mind. Again.

"I hate doing this on an empty stomach," she said as she fell toward the ground and into the vision.

"There are more people in the street than in all of Eire."

Great pillars of light held up the sunset sky overhead while great, glittering crowds of people pressed all around them.

* * *

Sammy estimated maybe a hundred small, long-haired cows munching contentedly on the lush grass in the pasture. Donal moved forward cautiously, getting in among the shaggy animals. Sammy signaled for Sean to join him after he was sure there was no one watching the cattle at this end of the field. When Sean didn't come to help, Sammy scuttled back through the woods to see what was keeping him. He found the older man kneeling next to Brianna.

"Oh, babe," Sammy said as he anxiously scooped the girl up in his arms. "This is no time to be having a vision."

The noise was deafening. They were waiting to be let inside a grand building. She would rather have stayed home and watched it on television.

Sammy, dressed all in black and white, his long hair tied back from his face, gave her a cheerful smile. His arm was around her shoulders, which were bare. What little clothing she wore seemed to be made out of pure gold. She should have been ashamed to be half naked, but no one seemed to care. She saw other women in far less.

Sammy glanced from the girl to the pasture and back to the girl again.

He could hear the herd dog yipping determinedly in the field, and the rumbling movement of the disturbed cattle. Donal called something; Sean answered. Brianna mumbled and clutched at his chest, bunching the fabric of his shirt up in her small fist. Sammy cradled her gently.

His heart knotted with worry for her. Okay, she did this all the time, but it couldn't be good for her.

"Don't worry," he whispered, "I'll take care of you."

"You mind the girl," Sean said. "She needs you more than the lad does." He took Sammy by the arm and led him under the sheltering cover of an ancient tree. Night was coming on quickly, and fog was rising from the wet ground.

"It's okay," Sammy promised Brianna. "I'm with you. Everything's going to be okay." He brushed his lips across her forehead in the gentlest of kisses.

She responded with a sigh to his encouraging murmur, and began to describe what she was seeing.

She and Sammy had been shoved to one side to let one of the unclothed women by. People were shouting for the Madonna, though this didn't seem to be a holy procession.

"Let's get you inside," Sammy said, giving her a reassuring squeeze. She felt small beside him but protected and very safe, even in the midst of the shoving crowd.

A great many cows passed by along the narrow trail while Sammy listened to Brianna's confused words. The herd dog wove in and out around their feet, bossing them around, oblivious to the difference in size between the cattle and the sheep it was used to dealing with. Donal mounted and followed the cattle off toward Ban Ean. The whole process didn't take very long. Sammy didn't pay that much attention; he was caught up in hearing about attending what sounded like some sort of celebrity bash. In his own time. With Brianna.

*   *   *

"Good luck, babe," he added, planting a kiss on the top of her head.

"I'm not going to win," she said. "No way I'm going to win."

"Not going to win what?" Sammy asked as Brianna opened her eyes.

"A little man named Oscar," she answered, trying to sit up and finding that she was cradled in Sammy's lap.

When she discovered where she was, she stayed put, snuggling closer. She moved her hand up to his shoulder and looked at him. In the darkness she could only make out the strong outline of his features. His muscles were bunched with tension. She wanted to run her fingertips across his face, but he spoke before she could quite make up her mind to do it.

"Oscar?" He didn't sound happy. He sounded as if he knew the name. "Like an Academy Award?"

"A slave, I think," she said, trying to summon up the essence of her vision. She knew what she'd seen, but that didn't mean she understood it. "He's given as a gift each year, I think, the way a king awards prizes for bards. Poor wee man," she added unhappily after a few seconds. "I don't know why anyone would want to give him to me, but if they did I would free him."

Sammy brushed some stray hair out of her face, then helped her to stand. "I don't know what you saw," he told her as Uncle Sean brought up their horses. "But it sounds really off the wall."

She didn't understand what Sammy meant, as she

hadn't seen any wall. She did know, as sure as she knew that she loved him, that he knew exactly what she had seen. She knew he could explain it all to her if he wanted to.

She can't help what she sees, Sammy reminded himself. He had no business being angry with her. She didn't know what it meant to see herself in his time. Brianna didn't belong in the twentieth century, he thought as he rode silently along the dark trail.

He heard her and Sean discussing the vision as they rode behind him, but he didn't add any comments. Maybe he wouldn't go back, maybe the spell wouldn't work. If it wasn't for his need to save Jerry Park's life, he almost wouldn't mind being stuck in the past. If he did he certainly wasn't taking her with him. She wouldn't survive half an hour in the insanity of the modern world.

Besides, he wasn't going to get involved in any dreams she might have of fame and glory and stardom in the future. What did a nice girl like Brianna need with all that artificial celebrity nonsense?

He didn't mind helping to save her village from Vikings, but he sure as hell wasn't going to help her make it in Hollywood.

"What do you mean this has been happening a lot lately?"

Sammy was so upset Brianna wished she hadn't told him about her most recent bout of visions. "I can't help what I see," she defended herself. "It's not my fault I keep seeing your world with me in it." She looked around the stable. Sammy had insisted they stay and talk after the horses were cared for. "This is my home."

"Damn right it is," he said as he paced up and down

the aisle between the stalls. "You're staying right where you belong."

"Of course I am. Where else would I go? If you think I want to go with you, you're mad."

Her words brought him to a halt. "Why wouldn't you want to go with me?"

Her own anger died as she saw the pain appear in his eyes. "I would go with you," she admitted. She looked away from him. "If I could," she added, bunching the fabric of her skirt in her fists.

The world was going to be so empty when he was gone. She knew now how empty it had been before he came. He was going to take all the light there'd ever been in the world for her back to the smoking city with him. She had no idea how she was going to survive his leaving.

He made a small sound, part sigh, part groan, all pain. "Good," he said. The humor was back in his voice, but she could hear what it disguised. "I'm glad we've got that settled."

Hearing his loneliness made her whirl back to face him. "They leave you, don't they?" He took a defensive step backward at her question. She followed him and went on. "All those women you make love to do not live in your house, do they?"

He gave a small shake of his head and a bitter smile. "I live alone. I like—"

"Nor do you live in their hearts," she cut him off, and saw that she was cutting his soul as well.

"Brianna," he said, the word a plea.

"They are fools, these women of your time. Fools, do you hear me!"

She stepped close to him. He stood before her, as rigid as one of Fergus's stone statues. Then his head shook once, slowly, in reply. His eyes were the color of deep bruises. She took his hands in hers. They were hard and callused, as a man's hands should be, but they were made of warm flesh and bone. This was no statue, but a man who'd wrapped a stone case around his heart to protect it from the wounds of others.

"I am no fool, Sammy Sam Bergen," she said as her hands slid up the long, sculpted muscles of his arms.

But for a sharp intake of breath at her words, Sammy kept still while her hands continued to move over him. She wanted to comfort him, reassure him, make him a part of herself, but she had no words. No songs. All she had was the sudden, overwhelming need to be close to him in ways she couldn't name.

Brianna had no control of her movements, all she had were the heady sensations that poured through her from touching him. Her fingers swept across the man's shoulders and traced the sharply defined lines of his chest. His fingers circled her waist, then glided upward. Then, as if neither of them had strength left to stand, they sank onto the stable floor.

Brianna put her head down on Sammy's chest, her ear over his heart. She absorbed its beating, its pulsing thunder, while her hands continued to soothe and explore beneath the thin material of his sleeveless tunic. Lord, but there was so much of him, and all of it so wondrous and fine!

She breathed in his scent and his heat. She rubbed her cheek slowly, catlike, against the rich fur of his chest. A sound came from her, deep in her throat, that was very like a purr. Again, catlike, she tasted him, running her tongue quickly along the line of his collarbone.

As his arms circled her she looked up at him and found herself saying in a voice thick with desire, "Were you mine to keep I would never let you go."

Then her mouth claimed his, demanding, possessive, with her fists clenched against his shoulder blades to pull him closer. She wanted him so close that they became one, for now if not forever.

Sammy couldn't have stopped himself if he tried. For once he didn't try.

Brianna was wearing just a dress with absolutely nothing beneath it. It was a simple matter to pull it over her head. It was all he could do not to hurt Brianna in his rush to touch, taste, and explore every inch of her. As it was, his caresses weren't gentle, but they were expert, arousing her as he pleased himself. They lay down together on the cool earth of the stable floor, surrounded by darkness and the soft noises of the stabled animals. Sammy took no notice of where they were; he was too much on fire with need to notice anything but the woman with him. She was small and round and perfect all over, her skin as sleek as white satin. Her hands danced with magic; her lips left burning memories where they touched him. The softness of her breasts intoxicated him.

He broke away from her only long enough to shed his own clothes. He was hard and ready, just barely in enough control to fish a condom out of his fanny pack.

While he tore the small square packet open with his teeth, Brianna sat up on her elbows to watch him. Her eyes were bright, her breathing ragged. He could have watched the quick rise and fall of her breasts forever if he hadn't been in such a hurry to make love to her. Her attention riveted on the condom as he prepared to slide it on.

"What is that thing?" she asked, a hint of fear in her voice.

He grinned. "Protection."

"From what? Why is it glowing?"

Sammy looked down at his penis. He didn't want to talk right now. He moved closer to Brianna. She shied away. "It's not glowing, it's just sort of shining."

He must have pulled out one of the ones Jane had given away as party favors at his last birthday. He vaguely remembered that there'd been a multicolored assortment available. This one was silver.

"Don't worry, sweetheart," he soothed as he touched Brianna's thigh. "I always practice safe sex."

Brianna swallowed nervously before she said, "Safe?"

He continued to caress her thigh while he wished that she didn't want to talk. Still, she needed some reassurance. "This it to keep you from getting pregnant."

Brianna pulled away from his touch. "'Tis the risk one takes. Sex is for the sake of having children, as I have been taught." She jumped to her feet before Sammy could stop her. "Sex without marriage is sin enough," she declared while Sammy groaned in frustration. "I know not what that thing is on your member, but I'll not have anything to do with it."

"Oh, God, you're Catholic. I forgot!" His body was screaming with need, but he got slowly to his feet and tried to be reasonable about the situation. "Listen, you don't want to risk getting pregnant. I don't want to take the risk."

She grabbed up her dress, then whirled back to face him, holding the cloth up to cover herself. "You don't want to risk responsibility. Aye, I see that about you. I think you're glad all those women leave you."

Ouch. "I—"

"Aye. It's easier to protect the world than it is to take responsibility for your own life, isn't it?"

"Ha. Look who's talking." Sammy hated himself the

moment the words came out, but anguish and frustration drove him. "You're just as bad, Bri. You'll take care of everybody in Ireland to avoid living life for yourself."

"Liar!" She struggled into her dress while she backed toward the stable door. Once she pulled her head through the neck opening she said, "To think I was about to give up my virtue for the likes of you. Go back to your smoking city and your empty life," she added just before she raced out into the night. "And be damned to you!"

"Yeah, you too!" Sammy called after her, his heart sinking as he leaned heavily back against the stable wall. He felt hollow and burned out as he added, "I can hardly wait to be out of here."

Rory was glad to be home from several days of hunting the Norse raiders. The time spent out in Eire's soft, rainy summer had left him eager for his roof and the glow of his wide hearth. He was by the peat fire, his hands held out toward the warmth, when Deirdre came into the hall. When he went forward to take her hands in his he brought the dark scent of smoke with him.

"My love," he greeted her after placing a quick kiss on her lips. "You look beautiful today," he declared. "As slim as a willow tree, and as fair." She was recovering quickly from the babe's birth, he'd been told by her women. He was looking forward to the day when he could take her to his bed once more. Meanwhile, he was glad to see her grow healthy and beautiful again.

She was beginning to long for him in her bed once more too; she told him so with a look. She said, "I trust you had good hunting, my lord."

His anticipatory ardor dampened somewhat. He led

her back toward the fire, where Cormac and Dillon the bodyguard waited. "Not the best manhunt I've ever had," Rory admitted. "Though it's true we caught one shipload of the raiders as they attacked Focarta." He cast a proud glance at the bodyguard. "My stand-in for battle even allowed me to take part in the fight for once."

Dillon made an elaborate bow. "A king's sword was necessary to turn the tide of this battle."

"We killed them to a man," Cormac said. "Our lord was truly a lion of battle at Focarta!"

A ripple of masculine approval went around the room at his words. Women clapped their hands and began to praise the warriors of Rory MacMurdo. Deirdre concentrated her attention on her husband.

"Yes?" she prompted him.

He squeezed her hands, glad that she sensed his disquiet. "I've ordered a feast for tonight, with cattle to be awarded to the bravest of my men."

"Yes," she said again. "But?"

"But there was a second Norse ship that never came to land," he told her. He rubbed his bearded jaw worriedly. "It put up its striped sail and sailed away. I heard the warriors on board laughing as they escaped."

"They're free to raid the coast," she concluded.

"Who knows where they'll strike next?"

"Perhaps the devils will return to wherever they came from," Deirdre said. She drew Rory toward his own high seat. Cormac and Dillon followed close on their heels. "Come and rest yourself, my lord." She gestured for the king's gold wine-cup and knelt to present it to him with her own hands.

"I'm sure you frightened the devils away from our shores," she added, taking her own seat by Rory's side.

"Perhaps," he said as he handed the drained cup to

a slave. "How is my son? How fared my lands while I was away?"

"Your son is very well indeed," she said. "Come see for yourself, my lord."

"I think I shall," he declared. "Yes, Brion?" he asked the steward who stepped up to the throne. He took his seat once more, his attention on the steward. Deirdre sighed.

"A cattle raid, my lord," Brion announced with a nervous bob of his head.

Rory's hands curled tightly around the arms of his chair with anticipation. Well, well, so the bait had been taken. He had to struggle to hide a smile. He feigned anger.

"What?" The room went still at the king's shout. "When?"

"Just yesterday, my lord."

Rory looked around him fiercely. "Have the dogs been hunted down?"

"No," Deirdre answered for the steward. "I didn't feel there was need."

"The herdsmen heard nothing at the time, my lord," Brion went on while Rory gave her an incredulous look. "But the cows were tracked to Ban Ean."

"Ban Ean," Rory said. He rubbed his beard.

"You do not look surprised," Deirdre said. She leaned toward him and whispered. "In fact, I think you are using your hand to cover a smile."

The woman knew him too well.

"What?" she demanded.

He ignored her as he rose to his feet. "My cattle have been stolen by the monks of Ban Ean?" With his hands on his hips he looked around at his staring retainers and servants. "Why was nothing done?"

"Perhaps nothing needed to be done," Deirdre said, also rising. "You did pledge fifty fine cows to the church, my lord."

"My pledge I will honor," he said. "But no man steals from me. Not even the abbot of Ban Ean."

"And I know exactly what you demand from the abbot in recompense," Deirdre said angrily. "Brianna!"

Rory looked askance at her. "Brianna," he agreed.

"She does not want you. She will not have you."

"She'll have no choice." At last Brianna would be his, though it stung his pride to know it was through trickery. He held his hand up to forestall any more argument from Deirdre. "Mind our darling child, my star," he said, "and give me peace on this matter." He planted a kiss on her lips before she could open them to protest.

Despite her fury, her touch was sweet. Her arms went around him, and he thought how good it would be to draw her to his bed. It had been so long since they had been together as man and wife.

But Rory knew he could not take her yet. The abbot's daughter would do until Deirdre was ready. He set his wife aside, patted her on the head as if she were a child and not a queen, and said, "I'll be back with my prize by tomorrow."

His confident words left her gaping as he gathered up his men. "What?" she called after him as he left. "Do you think to bed your wife and an unwilling bride on the same night? Well, come tomorrow night, Rory MacMurdo, you'll find that you're only half-right."

15

Sean was sharing a breakfast of cold honey-cakes in the main room of the abbot's house with his brother and nephew when the bellow sounded outside.

"I've come for my bride!"

They'd heard the horsemen ride up and a monk had rushed in to tell them who the riders were, but the man had no chance to speak before Rory MacMurdo's voice rang out in the square.

"I've come for my bride!" the great bull voice sounded again.

It was Donal, still full of himself from his exploits and the prospect of the marriage bed, who looked from one shocked face to another in the dim room and said, "Well, at least he hasn't come for mine."

To Sean's surprise, it was the usually mild and meek Colum who angrily chastised his son. "Rory MacMurdo would not be here now but for your foolishness. I've had to enter a devil's bargain to get the girl out of the house." He shook his finger at Donal. "But it was your greed that made Rory's plan work."

"Bargain, Colum?" Sean asked his brother the abbot. "Rory's plan? What have you done?"

"Forced the issue of Brianna's marriage," Colum answered.

Sean didn't understand but had no time to ask for further explanations as the door to the house was slammed open by Rory's guard captain.

"The king will speak with you, Abbot," the man announced gruffly. He grabbed Colum by the sleeve of his robe. "Though your hospitality will be most welcome," the man said as he hustled Colum outside, "my lord will conclude your business in the daylight before the church door."

Sean exchanged a look with Donal as they followed the men outside. "Perhaps the king's called a court to execute you over the cows," he said.

"It sounds like it," Donal agreed. The lad checked the window in the bedroom at the back of the building. "Rory's men have surrounded the house. This could interfere with the wedding."

"Wedding," Sean repeated, and ran his fingers through his graying beard. "The man's calling for his bride, not his cattle. Let's go see what this is about."

Donal looked reluctant, but he nodded. "Brianna might need my help," he agreed. "Where is she, anyway?"

"So," Sammy said, as he pushed the silent black beast into the oak grove. "What about forever?"

Brianna might have run at the sight of Sammy, but her sense of duty kept her from moving. She was carefully mixing herbs in a small iron pot hanging over the fire and didn't dare get the ingredients wrong. Sammy left the beast under a sheltering tree and came to sit beside her.

"I ended up sleeping at your uncle's place. Not that I slept much," Sammy added. "He kind of kicked me and the bike out this morning. I don't think he likes my Harley. Why did I keep hearing you say 'forever' in my head all night?"

Brianna glanced up from her work, giving Sammy the briefest of looks. "I do not know what you mean."

She'd spent the night in a makeshift shelter of twigs and bracken on the edge of the sacred grove and then come to the oak grove to sing her songs and think. It was easier to think and work in the ancient, holy place than to return to her house, and the chaos Donal had created by bringing home the cows.

She had decided not to go home at all for a while. She didn't want to hear about her brother's wedding plans or hear her father procrastinate about the date of Donal's marriage ceremony. Nor did she wish to be fussed at, prodded and prayed over about her own wedding. Most of all she wanted to avoid Sammy.

Sammy, the last person she wanted to see, was the first to put in an appearance. She hadn't slept, of course, and she didn't know if she'd ever be able to sleep again. She knew she didn't want to. She was tired of dreams of a world far from her own, tired of dreams of making love. She was tired of visions of the future. In fact, she was just sick and tired of everyone and everything that made up her life.

"Go away," she said to Sammy. "I don't want you here. And don't worry about your spell," she added bitterly. "No one wants you back in the future more than I. The right words will come to me soon enough. You need not fear for saving your friend's life."

Sammy didn't move from his spot across the fire. Brianna sighed and tried to ignore him. Only, his very presence stirred memories, and the memories brought an unwanted, but pleasant tingle to all her senses. Her longing for him only intensified with his nearness, but she was too disciplined to let the longing disturb her concentration.

When she was finally finished she wiped her hands on the cool grass and gave her attention to Sammy. If he wasn't going to go away, she supposed she'd better talk to him.

"What about forever?" he repeated when she looked at him.

"Forever?" While fragrant steam rose from the pot to fill the grove, she spread her hands on the stained white linen of her skirt. She looked everywhere but at Sammy. "If you dreamed the word so strongly, it has meaning."

"I figured. What do you think it means?"

Brianna's fingers tangled together in her lap. She hadn't meant to scream her anguished cry into his mind but supposed it was best to own up since the man insisted on knowing. "It means that I will love you forever."

Sammy took a deep breath. Then there was silence for a long time. Brianna found herself counting the heartbeats slamming wildly inside her chest.

"That smells nice," he said at last. His voice sounded so normal she almost thought he hadn't heard her confession of love.

She wished she'd never heard it herself. A few days ago she had never expected to know what love felt like.

Now that she did she wasn't going to let the man she loved get away with pretending it hadn't happened, that it didn't matter, that he didn't feel something himself.

She looked at Sammy. "I love you," she told him. "I will never love another."

Sammy knew they shouldn't talk about this. He wished he'd kept his mouth shut. He didn't know why he'd thought he'd be able to tease her about the word she'd chanted in his head all night. For some stupid reason it had seemed important to confront her, to straighten things out.

He was crazy. There was nothing to talk about. There was nothing between them. There couldn't be. The problem was, he strongly suspected that he wanted there to be. That the *forever* hadn't been coming only from her.

"This is crazy," he said. "I have to leave you."

"Aye," she agreed. "But I still love you."

Damn, but she was a brave woman. The *L* word didn't seem to give her any trouble at all.

"You love me?" he asked. Even as he spoke he was telling himself to shut up, to leave it alone. That he was setting himself up for bigger hurt than he could handle.

She nodded. From his hungry look Brianna began to believe no one had ever told him so before. "Those women of yours are such fools."

"You said that before. What's love got to do with it?"

"The movie or the song?" she asked.

"What?"

Brianna shook her head to clear it of the images from the future that suddenly intruded. She didn't have time to deal with Tina Turner's life story when her own life was such a mess. Tina who? She blinked away the question and focused her attention on Sammy.

"I love you," she said, voice strong and firm, and a bit wary. "There. Take it for what it is worth. You are loved. Now, go back to your world and leave me to mine."

Sammy jumped to his feet. She had a long way to look up to see his angry expression. "Great," he told her. "Typical. I love you." He wiggled his fingers at her. "Bye. I've heard that a few too many times, you know? That's why I don't need any emotional involvement in my life."

Brianna got up and stalked over to him. She pointed a finger stiffly at him—rather like the way Harrison Ford showed angry determination in all his movies. "Who's Harrison Ford?" she asked when that had not been what she'd meant to say at all. Before he could answer she regained the thread of her anger. "I'm not the one leaving you. Know this, I'd never leave the man I love. You are the one who will leave me."

"I can't help that!" His voice thundered across the grove. She was being psychic again, and it terrified him as much as knowing she loved him did. He could not deal with psychic women in his life. Couldn't deal with being loved by—

"It's not my fault I have the Sight!" It was Brianna who thundered this time. "I am not Karen!"

Sammy's legs collapsed under him at the impact of her words. He sat as quickly as he'd risen and put his head in his hands. Brianna was by his side instantly, kneeling next to him, a comforting hand on his arm.

He looked at her, knowing every moment of pain he'd ever had was clear on his face. "No," he said, voice an aching rasp, "you're not Karen."

But the situation was just the same. Circumstances were going to pull them apart.

Forever.

There was nothing that could be done about it. The situation was completely impossible. It wasn't anybody's fault. It hadn't been Karen's fault, either. Somehow this was worse, though. This time he was the one doing the leaving.

And God knows, this time he really was in love.

"So," Brianna said. Her voice was calm, though he could feel her hand trembling on his arm. "Who is this Karen, anyway?"

"A girl," Sammy said, and looked Brianna in the eye at last. "A girl like you. Psychic."

"She had the Sight?"

"Well, not exactly. What she had were nightmares. Oh, she could see ghosts and auras and read tarot cards. Before the nightmares got so bad she used to help the police find missing people, and stuff."

"You loved her."

He gave a slight jerk of his head. He didn't know if he'd meant to shake it, or nod. "I lived with her. I found her on the streets when she was a teenage runaway. I took her in, took care of her. This was just after I got back from—Ireland, here, in my time. I was just getting the school started when we met. I don't know if I paid as much attention to her as I should have at first. She came in and out of my life for a long time. It wasn't like I had any hold on her."

"Ah, but she had a hold on you."

"Yeah. She sure did. She was beautiful, and different. Really wise and caring when her head was on straight. She's the one who got me into Buddhism." He gave a hollow laugh. "Little did I know just how into Buddhism she was going to get. The mystical, tantric Tibetan kind. Me, I'm into Zen. Keep it simple, accept what life throws at you."

"What was it life threw at you? With Karen?"

Sammy ran his fingers through the snarled tangle of his shoulder-length curls. "This is heavy. Really heavy." Then he laughed. "Here you are renting movies from the ninth century and I'm worried you won't understand what happened to Karen."

"Well, what happened to her?"

"You know about reincarnation? About one soul slipping from body to body, life after life?"

"Of course," she answered. "'Tis a druid belief."

"Well, what happened to Karen is she remembered who she used to be. The process of recovering those memories nearly drove her crazy. She nearly took me along for the ride."

"Why would anyone want to remember who they used to be?"

"I didn't say she wanted to remember. She needed to remember. See, she used to be this holy man, a Tibetan monk. She used to have these dreams about a monster coming for her through this yellow silk wall. Turned out she was picturing an abominable snowman and saffron monk's robes. Her subconscious was trying to tell her to get back to Tibet. Of course she ended up in a monastery in Nepal, but that's pretty close to Tibet, I guess."

"Your Karen is a monk?"

She didn't sound like she believed him. He wasn't sure he believed the story either. He put his hand over his heart. "It happened, I swear. One day these monks showed up at my place. She recognized them. Turned out they'd been hunting for this monk's reincarnation for years. She went off with them. Sometimes she writes," he added, and realized he didn't feel as bitter about the crazy situation as he used to.

Brianna turned back to stir the bubbling pot while she considered his words. She knew that men had trouble distinguishing between what their heads, hearts, and manly members wanted, so they often couldn't define whom or what they loved. They tended to blame women for their own confusion and a great deal of trouble came from that. Sammy blamed Karen, used her as an excuse for his own problems.

Men were, of course, complete fools. Sammy was dear and kind and compassionate, but he was no exception.

And Brianna was a healer. She wondered if there was any way she could heal him of the pain Karen had given him. Heal him so he could love some woman in his own time?

"No," she said firmly. "I don't think so."

Even she wasn't that much of a martyr.

So, she stirred the pot as silence grew between them, and tried to decide what she could do. About anything. Her problems. His problems. Theirs.

"Oh, well," she said at last, "at least I can do something about Donal's."

Sammy suddenly looked at her. She wondered if he had anything more to say about Karen, but she didn't ask. His eyes were full of worry, but also a hope he probably didn't know he felt. It made her feel hopeful, though she didn't know why.

She could sense his urge to drown his questions in kisses and caresses. She wanted to do the same, to run into his arms and forget everything but the wonder of his touch. Instead, she held herself still and respected his silence. He was a thinker, this mighty creature she loved. He looked like a warrior, he moved like a warrior, but he was more head and heart than he was muscle and menace.

Brianna loved him for his strength of mind more than his strength of body. She wanted more with each passing second to reach out to him, but she remained still.

The fire sputtered and the pot bubbled, gulls and ravens circled overhead while a breeze rattled the branches of the surrounding oaks. The herd dog barked out commands in the nearby meadow. Despite the noise of the world around them, the grove was filled with the silence between them.

Oddly enough, Sammy realized, it was a comfortable silence, despite last night's sexual fiasco. And despite the insistent drumming of her voice in his head all night long, he liked hearing her voice. Being near her was wonderful.

When he'd first seen her as he came up the hill he'd felt as if he'd just come home. All he'd done for the last few days was think about her; now he couldn't understand why he'd thought he'd needed to leave her. He should have known better than to pull that kind of silently suffering, uncommunicative guy thing. He'd seen a lot of beautiful countryside, but no Vikings. He hadn't been anything but confused the whole time.

"I loved you before I met you, I think," he said at last. He hadn't meant to say the *L* word out loud, it just came out. He promised himself he wouldn't say it again.

He wanted to take her in his arms, but he drew up his knees and wrapped his arms around them instead. "I heard you singing to me. It was the most beautiful sound I ever heard. I never wanted anything more than I wanted to meet the voice singing in my head. And now that I have, I don't want to leave you. That's what I've been thinking about for days, leaving you. Keeping you safe."

"But you have to."

"Yeah. I have to."

She looked at him through the mysterious steam rising from the pot. "Then we'll not discuss it again." Her voice was firm, but she looked as if she was on the edge of tears.

Sammy supposed that was for the best. He nodded.

Brianna heard the fear of betrayal in his voice when he spoke of loving her, and flinched inside. It wasn't just betrayal, was it? It was her.

"What is it you fear?" she couldn't help but ask. "The magic?" It would be awful if he feared her magic. She was nothing without her magic. "I will give it up for no man," she said, though it hurt to put her needs before those of the man she loved. Not that it mattered. He was leaving her. Her magic would see to that.

"You *are* magic," he answered, and her heart sang at his understanding. "You couldn't stop having visions if you tried."

"But they frighten you," she said, petulant when she knew she had no cause to be. "They frighten everyone. Even Donal." She realized she was confessing her fears to the one person she trusted utterly, not really accusing him of being like the rest.

"Sure they do," he agreed. He moved to her side. He took her hand and kissed the back of it, then the palm. It sent shivers through her. "But I get scared for you, not because of you."

Brianna felt immense relief at Sammy's words. Not just relief, but a flicker of hope that this wasn't a completely hopeless situation after all. Perhaps her visions of herself in his future place were not so frightening as they seemed. Perhaps there was some way to work out—

No. That was ridiculous. Her place was here.

She turned from him abruptly and busied herself with stirring the pot. Sammy didn't say anything, he just stayed seated beside her. She could feel his gaze on her, but she didn't look at him. After a while, she stood.

"Where you going?" Sammy called after her as she started out of the grove.

She looked back over her shoulder. Sammy had gotten to his feet. "I'm going to see Moira and Bridget."

"Why?" he asked as he followed her.

"I need a lock of their hair."

"Oh." After a moment, he added, "Huh?"

16

"*You're working on* a love spell?"

"Not exactly."

"But you said it was to keep Donal and the girls together," Sammy said as they entered Ban Ean. "Sounds like a love spell to me."

"Well, it's not." She saw his confusion and said, "Trust me, I know the difference between a love spell and what I'm brewing."

"Oh, yeah?"

"I know the difference between love and—and other things. Bridget and Moira love my brother, but they have ever been flighty girls. The potion I'm brewing for them will keep their attention fixed on Donal. It's not a love spell. Not really."

"Oh," he said, a note of teasing in his voice. "I see. It's not a love spell, it's a memory aid." He took her hand in his as they walked along. "You know," he added, "I think Donal can handle the girls on his own."

"Oh, aye, Donal thinks so as well."

"Then why not let him have his shot at it without any chemical enhancement?"

"Chemical?"

"Magical, whatever."

"Because Moira and Bridget asked me for the potion, of course."

"*They* asked—but how can they start a marriage under false pretenses like that?"

"False?"

"They'll know that they don't really love Donal."

"Of course they love Donal." She saw no reason for Sammy to be upset about someone else's marriage plans. "Bridget and Moira asked me to help them make a commitment they aren't sure they can keep to on their own. At least *they're* willing to *try* to make a commitment."

Sammy's face went red, and he pressed his lips together as if struggling not to comment. Brianna felt a slight hit of shame at having touched his sore spot, but she didn't apologize. She would concentrate on Donal's wedding for now, she decided as they came around the corner of the church and into a crowd. Perhaps she'd continue to fight with Sammy later.

Rory MacMurdo was standing on the church step looking as if he'd just won the keys to heaven and the bottomless cauldron of fortune for his very own. When he saw Brianna his smile widened, and she knew exactly what it was the king felt so triumphant about.

Rory waved away the people in front of the church as he called out, "Make way for the bride of the MacMurdo!"

Sammy looked down at Brianna and asked, "What's he talking about?"

"Me," Brianna answered, and stalked forward angrily, practically dragging him along with her.

"Thought so," Sammy said as they approached the church step. Maybe he didn't understand the king's words, but he didn't have any trouble understanding what he was up to.

He noticed that Brianna's father, Sean, and Donal were standing near the king, all looking at Brianna with various expressions of concern. Just about every member of the monastic community was in the square, waiting in curious silence. Sammy saw that the king had brought a lot of his own people with him, including Cormac, the man he'd left to look after Deirdre when she was in labor. Sammy gave the man a friendly nod in passing, but he got a hostile look in response. In fact, all of Rory's men were glaring at him. Sammy figured it was because he was holding hands with Brianna.

Things did not look good, especially for Brianna. Rory had come to take her away, and Sammy knew she didn't want to go. Well, he certainly wasn't going to let her be taken anywhere against her will.

He felt himself tensing in anticipation of a fight, and hoped his muscles were stretched enough by the brisk pace Brianna had set on their walk back to Ban Ean.

Brianna could have screamed with frustration. Instead she looked up at the red-bearded king and demanded, "What are you doing here, Rory MacMurdo?"

Rory stepped down from the church entrance and put his hand on Brianna's shoulder. "It's the cows, darling girl," he told her, completely ignoring Sammy's presence. "Your brother took them and I've come to either behead him for the theft or marry you in reparation. It's up to you to save Donal's life. Your father has agreed, and this time you will marry me. No more excuses, my dark jewel." His smile widened. "See how simple it is?"

"You owed my father those cows," Brianna replied.

Rory gestured toward the abbot, who was cringing in the shadow of the church door. "Ah, but Colum agrees that stealing is a great sin. And stealing from a king is an even mightier sin than stealing from a common man. My honor has been stained. It's up to you to redeem it for Donal's crime."

"What Rory means," Sean said, stepping up beside the king, "is that he and your father struck a deal before the cattle was even stolen. Donal was tempted—"

"He did not have to yield to temptation," Brianna's father broke in. "It was the sins of the flesh that called to him."

"All you ever worry about is sin, Colum. Be quiet, now, while we work this out," Sean said.

"I'll not be silent, you wicked pagan!" her father shouted.

Brianna knew her meek and loving father had to be upset indeed to speak so to her uncle. Still, she couldn't stop herself from defending Sean. "Wicked! Who is it who tends the sick? How dare you call Uncle Sean wicked?"

Sammy squeezed Brianna's hand gently. "Uh, babe, I don't exactly know what this argument is about, but I don't think this is the time for it."

"Aye," she agreed. She looked up at the tall giant beside her, and her expression softened. "You're right, Sammy, my love."

"Your love!" Rory stomped up to them and stood toe to toe with Sammy. "She's not yours to be loving, stranger."

While Brianna translated Rory's words, Sammy took his arm from around Brianna and did a quick

assessment of the angry king. He was a broad-shoul-
dered man who measured maybe six feet, which was
tall for this era. He was muscular—a trained fighter,
Sammy supposed, and probably not used to losing.
Vain, too, he added after carefully noting the man's
finely worked clothes and heavy gold jewelry that
included a thick torque and wide bracelets.

"Actually, she is my love," Sammy told the king.
While Brianna gasped at his words, he added, "We're
engaged. Tell him, Bri."

She blinked, and had to open and close her mouth a
few times before she could get any words out. "Tell
him what?"

"That we're engaged."

"In what?"

"Just tell him you and I are getting married."

"We are?"

Sammy sighed heavily. "No, of course not. But if he
thinks we are he'll leave you alone."

He expected her to be shocked or upset by his
words, but instead she gave him a conspiratorial smile.
"Ah, of course. I told my father the same thing a few
days ago."

"That's what Donal told me."

Brianna blushed. "You knew?"

Sammy nodded. "Donal said he'd figured that you
didn't mean it. So I didn't think it was necessary to
bring it up."

Rory glowered at him as he spoke, then he looked at
Brianna. "What's the man saying?" he asked. "I can't
understand a word. Is his tongue made of oatmeal?"

Several of Rory's men laughed at the king's words.
Brianna just smiled wickedly and answered, "Oh, no,
my lord, it's more of a cat's tongue, clever and quick

and very pleasing to the touch. I've inspected it myself and know this to be true. 'Tis a kiss like fire and honey mixed with poteen and storm that my Sammy has."

"Thanks, babe," Sammy answered with a modest duck of his head.

He chuckled to himself at her description while Brianna looked pleased with herself. Laughter erupted from Donal and Sean while the abbot and just about everyone else present gasped in shock. Silence reigned among the king's followers. Rory's face went red with fury as his hand flew to his sword.

Sean hurried forward before the king could draw his weapon, "Would you offend my honor and yours by harming my guest?" the druid shouted as he halted before the king.

The crowd murmured worriedly while Rory looked more confused than angry. The king eased his hand away and took a step back, fixing his attention on Brianna.

"You're mine," Rory told her. "I don't care if you have been kissing the wrong man."

"I'm not yours, and I'll kiss whom I please."

"You've been kissing him?" her horrified father asked, pointing at Sammy. "You've been kissing the fairy lord?"

Despite Sean's timely interference Sammy still thought there was going to be a fight. He hustled the older man to the edge of the crowd and turned back to Brianna, who was confronting her father.

"I'll do more than kiss him." She took Sammy's arm. "This man is the one I'll marry."

Rory's face turned even redder and he opened his mouth to give an angry howl, but a group of riders came into the square before he could.

When he saw who the lead rider was he took his frustration out on her. "By St. Tigernach of Clones, woman," he swore at Deirdre, "Can't you let a man go anywhere by himself?"

Cormac hurried forward to help the queen down from her gentle pony, and she marched up to her husband with a falsely sweet smile. "I've come to help you retrieve your cows, my lord, just as Queen Maeve helped bring home the Cow of Cooley. It was the cows you came for, was it not?" she asked, then knelt before the abbot for his blessing.

Rory turned and followed his wife. "I—" he began, but she took his hand in her own soft, slim one and drew him down to kneel beside her.

Within moments everyone in the square but Sean the druid was on their knees and Colum had launched into a long, rambling prayer. Rory could do nothing but let the praying go on. By the time everyone got back on their feet, his pleasure in his triumph was gone, but his fury was still bubbling close to the surface.

Deirdre kept his hand in hers and turned her shining gaze on him. "Shall we take our cows and go home now, my love?"

Oh, she was being clever with her gentle, persuading demeanor, trying to show him that he needed no woman but her. He loved her, and perhaps she was right, but this game had gone too far. He wasn't going to let her win so easily. He wasn't going to let Brianna win. He was king and he would have his way. He would have the two most beautiful women in all Eire as his legal wives, and he would have them today!

He growled at his smiling Deirdre and turned on the man whom Brianna would claim as her own. "You're a great and ugly bull, and I don't care if you were sent from the fairies by way of the king of Tara. Step away from my woman."

Brianna had been amused and quite pleased by Deirdre's interference. She'd hoped that Rory would say his prayers and go home with his wife like a good lad, but apparently he had no intention of giving up his claim to her.

"Your woman is by your side," she told him. "My man is by mine. I'll not have you. My visions do not lie. We will be man and wife and you cannot stop it." There. She'd given the king an honorable retreat. He could go away saying that even he could not argue with fate. His face would be saved, and she would be rid of him.

The king crossed his arms on his broad chest. "If you do not marry me, then your brother dies." At Rory's nod two of his guards moved to seize hold of Donal.

Donal kicked one in the back of the knee, knocking him off balance. Then he toppled the second man with a flat-handed smash to his throat and grabbed one of the downed men's swords. Meanwhile everyone else stared at him in consternation while Sammy gave his student a very small, approving nod.

"You are outnumbered," Sammy reminded him as Donal edged up to where he stood with Brianna.

"How'd you do that?" Brianna asked her twin.

"Sammy taught me."

"Oh, aye." She gave Sammy an adoring look. "I should have guessed."

"I could teach you if you want," he said. "If we get out of this alive."

"You would? You could? Could I be a warrior woman like the great queens of old?"

Her eagerness almost made him forget that the rest of Rory's men now had their weapons out. Sean and the monks had retreated to the shelter of the wide church door. Deirdre was clinging to her husband's arm, but her servants were quickly backing away from the center of the square.

Sammy shook his head. One moment everyone was praying, and now here they were getting ready for a fight. He had no intention of letting all these people get into a fight. He figured a simple skirmish between just two people would be enough to settle this nonsense. He knew it wasn't going to be Rory.

"Translate for me," he said as he took a step toward Rory. He bowed formally, his palms flat against his thighs. "Okay, dude," he said. "Let's talk this over. Basically, it happened like this," he went on quickly while Rory frowned at him and Deirdre clung tenaciously to her husband's sword arm. "You called Brianna's bluff over the cows and you lost. The cows were owed to the monastery, you agreed with Brianna's dad that we'd pick them up and it would look like a theft."

After Brianna finished turning Sammy's words into understandable Gaelic, Rory said, "I did?"

Sammy nodded. "We both know it was a conspiracy to get Brianna to agree to marry you. It didn't work. Why don't you just drop it?"

"Indeed," said the abbot from the door of the church. "Our agreement has troubled my soul since we made it. There's been enough trouble over the cows. I agreed to allow my son to marry two women instead of entering the priesthood in exchange for my daughter entering the house of a king."

Rory turned on the abbot. "You thought it a clever plan when I proposed it, old man."

Colum gave a regretful shake of his head. "It was vanity to wish my child to marry so high. She has told me many times that she will not have you, Rory Mac-

Murdo. I will no longer try to force her. Let her follow her vision."

"You're a weak fool!" Rory snarled. He shook off his wife and spun back to face Sammy. "I will have her!"

"No, you won't!" Brianna countered fiercely after she'd translated everything that had just been said to Sammy.

Sammy gestured for Brianna to stay out of this. "Listen," he said to Rory, "I want to marry her, you want to marry her, she wants to marry me, but you don't want to give up. Right?"

Rory puzzled through this muddle and answered, "That is so, outsider."

"You believe in challenges, right? In trial by combat? That sort of thing?"

It was Cormac, the guard commander, who answered. Brianna repeated, "We surely do, giant. A man's honor is measured in contests of all sorts."

"Cool," Sammy said, and turned a bright smile on Rory. "You want Brianna, Rory? I'll fight you for her."

Brianna gave him a worried look, but translated. As Sammy's meaning was made clear a collective gasp went up from the crowd. Deirdre squeaked in shock. Hands that had been relaxing, tightened on weapons once more. The abbot began to pray loudly. Sean began to recite one of his spells. Brianna tugged urgently on Sammy's arm, and Rory looked as if he was about to have a seizure.

Sammy looked around at the shocked crowd. "What'd I say? I thought that was how you people operate."

It was Donal who answered. "You can't challenge a king!"

"Why not?"

"Because he's the king," Brianna told him. She didn't seem at all happy about his offer to fight for her. "Rory's honor is the honor of his people. If he loses, the people lose. A king should not be challenged directly." She pointed to a big man standing next to Cormac. "Dillon is the king's champion. He answers challenges for the king."

"Oh." Sammy considered for a moment, then said. "It's like the concept of face, right?"

"Aye," she said. "Exactly. The king cannot lose face himself."

He bent down and whispered in her ear, "Why not? Just this once? To get him off your case."

Brianna looked thoughtful, then a slow smile spread across her features. "Oh, wouldn't it be lovely to be rid of the man at last." She kissed the tip of Sammy's chin, then faced the king with a wicked glint in her eyes.

"If you want me, Rory MacMurdo," she announced loud enough for the whole village to hear, "then you'll fight for me yourself. I'll accept the marriage no other way."

It was Deirdre who rapped out an angry response. "No woman is worth a king's honor!"

"I know that," Brianna agreed. She pointed at Rory. "But does he?"

Rory slapped his sword into its sheath and strode up to where she and Sammy stood. "By St. Scuithin of Slieve Margy, I'll not let you and this great yellow gelding of yours win!"

"And by the Wise Woman of Wicklow herself, I'll not let you win, you flame-haired fool!" Brianna swore back.

Sammy scratched his jaw. "Frankly, Rory," he said,

studying the animosity between the pair, "I don't know why you want her."

Rory gave him a venomous look and stomped off to talk to Cormac and his stand-in. Sammy put his arm comfortably and conspicuously around Brianna's shoulder and waited.

Rory was so angry the whole of his vision was tinted with red. "Well?" he said to his men. He consulted them out of habit, even though he'd already made his choice.

Dillon looked him over, and with a fine reading of his mood gave the reply Rory wanted. "In matters of love, it is best to fight your own battles, my lord."

Cormac looked from Rory to the stranger. "You are a bull of battle as all know. He's big, but is he a warrior? I'm told he's a fighter, but I've seen him at practice. All he does is stretch and exercise and dance across the sand. What kind of fighting practice is that?"

Rory put a hand on his half-brother's shoulder. "Then you say I can take him?"

"Aye," Cormac agreed after a slight hesitation. "You are the king. How can you not win a fight with a man who acts as a midwife and eats only roots? The day will be yours."

"The girl will be yours," Dillon added encouragingly. "To accept the challenge will only increase your honor."

Rory gave a decisive nod and drew his sword once more. "I accept your challenge," he called out to the stranger. "Arm yourself!"

Donal offered Sammy a sword, but Sammy just waved it away. "Don't need it," he said and moved at a graceful lope into the empty center of the square.

Brianna watched him as she was urged backward by her twin. "We need to give them room," Donal said as Rory moved forward to face Sammy.

She didn't know whether to be worried or confident in the outcome of the fight. "I wish he had a sword," she said, looking at the polished blade in the king's right hand.

"He needs a sword," Rory said, echoing her thought.

Sammy shook his head as Cormac tried to hand him his. "No."

"Does he intend to be slaughtered where he stands, then?" Rory questioned. He gave a taunting laugh. "Perhaps he is looking for death to escape Brianna's sharp tongue, then?"

The crowd laughed. Brianna even smiled a little, then her gaze met Deirdre's. The queen was looking at her from the step of the church, with Cormac and Dillon flanking her protectively. Brianna saw none of the hostility and resentment she was used to from Rory's wife. She did see concern that she shared. Deirdre shook her head sadly, Brianna did the same, exchanging the knowledge that men are stubborn fools.

"Sometimes we need to conspire together against them," Brianna whispered, and felt as if Deirdre heard her. The queen nodded, and Brianna knew that Deirdre did not hold her accountable for the upcoming battle, even if she was the prize.

Brianna nervously laced her fingers together and stood perfectly still while Rory continued to scoff at the uncomprehending Sammy.

"Do you plan just to stand there and be cut down?" He raised his sword while Sammy merely tilted his head to look at him. "Fine with me."

Sammy took a step back, Rory charged forward. The crowd drew in a collective gasp of breath. The fight was over in the space of that breath.

Rory's head was tilted up to watch his enemy's eyes. Sammy held Rory's gaze and hardly seemed to move as his right leg shot straight up. In two smooth motions he kicked the king in the jaw, then in the chest as his foot came back down. The sharp jab pushed Rory backward. Rory's sword fell from his hand, hitting the packed earth with a dull thud. Rory followed the sword down, crumpling into a coughing, groaning heap at Sammy's feet.

"No problem," Sammy said, and turned to Brianna.

It had happened so fast Brianna hadn't quite grasped that the fight was over. "But—"

Deirdre screamed and rushed forward, closely followed by Cormac and Dillon. She knelt beside her husband. The king's men rushed at Sammy, and Donal and Sean stepped in front of him.

Donal had his sword, but Sean had authority. "The victory was won fairly," he said. "You would offend Rory's honor more to harm the man who bested him."

Dillon lowered his weapon. "Aye," he agreed with a defeated sigh. "This is a sad day." He and Cormac went to stand over their fallen lord, whom Deirdre was already learning over.

Sean went to carefully examine his bruised jaw and chest. "You'll be fine," he said as the crowd drew near. He looked up at the king's men. "What are you waiting for? Help him to his feet."

They did, and Sean helped Deirdre up. She glanced at Rory, and Brianna thought the lady hid a smile behind her hand as her husband shook off his men's support.

Rory rubbed his jaw and said in a voice slurred by the rising swelling, "In matters of love it is best to fight your own battles, my lord." While Dillon flinched, Rory swung his angry gaze to Cormac. "The day will be yours. And what was mine?"

While the crowd watched in stunned silence, the men went down on their knees before the king. He slapped his hand hard against the crouching Cormac's ear. His furious face was nearly as red as his hair.

"Nothing!" he went on. "I've gained nothing from this day's work. My pride is broken. The girl is given to another."

He rubbed the spot where his beard covered his bruised jaw. The fire of his anger blazed down on his disgraced servants.

"Oh, dear," Brianna murmured, fearful that he was about to order Dillon and Cormac's executions.

"You are no longer in my service, or kin to me," he declared. "I never want to see the faces of either of you again. You are banished from my land. Outlaw. Masterless." Both men cringed, but neither begged for mercy. Rory pointed toward the rolling hills beyond Ban Ean. "Be off. I will send my huntsmen and my hounds after you if you are seen within my lands after this day."

The men scrambled up off their knees and hurried to disappear from the square. The crowd parted to let them pass, cringing away from their disgrace. Rory, looking at no one, mounted his horse and rode away. The rest of his retainers scrambled to follow him. Deirdre looked after her departing husband but seemed in no hurry to leave Ban Ean.

"Well," the queen said as her gaze swept around the gathering. Her attention came to rest on Sammy and

Brianna. "We have a wedding to get on with, do we not? Right now," she added, speaking to the abbot.

Sammy tugged on Brianna's sleeve. "What?"

"We're getting married," Brianna told him.

He grabbed her by the shoulders. "What?"

"Married. Right now."

Sammy looked around wildly. The square was full of people, and they were all grinning at him. Even Brianna's eyes were full of merriment. "Now wait a minute."

"You won me fairly, Sammy Sam Bergen."

"But—I was hoping for a long engagement. You, know, like—"

"Forever?"

"Brianna!" He gave her shoulders a slight shake. "The point was to protect you from Rory."

Brianna's heart was breaking at the thought of the sham marriage she'd brought on herself, but she refused to let it show. He had started this; she was going to see it carried through to the end. For her honor, for Sammy's, for Deirdre's, and even for the king's.

She gave Sammy a brisk nod and kept her tone slyly amused as she said, "And I thank you for it. But would it not be safer for me if I was indeed your wife." She brushed her hand across his cheek. "Oh, I know you're going away, but they do not. It would only be for a few days, then the fairy lord and his beast will disappear into legend." He looked at her thoughtfully while she forced herself to keep an amused expression on her face.

"You don't mind?" he asked. "That it's not real?"

"I do not mind," she lied. She looked at the queen, at her father, at the villagers. "Besides, I do not think we have a choice."

Sammy looked around as well. "Yeah, I see your point. Oh, what the hell?"

Sammy laughed, throwing back his gold-maned head and letting out a deep roar. Brianna's forced laughter joined in harmony with his a moment later, followed by the laughter of everyone else in the village square. There were shouts of joy and congratulations from the onlookers. While amusement bubbled around them, Sammy grabbed Brianna around the waist, lifted her, and swung her around.

"Yes!" he crowed as he twirled her. "Let's do it right now!" He pulled her to him and covered her mouth with his.

If she'd thought the kisses they'd shared before had been exciting, she'd been mistaken. This kiss, for all that she was aware of the bittersweet irony of the moment, took her out of herself and sent her soaring right out of this world.

After a while, somewhere in the distance, she heard people cheering. And her father denouncing the wicked ways of the flesh. And Sean defending them. And then she felt a hand that she knew couldn't be Sammy's, because Sammy's hands were shamelessly wrapped around her behind, tugging on the long braid of her hair.

The hand tugged hard enough to hurt, and it broke the spell Sammy's mouth put her under, and she looked up. It was Donal. "What?" she growled at her twin.

He was giving her his usual teasing grin. "Do you want to get married, or do you want to make love?" he asked. "Personally," he went on, "I think you might want to consider the lovemaking first."

As she gave an embarrassed gasp she noticed Bridget and Moira stood next to him. "Is it marriage or lovemaking you have on your mind, brother?"

"Both." He draped an arm over each girl's shoulder. Moira and Bridget giggled in unison. "What my twin does, I do," he said. "Let's make it a double wedding."

17

"So this is where you slipped off to."

Brianna didn't look up as Sammy came into the abbot's house. She continued mixing the honey posset.

Sammy stepped up to the glowing peat fire while she crumbled herbs into the pottery cup. "It's started to rain. Again."

She nodded at his casually spoken words, but did not reply. She poured a measure of poteen into the cup.

"How come you disappeared right after the ceremony? I didn't even get a chance to kiss the bride."

Sammy and Donal had been surrounded by the men of Ban Ean almost before they'd spoken their marriage vows to offer congratulations and advice. The women had clustered around Brianna and her new sisters-in-law. Deirdre had taken off one of her gold bracelets and presented it to her as a wedding present, satisfied to be rid of her rival at last. Then the queen had bowed to the holy abbot and gotten onto her pony. Brianna had noticed her father beginning to cough as the queen rode away.

Brianna had slipped away as they watched the queen go, knowing that she had to be alone for a while or she would fall apart in front of all of Ban Ean. Oh, they would not have minded her tears. The women would soothe and reassure her, the men would offer gentle jokes. Donal's words would be barbed, but he would mean well in his own way. And they wouldn't know they were comforting a sinful, lying woman whose vows before the church door had been no more than an expedient jest.

"My father is ill," she finally answered Sammy. She held up the cup. "This will help his cough."

Brianna was definitely bent out of shape, but Sammy wasn't quite sure why. Second thoughts? Prewedding-night jitters? Was there even going to be a wedding night? If he had anything to say about it there was going to be. He wanted her more than he'd ever wanted anyone in his life. There was no reason they couldn't have at least a few days of happiness together. Hell, even one night with Brianna would be worth the whole trip back to ancient times.

He came toward her, but she took a step away. She was definitely jittery, he decided. He put his hands behind his back and gave his most nonthreatening smile. "Donal tells me they're giving us a party in the common house. Why don't you put on your best dress and we'll dance, or whatever you do on a date."

"I have to see to my father."

Sammy did not like the flat tone of her voice. He wondered what it was covering. "Did I miss something back in the square? When you talked me into marrying you?"

Her lower lip trembled for a moment. So did the hand holding the cup. She looked up at him, tears in her eyes. "'Tis not a marriage."

Sammy swore under his breath. He felt that a certain amount of 'this wasn't my idea' recrimination might be justified on his part, but he could tell she wasn't up to that kind of useless quarreling. Besides, he had gone along with it.

She started to walk past him and he put his hand out to touch her. He ran his finger along her jawline, then down to caress her neck. "You're beautiful," he told her. "I want to make love to you." She turned her head slightly and rubbed her cheek against his palm. Her skin was warm and silky against his hand. "You want to make love to me."

He started to take the cup from her. He wanted to pull her close and kiss her. Instead, she moved away, toward the door. "No," she said. "I do not want to make love to you."

"Brianna." He took a deep breath. Without making the words an accusation he reminded her, "You wanted to last night."

Brianna choked down a sob. She forced herself to look Sammy in the eye. "What I wanted to do last night was wrong."

"Why? Because we weren't married?"

"Yes," Brianna said, louder than she intended. Her finely trained voice carried throughout the house, rising as she spoke. "I thank God I woke up this morning still a maiden despite what I offered you last night."

It was not Sammy she was angry with, but she was in pain because she knew she would lose him. Even with a wedding vow, he could never be hers. She would have given herself to him and been glad of the memory last night. Now the thought of a few hours of pleasure with nothing to follow was too much to bear. Better never to know what loving was like than to pine for it—forever.

"I'm sorry about last night," he told her.

"So am I."

"We can start—"

"No!" She shook her head wildly. "I'll not have you in my bed. I'll wake up a virgin tomorrow as well. This is no true marriage!"

She shouted the last words, which was unfortunate, considering that the door banged open while she was speaking. And that the men standing in the doorway with their mouths hanging open as she whirled to face them were Cormac and Dillon, Rory's exiled men. She went hot with embarrassment at knowing they must have overheard her words. At least the embarrassment drove out some of her self-inflicted pain.

"What do you want?" she demanded before either of them could speak. Their mouths opened, but no sounds came out.

Then Dillon took a deep breath and spoke to Cormac. "The marriage not to be consummated? We must—"

Cormac elbowed Dillon in the ribs before he could finish. While Brianna blushed from head to foot, Cormac said hastily, "We've come to see the abbot. We're here to join the holy brothers."

"To become monks," Dillon added, as though anyone from Ban Ean might be confused about which holy brothers they meant. Dillon, Brianna well knew, for he was her mother's brother by their father's third wife, was strong and handsome, but not particularly intelligent.

"You're joining the monastery?" Brianna asked. "Why?"

"Your father?" Cormac asked again, ignoring Brianna's question. "We must speak with your father."

Brianna decided not to pry further. She needed to get away from Sammy. Besides, she still held the cup of posset for her father. She would take the men to him, but they had better not ask her any more questions about what they'd overheard. She favored Cormac and Dillon with a warning look.

"You will be taking vows of silence, I hope," she said. "Starting today."

Dillon looked at Cormac mournfully. "Will we have to?" Cormac just looked long-suffering instead of replying.

"Come along," she said to Rory's men as she stepped outside, eager to escape from Sammy's all-too-tempting presence. "You can come with me to see the abbot."

"At last. You've been in the church for near two hours. I mean, I'm glad I found you."

A jolt of anxiety passed through Brianna as she responded to the concern in the speaker's voice. She had been hoping that it was Sammy, but the voice was no where near as deep or as caring. She looked up into the face of one of the men her father had sent to the novice master earlier in the day.

"Yes, Dillon?"

"A healer is needed." The man who'd spoken was tall, dressed in a new brown monk's robe, and a fresh tonsure revealed much of the scalp above his forehead.

"Who is ill?" she asked as he hurried toward her.

He took her by the arm and urged her away from the square. Almost everyone in the community was already in the common house. She had lingered in the church for a long time to offer up prayers, and to hide from her husband. She'd been planning to go up to the oak grove later and offer a few prayers to the older gods, but now it looked as if she would have to postpone worship and hiding in order to work.

A steady rain was coming down outside, and she pulled her shawl over her head for protection. The smell of roasting beef filled the air, and laughter came from the hall as she and Dillon passed it by. A harper began to play. She had to raise her voice to be heard above the festivities inside.

"Who is ill?" she asked Dillon as he hurried her past a monk carrying a platter of fresh baked bread from the bakehouse. The monk gave one glance back before continuing on his way.

"Cormac," Dillon told her. "This way." He steered her toward the stables. "We must hurry."

"What's wrong with him?"

"A horse—it kicked him. Bit him. Stepped on him. In here."

Brianna thought that Dillon sounded singularly unsure of just what had happened to his friend. She tried to pull away. "I have to get my bag of medicines."

His grip tightened on her arm. "No," he said, and shoved her inside the stable. "I've got her," he called out.

Cormac stepped out of the shadows of a stall. "The horses are ready," he said. He looked at her and said sternly, "Not a sound, lass."

Like Dillon, the former soldier wore the robe and tonsure of a monk, but there was nothing of the humble novice in the man's alert bearing. Nor did he look as if a horse had done anything at all to him.

"What do you mean not a—"

Before she could finish, Dillon grabbed both her

arms from behind, and Cormac gagged her with a piece
of cloth. She kicked at both of them, but they ignored
her. Cormac mounted a horse while Dillon tied her
hands behind her. When he was done he passed her up
to Cormac as though she weighed nothing. She soon
found herself slung sideways, head down, in front of
Cormac. When she struggled, he slapped her rump.

"Be still," he commanded. "It's not such a long
ride. You'll be fine," he added in a gentler tone. "Hurry,
Dillon."

Dillon mounted a second horse and they rode out.
All Brianna saw of their departure was upside down.
They traveled swiftly, at a jarring gallop. It reminded
her of riding in a boat on rough seas. And her reaction
was the same as when she was in a boat. She soon
became desperately ill from the motion. Fortunately, it
wasn't long before she passed out.

"What has gotten into that woman?" Sammy muttered as he entered the common house. Oh, he had a
few answers to the question, and a lot of things he
needed to say to Brianna. He had to find her first,
before he could talk to her. Or maybe he should wait
and let her find him. He didn't know.

He did know the moment he stepped in out of the
rain that it was a great party. Everybody in the village
seemed to be crowded into one smoky room, even
some ladies he hadn't seen before dressed in nuns'
habits. Tables were piled with hastily prepared food.
Musicians were playing on opposite ends of the room.
Some people were dancing, some were singing. Donal
and his brides were standing by the fire, surrounded by
a crowd. It was a very noisy, happy gathering. Donal,

grinning proudly, waved and gestured for Sammy to join him.

Sammy decided, almost defiantly, that he was going to have a great time, with or without Brianna. He'd gone for a walk in the rain after she'd left, feeling furious at her behavior and confused at his own less than helpful reaction to her. He didn't like being furious or confused, so he'd waited until he was under control before returning to the party. He hoped Brianna would be there, and that they could go somewhere private as soon as possible.

Standing head and shoulders above just about everybody, he now had no trouble looking around. Brianna was nowhere in sight. After a while he made his way back to the door, leaned against the wall next to it, and waited. Okay, so she hadn't shown up yet. Eventually she would. She wasn't going to miss her own wedding reception. He figured she was too dutiful for that.

Eventually, Ailill came up to him. The boy was holding an earthenware cup, and his cheeks were bright red. His eyes were bright.

"You're drinking poteen?" Sammy asked. "Aren't you a little young for that?"

Donal came up behind Ailill and plucked the cup out of his hand. He sniffed it. "I thought so. You're too young for this." While Ailill looked on, crestfallen, Donal drained the cup himself. He gave a satisfied sigh. "Uncle Sean makes the finest brew in all of Eire." Donal patted the boy on the shoulder, then pointed toward the long table. He nudged him toward it as he said, "Off with you."

Ailill gave his foster brother a jerky nod and headed for the food. Sammy chuckled.

"I haven't seen Brianna," he said. "Do you know where she is?"

Donal turned around and asked everyone nearby, "Has anyone seen my sister? Her husband here is seeking her."

One of the monks came up and said, "She was with the abbot. Then one of the new novices told her someone was sick."

"You mean she's making a house call?" Sammy asked after Donal translated. He tried to conceal his disappointment at Brianna's absence. "Too bad." He'd almost forgotten he'd married a doctor.

Donal went back to his brides, leaving Sammy to sulk by the door. He leaned against the wall for a while and tried not to fret too much about how long Brianna might be gone. He spent some time mentally kicking himself for last night's fiasco, for today's fiasco, and for what might turn into tonight's fiasco if she didn't turn up pretty soon. He should never have let her leave the house still angry and with things unsettled.

"I'm an idiot," he muttered. "A complete bozo where women are concerned. Always have been. Always will be. I should get out of here and let the woman get on with her life."

The problem was, he didn't want to leave anymore. For when he did, his heart was going to stay right here with Brianna.

He decided to find out just where Brianna was making her house call and wait outside for her until she was done. Then he saw Sean over by the fire, pouring rich gold liquid from his whiskey jug. It looked like the crowd was getting ready to begin toasting the marriages. The poteen suddenly looked inviting. And if he was going to hang around outside a hovel in the rain, a little fortification first wouldn't hurt.

Why not? Sammy thought with a shrug, and went

over to get a cupful and join in the celebration for a while. Then he'd get Donal to find out where he could find his wife.

"And just how," Rory demanded of the men standing in the middle of his hall, "did you come to be here?"

He was leaning against the gallery rail, half-dressed and furious. Dillon and Cormac looked up at him with pleased smiles on their faces. Their newly shorn pates gleamed in the firelight, telling Rory the pair had come from Ban Ean. His retainers surrounded the men he'd exiled, but at a fair distance, with no weapons drawn. Something bundled in a cloak lay at their feet. Rory had been woken from a sound sleep in his wife's bed, and he wasn't at all happy about what had disturbed him.

"Well?" he demanded when neither man gave him a quick answer. "What are you doing here?" Rory stared at his new guard commander. "Who dared let them in?"

Cormac gestured at the bundle. "Peace, brother," he called up to Rory. "I bring you a present."

"We took refuge at the monastery," Dillon went on. He ran his hand over his tonsured head. "We would have stayed and done penance for the wrong we did you. But our luck turned and we saw a chance to make everything right again."

Deirdre came out of her room. Coming up beside him, she asked anxiously, "Is there danger, my lord?"

"No," he assured her. He had left her sleeping when the slave had woken him. "You've disturbed my wife," he called down to Cormac and Dillon. "Be off with you before I have you beheaded for the offense."

"But it's a wife we've brought you," Cormac called back.

"What?" Rory shouted, leaning further over the carved rail to peer down at the shadowed hall. Deirdre's small hand clutched his arm as he spoke.

Grinning, Cormac twitched back the cloak. In the glow from the fire Rory got a glimpse of raven-colored hair and milky skin. "Brianna," he breathed, his groin tightening at the sight of her as she stirred and stared at him.

She was bound and gagged, and Rory thought perhaps he liked her that way, as it prevented her from sharpening her tongue on his hide.

Beside him, Deirdre stiffened. She repeated, "Brianna!" Her tone was far from pleased, and her nails dug *painfully* into his arm. "What is she doing here?"

"I know not," Rory answered her, truly innocent, though certainly pleased. He looked down at his exiled men. "What is the meaning of this?"

"You had no right to have her kidnapped," Deirdre told him in a fierce anger he had done nothing to provoke.

"Hush, my heart," Rory soothed. While he patted her on the shoulder he once again asked his men, "What is the meaning of this?"

"Brianna can still be yours," Cormac declared. He pulled her to her feet and held her before him. Dillon held up a torch so that the dark-haired beauty could be seen more clearly.

"Can she, indeed?" Rory asked. He rubbed his chin as he looked the bound woman over. He slapped Deirdre's hand away when she would have hit him. "Peace, my heart. This does not concern you."

"Not concern—!" Deirdre sputtered in anger for a few moments, then she pointed out, "She's married to another! I witnessed the wedding. You lost her."

"I lost her," Rory agreed, speaking quietly to his wife. "But now it seems I have her back."

"But she's married to another. You have no claim."

He knew Deirdre was right. He knew the jurists who interpreted the laws for him would say the same. Disappointment curdled in his stomach. Cormac and Dillon had made a fool of him again by bringing him this fine present. Maybe he would have them beheaded this time.

"Take her back," he told them. "She's not mine to marry."

"But she is, brother," Cormac replied quickly. "I would not bring another man's wife to you no matter how much you desired her." His face darkened with justifiable anger. "Am I not the son of a king? I have honor of my own, Rory MacMurdo."

"Aye, that you do." He left Deirdre in her anger standing by the gallery rail and hurried down the stairs. "So," he said, coming up to where his brother stood with Brianna, "what have you brought me?"

It was Dillon who answered. "A virgin who refuses to lie with her husband. She will not have the gold bull."

Rory didn't believe it. She had acted as though she adored the man, or fairy, or whatever the giant was. "I would have sworn they had lain together before the wedding."

"Not true. She is a virgin," Cormac insisted. "I heard the words from her own mouth when we went to join the monks." Brianna struggled in Cormac's hold while they discussed her, but they paid her no mind. "We truly meant to join the monastery. But when we heard her angry words we knew we had a way to redeem your honor."

"What? Is the bull incapable?" Rory laughed. "I would

wager it is so. But what has that to do with me?" he added. "She's still his wife."

"The Roman church would say that she is not a wife," Cormac said. "The Roman priests say that marriage is for the procreation of children only. So it must be consummated to be a true marriage."

Though religious discussion raged hot and heavy in every corner of the land, Rory had no taste for theology, whether native to the monasteries of Eire or the Roman rites brought back from traveling clerics. He kept priests and he let them talk all they wanted, but he never paid any attention. He'd always thought the church founded by holy Patrick was good enough for him, but if these new ideas would be of any help to him, perhaps the Roman way was correct after all.

"Well?" he demanded, turning to the nearest priest. "What says the church on the matter of virgin brides? The Roman church," he added before any debate could get started.

"Cormac has the right of it," the priest answered hastily, and correctly for Rory's purposes.

"When we realized you could still claim her, we brought her to you," Cormac said.

"But Brianna doesn't want him!" Deirdre called down from the gallery.

The men paid no attention to her protest. "You are the king," Cormac went on. "The girl is rightfully yours."

"Yes," Rory agreed with a nod. He reached out a hand and touched Brianna's cheek. His fingers came away wet with her angry tears. "All will be well, dark star," he assured her. "You've nothing to fear." She tried to kick him, and he chuckled as he backed away a step. "She may not want me," he told his smiling courtiers, "but she's mine and I'll keep her."

"No, you won't!" Deirdre shouted. "I'll not share this house with another woman."

Rory felt the back of his neck grow hot with embarrassment. He was used to Deirdre complaining to him in private, but it rankled that she would dare to speak out in front of everyone. Her public protest hurt his honor. He chose to ignore her rather than acknowledge her inappropriate behavior.

"I mean what I say, Rory MacMurdo!"

Rory concentrated on what was before him. "I thank you for this gift," he told the men. "I forgive you both, and restore you to your rank in my household."

Dillon bowed in thanks. Cormac would have, but he had the squirming Brianna to deal with. Rory gestured to a pair of slaves. "Take her and clean her up," he told the women. "And watch her closely." He stroked Brianna's cheek again. "I will be seeing you soon, my dark heart."

As Brianna was taken away, the priest spoke to him. "You should not bed her tonight," he said. "Not if you intend to marry her."

"What?" Rory stood very still, stiff with growing anger. He glared at the priest. "I've waited too long for this girl."

The priest did not flinch from his wrath. He pointed at Brianna as the slaves hustled her away. "The woman is clearly unwilling."

Rory clenched his fists at his side. "What of it?"

"It would be rape to force her before marriage."

Rory's jurist stepped forward. "In which case the woman might be able to have your marriage to her annulled under the Brehon Laws."

Rory was quivering with outrage, but he managed to keep his voice steady when he spoke to priest and lawyer. "Are you saying that I cannot bed her this very night? In my own house?"

Both nodded. "It would be wiser to wait until an annulment has been declared from her first husband," the priest said.

"And after you marry her yourself," the jurist added.

"And how long," Rory asked, his voice still mild, "will that take?"

The men gave each other hasty, nervous looks. They obviously recalled times in the past when Rory's anger had turned deadly cold.

"A few days," the priest assured him. "Just a few days, my lord. There are letters to be dispatched to the bishop of Armagh. He will surely grant his permission within a few days."

"Very well," Rory said, the two words coming out in a slow growl.

He had difficulty turning away from the men without striking them. He was a man of hot, swift passion, but he'd trained himself to act as a king, to think even when he'd rather give way to rage. Frustration burned in him as he walked up the stairs. When he looked up and saw Deirdre waiting for him at the top of the stairs he welcomed the coming argument with his queen. It would be a fine way to vent his rage, his passion. He smiled at her as he drew near, a fine, feral smile, to tell her how he would claim her on her own bed and ride out his fury deep inside her.

Oddly enough, his gentle Deirdre gave him his dangerous look right back. He didn't see the heavy silver dish she was holding until she brought it down hard on his head.

18

There were two things Sammy knew for certain when he woke up. One was that he shouldn't have drunk more than one toast to the happy newlyweds. The other was that the warm body stretched out beside him wasn't Brianna's. Fortunately, when he did manage to crack his eyes open enough to take a look, he discovered his sleeping companion was Ailill's wolfhound, and that he was lying on the floor of the common house. Weak morning light was filtering in through the windows. He could hear rain pounding on the roof, which only added to the jarring pain in his head.

He knew he hadn't had more than two cups. He knew he had a hard head for liquor. But he also knew he had the hangover of his life, and it was from only two cups of whiskey.

His brain, however, was back in working order, even if his body was content to shut down and go back to sleep. Now Sammy supposed he'd better get up, clean up, and go looking for his wife.

His wife. Oh, Buddha, what a fiasco! Maybe she'd forgive him, though he wasn't sure what he had to be sorry about. Maybe they could work things out, though he wasn't sure what they needed to work out. To tell the truth, he wasn't all that sure of his name, rank, or social security number right now.

"Aspirin," he said, fumbling with the zipper of his fanny pack. "I need aspirin."

He sat up very slowly, opened his eyes all the way, and looked around. Brianna was not in the common house. He could only suppose she hadn't made it to the party at all. Maybe she'd gone back home after tending to her patient. Maybe she was still with her patient. He was going to have to get up and find out. It wasn't going to be pretty.

"Okay," he said, "I can deal with standing. Sure I can." He wasn't sure at all, not with the way his head and stomach were making war. "What does Sean put in that stuff?" he grumbled as he closed his eyes and cautiously crept to his knees. Maybe, he hoped, his magical Brianna would have a cure for what ailed him.

"And the hangover, too," he said as he finished the slow ascent to an upright position.

Once his feet were planted under him he opened his eyes again and found Donal standing before him. "You look like death itself would be better," he said.

Sammy took a step toward the door. "It would," Sammy agreed. "What are you doing here? You should be on your honeymoon."

"I took an oath to serve you," Donal reminded him. "I thought you might need my help this morning."

"You got that right."

Donal laughed in response. The sound was high-pitched enough to go straight through Sammy's head. He hung on to the door frame for a few moments until the pain settled down to a dull ache again.

"Don't make any loud noises, okay?"

Donal put his fingers in front of his lips and nodded. A wave of affection for the man who was now his brother-in-law, sort of, went through Sammy, but he wasn't up to expressing it at the moment. He gingerly opened the door instead. It was pouring rain outside. Sammy stepped into it and tilted his face to the flooding sky, letting the cold water rush over him. The shock of it helped to clear his head. Donal, Ailill, and the wolfhound followed him outside. It didn't help that the dog started barking as someone came riding into the square.

Sammy had to jump back against the wall as the horse was reined to a halt right in front of him. The rider threw back her heavy hood and glared down at him. Sammy didn't think he'd ever seen anyone so angry in his life. The horse pawed the muddy ground while the wolfhound growled warningly. The woman on the horse pointed an accusing finger at him. She spat out furious words while she glared into his eyes.

His head was still pounding from the aftereffects of the poteen. He wanted to find his wife. He didn't need an angry queen yelling at him. "What's my fault?" he asked her after Donal repeated what she'd said.

"She wants to know why you didn't make love to your wife," Donal explained as Deirdre continued to

berate him. "She says that both she and Brianna had
the man they wanted—then you turned out to be not a
man at all."

"Wait a minute!"

"And now Rory has her. What?" Donal demanded
as the queen got off her horse. "What do you mean
he's got my sister?" He grabbed Sammy's arm. "Do
something!"

Sammy found himself studying Deirdre as he took
in the situation. She was a little thing, smaller than Brianna, with auburn hair and flashing eyes. An angry little redhead. She yelled at him some more while Sammy
stood rock still, an angry fire growing inside him.

"She says she'll not go back to Rory MacMurdo's
hall while he has another woman there," Donal
explained. "She claims this is your doing, and you'll be
the one to make it right." Donal put his hand on his
sword hilt. "She's right, Sammy. You've got to do
something."

His wife had been kidnapped by the king.

His wife! Never mind what either of them had said
yesterday. In his heart this was no joke, no trick, no
small inconvenience. Brianna meant more to him than
he'd realized, and now she was in danger.

Sammy had thought Rory would give up pestering
Brianna when he beat him, but he'd been wrong about
that. It looked like Rory was the type who got even
instead of giving up.

Sammy didn't like himself when he got angry. He
didn't like the things he did to people when he lost
control. When he did, it wasn't pretty. Right now he
was angrier than he'd ever been in his life.

"I'm going to kill him," he said, and it wasn't an
empty threat.

*   *   *

"You can't kill him," Deirdre said again as she paced back and forth before the central hearth.

It seemed to Sean that the woman had absolutely no comprehension that the giant couldn't understand her. Not that Sammy was paying any attention to what anyone in the room was saying anyway. Donal had given up translating some time ago to go off on his own furious tirades about the king's impending doom. Things had not been peaceful in the abbot's house since Deirdre, Donal, and Sammy came trooping in with the news. Sean almost wished he'd gone home last night instead of accepting his brother's invitation to pass the night with him in Ban Ean.

"You can't kill him," Deirdre repeated. She came up to Sammy and gave him a pleading look. "He is my husband and I love him."

Sammy didn't need a translator to understand what she meant. "Brianna's my wife. Even more importantly"—Donal stopped grumbling so he could translate—"the man's a menace. He's acting like a spoiled child who has to have everything he sees. Only he's a kid with power, and that makes him dangerous." Sammy looked from Deirdre to the other people in the room "He's a danger to all of you. Who knows what he'll want next?"

Sammy was sounding civilized out of habit, but in truth he was ready to kill Rory simply because he'd taken Brianna.

"He took my wife," he said to Deirdre. Donal translated. "What would you want Rory to do if somebody abducted you?"

"It is his right to kill Rory," Donal added. "You know it is."

Deirdre lowered her head but not before Sammy saw the tears spilling from her eyes. "Don't do that," Sammy pleaded. There was nothing more dangerous than a crying woman.

She dashed away tears with the back of her hand and looked at Sammy again. "He didn't take your wife. He had nothing to do with abducting her."

She'd explained this before, but Donal repeated it again. She said that Brianna had been taken by the two men Rory had exiled.

Sammy remembered seeing them at the door yesterday. They'd done it in hopes of returning to favor. He'd noticed them looking speculatively at each other, but hadn't suspected they'd been a threat to Brianna. He should have. Somehow, he should have. He should have been there to protect her.

"Okay, Rory didn't do it himself," Sammy conceded, "but he still plans on keeping her."

"That's your fault!"

Deirdre had said that before, too. The reasons Rory was keeping Brianna, besides just wanting her, had something to do with several sets of conflicting religious and civil laws about just what made a marriage legal. Sammy didn't care.

"Listen," he told the queen and Brianna's watching family, "she doesn't want him. Rory doesn't have any legal case. I'm going to get my wife back. And I'm going to kill him." He looked around the room as Donal finished explaining for him. "Now, will somebody please show me the way to this dude's house?"

He and Donal had spent time wandering along what passed for roads in this place when he'd been scouting for Vikings. They'd skirted isolated farms and seaside villages but hadn't once passed anything that looked like it might be the local king's stronghold. They hadn't even gone near the pasture where they'd taken the king's cows.

He got nothing but silence in answer to his question. Sean considered the problem for a while, then finally spoke. "Donal, tell him there is another way."

"Another way?" Sammy stared in puzzlement at the druid. "Nobody's even told me the regular way of getting there yet."

"Another way of defeating Rory," Sean said. He came to stand in front of Sammy. He hoped Sammy would pay attention to him. "No one has to die."

"He has soldiers," Donal told Sammy after repeating his uncle's words. "Swordsmen and spearmen and archers. Even you and I together will have trouble defeating them to get to Rory. He'll have set a watch for you."

"I have to give it a shot," Sammy said. For Brianna's sake he didn't want to be reasonable. He wanted to prove himself to her. But he was, at heart, despite his deadly skills, a man of peace. "What else can I do?"

"Listen to Sean," Donal told him. "He's a druid. Druids are wise."

"Fine," Sammy said. It wasn't as if he could rush off to the rescue until he knew where he was going. "If you've got a better idea, Sean, let me have it."

Sean fingered his beard for a few moments while he looked gravely into Sammy's eyes. Sammy was not impressed by this Merlin imitation. His anger reasserted itself as the silence drew out.

He'd started to turn toward the door when Sean spoke up. "It's a matter of honor, isn't it? Honor is the strongest weapon you have in a battle against a king."

"That's true," Donal said after translating.

Sammy remembered just how important a king's honor, his prestige and dignity, was to all his people. He'd already used it against Rory once. Honor was definitely a dangerous weapon. Maybe he could use it against Rory again.

A weight lifted from his mind as the killing anger suddenly faded for good. Deirdre was still crying. He didn't want to have to deal with making her a widow. It would be better if no one had to die.

"Honor," he said. "How do I get Brianna back with that?"

"He's going to kill you."

Brianna could tell Rory was disturbed by the pleasure she took in her prediction. He drained his gold wine cup and looked as if he was considering throwing it at her. She was seated in his wife's place at the king's table. Rory had forced her into this breach of manners because of his fury at Deirdre's leaving him. Brianna was pleased by the sight of the bloody, bruised lump on his head, proud of Deirdre for putting it there, and hoped it hurt like the devil's own fire.

She was still tied, but her hands were fastened in front of her now, and the gag was gone. At least for now, she added to herself as the king gave her a warning look. She only smiled, then accepted another spoon of stew from the slave who'd been assigned to care for her. It was dinnertime in Rory's hall.

After hours of angry, spitting fury, she had calmed to a cold, certain rage. The rage was welcome, and it drained away her fears and uncertainties of the day before. It made her thinking clearer and gave her perspective on everything that had happened in the last few days. She knew she'd acted like a fool, and that she'd love Sammy with joy instead of regrets—forever.

She was certain Sammy would rescue her, or she'd make Rory's life so unpleasant he'd have to let her go. She also knew that if Rory dared touch her, she wouldn't wait for her husband to avenge her; she'd find a way to kill the king herself.

She watched him fidget with his wine cup, running his thumbs along the jewels set along its outside edge. "Perhaps he'll hold Deirdre as a hostage," she suggested, guessing where Rory's thoughts were. "You can exchange me for her."

"I'll not give you up." Rory slammed his fist on the table. "I'll kill him if Deirdre comes to harm."

"She won't," Brianna replied quickly. "Sammy is kind and loving. She'll be well treated by him."

Her words only made him angrier. "I'll kill him," he repeated.

"But Deirdre left of her own free will," Brianna reminded the king.

The queen had ridden away shouting that she would enter Ban Ean as a nun before living under Rory's roof again. No one had made an effort to stop her. Rory had not been pleased to find Deirdre gone when he regained consciousness after the blow delivered by his queen's hand. Brianna had been delighted when she heard the story.

She looked around her. The hall was crowded, but everyone seemed to be pretending they were somewhere else. The room was silent but for her and Rory. Not even a harper was playing in the gallery. The poet seemed to have run out of verses. The soldiers stood stiffly at the door, and the courtiers ate with their gazes on their food.

She gave Rory the mildest, meekest of smiles. "Your true wife wants you no more than I do. Or so the gossip runs among your court and servants, though none seems willing to speak of this day's events in your presence."

Rory threw the cup at her head and jumped to his feet. It missed, hitting the wall, then clattering loudly to the floor. Rory stood over her, his hands gripping the edge of the table, the knuckles white with the pressure. His face was redder than his hair. Brianna merely blinked when she would rather have flinched from his dangerous regard.

It was Cormac who stepped forward and put a hand on her shoulder. "Should I put the gag back on her?" the reinstated guard captain asked the king. "It would make all our dinners go down easier, I think, if the druidess was silenced."

Brianna looked up at Cormac and told him in a chilling whisper, "This is a druidess who can curse you with or without a voice. Even with my hands tied so I make no magical signs I could conjure harm to you." He stepped back as though his hand had been stung.

Rory made no comment but eased away from the table and turned his back on Brianna. "Where is that priest?" he demanded of Cormac. "Why hasn't he come back from Ban Ean?"

Brianna laughed at Rory's words. "Did you send another in your place to plead with your wife?" she asked. "Must you always send others to do your work? Even my Sammy helped deliver your babe."

He whirled around angrily. "What choice do I have in how I conduct my life? Am I not a king?"

Brianna looked at him steadily. "If you love her you'll be a man."

He gave an angry snort, followed by a vicious laugh. "A *man* like the one you wed, virgin wife?"

Brianna only smiled smugly at his mockery. "'Twas not Sammy's fault. I will make it up to him with long, glorious nights." *For as long as we have,* she added to herself.

His fist banged down on the table again. It rattled the plates of the courtiers. Some stared openly now, some still pretended not to notice the confrontation. Some had wisely slunk away.

"You'll not wait for me much longer!" Rory bellowed. "I'll make you forget that golden ox you chose to marry."

Brianna had never known why Rory kept insisting she would want him someday. Oh, she understood why he wanted to marry a woman with the Sight, so he could pass the gift along to his children. She understood why her grandfather the bishop thought it would be good to ally her family to the MacMurdos. She knew she was fair to look on and that men said they wanted her because of it. That didn't mean she wanted them. She had only ever wanted Sammy. She certainly didn't want Rory. Didn't that amount to something?

Of course not. To Rory it mattered not at all. She knew that it would matter to Sammy. If she had told him she didn't want him he would have listened. He would respect what she wanted, always. He had already proved his honor and integrity, though he had been sorely tempted several times to make love to her.

"Sammy," she said, getting back to an earlier point, "will kill you."

Actually, she didn't believe he would quite kill the king. She knew full well that Sammy could kill but wouldn't. He was a warrior who understood restraint. No, he wouldn't kill Rory, but he would hurt him enough to teach him a lesson.

Rory did not acknowledge her words, but he had a look on his face that was more than thoughtful as he absently rubbed his chest. She was willing to wager he touched the exact spot where Sammy had kicked him when they last met.

He gestured and a slave brought back his wine cup. It brimmed with dark gold mead, but it also had a deep dent from where it had hit the wall. As he started to take his seat once more several of his guards came into the room. A priest was with them. To Brianna's surprise, so was her Uncle Sean.

Rory didn't seem to notice Sean at first. "Well?" he demanded of the priest. "Where's Deirdre?"

The priest opened his mouth, but it was Sean who answered. "Your lady is safe in my brother's house," he told the king. "She misses her son, but is otherwise happy and well."

Rory banged his mistreated cup down on the table. The wine spilled over and fled away down the grain of the wood. "I'll have her back!" Rory shouted. "If I have to raid Ban Ean with all my men and burn the place to the ground. Tonight," he added. "I'll raid the monastery this very night."

Though the guards flanked him, Sean approached the king with quiet confidence. Brianna kept still. She liked the clever look in her uncle's eye and wondered what he would do. There had to be a plan, and she knew her Sammy would have the major part in it. A heavy, expectant silence took hold of the hall. No one moved but Sean; no one seemed to breathe but the king, and in sharp, angry huffs.

"You will have to raid Ban Ean another time, Rory MacMurdo," Sean said, voice piercing the silence. "For tonight honor binds you to stay within your own walls. Tonight and for however long it takes for justice to be done."

Rory put his hand to the dagger on his belt. "I go where I choose."

The priest slowly came up behind Sean, a black crow in contrast to Sean in robes as white as a swan's wings. From outside came a rumbling like distant thunder. No one seemed to notice it for the moment but Brianna, and she smiled.

"Samuel the son of Bergen brings an accusation against you, my lord," the priest said.

"Impossible! None may accuse a king," Cormac objected.

"Oh, aye," Sean said. "A king's person is sacred, as we all know. So some kings think they have free reign to do what pleases them." The druid swept his gaze around the room before bringing it back to Rory. "There is a way," he reminded them.

He pointed accusingly at the king. There was a collective gasp, as though the courtiers expected the druid to draw down a curse on their lord. He did not speak a curse, though, but merely voiced a promise. "Samuel the son of Bergen comes to shame you into seeing justice done."

Before Rory could draw breath for an outraged shout, the priest hurried on with his own message for Rory. "Your queen will not return to you unless you release Brianna Nariade."

It seemed to Brianna that Rory did not know whether to draw a weapon, bang his fist on the table, or howl his frustration to the sky.

"Listen," she said.

Inside the hall silence followed. Outside, the growling, deep-throated howling thunder of the black beast grew nearer. Slowly, the unnaturalness of the sound penetrated the minds and bones of the people in the hall. Gazes turned inexorably toward the door. A growing fear swept through the room. People rose to their feet, some slowly, as if pulled on strings. Others jumped up from the table and ran, afraid for their lives. Only a few brave souls remained to guard their king.

Rory looked from Sean to Brianna. "What is it?" he demanded.

Brianna stood and held her hands out. "My husband is coming for me. It would be wise to release me."

The priest was trembling. He clutched at Rory's sleeve. "Release her, my lord, I beg you for your soul's sake."

Rory brushed him off and he gave a stubborn shake of his head. "I don't care if the banshee itself is coming for Brianna. It can't have her. The woman is mine."

Cormac ran back in from the courtyard. "A rider on a black beast, my lord! The archers will not fire at it. They dropped their weapons and ran."

They heard the beast halt just outside the door where it snarled and roared for a few moments more, then gave a sputtering cough. After that was silence. The people in the hall stood frozen, waiting.

Brianna, familiar with the ways of beast and rider, could picture what was happening outside. She imagined the way Sammy gave the beast a fond pat as he brought his feet to the ground, then silenced it and ordered it to await his return with a nudge of his booted foot. Then he would swing out of the beast's saddle and walk away with his loose-limbed, graceful stride up to the king's door.

Everyone in the room jumped as the muffled sound of knocking penetrated into the hall. Everyone but Brianna. She threw back her head and laughed.

"Ah, Sammy, my love," she cried, "you've come to take me home!"

19

Sammy was ready for the attack when the door opened and Cormac came lunging out with a sword. It took a couple of kicks and a well-placed punch in the kidneys to ensure that the guard captain wouldn't be getting up for a while. Then Sammy took the man's sword and strolled into the king's house.

He'd been expecting a proper castle, with crenellated stone walls and towers and stuff like that. Rory's stronghold turned out to be a large, two-story house with a few outbuildings making up three sides of a courtyard. The door opened onto a wide room lit by a central hearth and a few torches around the walls. It was bigger, but dim and smoky like every other room Sammy had seen in this time.

It wasn't so dim and smoky that he didn't see armed men lurking in shadowed corners. He counted enough to know he couldn't beat all of them, but he walked up to

Rory as if it didn't matter. He just had to accept that Sean was right about how he had to get Brianna out of here.

Before speaking to Rory he took a long, hard look at Brianna. The fist that had closed around his heart eased open at the sight of her. She was grinning at him with delight. She didn't look any worse for wear, though her hands were tied. She took a few steps forward, stopping when Rory grabbed her shoulder. Ignoring the man's interference, she held up her wrists, and Sammy cut through the rope that bound her.

"Better?" he asked.

She nodded. "Much."

"Did he hurt you?"

Brianna shook her head. She kicked away the severed rope that had landed at her feet. "That was to keep me from hurting him."

Sammy gave a quiet laugh. "That's what I figured."

Following Sean's instructions, he carefully refrained from touching her. The longing to take her in his arms nearly drove out any interest in the rescue plan. He just wanted to grab his wife and get out of here.

Rory had been scowling at him while he talked to Brianna. He finally spoke. Brianna translated, "He says he will have you killed if you try to take me from his house."

That pretty much stalled any negotiations before they could even get started. Sammy hadn't expected anything else. The dude was totally obsessed, totally self-involved. Maybe it would be better just to punch him out and leave, but there were the swordsmen to consider, and the chance Brianna might get hurt in the fight.

Sean decided it was time to speak up. "This man comes to the king for justice," he announced.

Rory pulled Brianna back and held her tightly to him, with his arm around her waist. Sean watched with admiration as Sammy controlled the urge to stop him. The big man's muscles were tense as though they'd been carved in stone, but he made no move. His dark eyes, however, blazed.

"I have what is mine," Rory said. "Tell the gelding to leave or he dies."

Brianna clamped her lips tightly together and shook her head.

"You're going to have to listen to me," Sammy said. Brianna translated his words. He looked at no one but her as he spoke. "I've come to fast against you, Rory MacMurdo, until you grant the justice and wisdom of giving me back my wife."

What he was proposing would shame Rory into leaving them alone once and for all. It would work much better than fighting the fool, Sean had assured him. Sean had better be right.

Rory gave Sammy an amused look after Brianna translated. "Fast away, then," he said. "You can sit outside my door and starve yourself to death for all I care. Brianna is mine."

"But my lord—" the priest began.

Brianna cut him off with a laugh. "You have forgotten the other half of the old custom I see, Rory MacMurdo."

Sean nodded as Rory gave the priest and two druids a puzzled look. "When a man fasts against a king, a king must fast as well," Sean said. "That is the ancient law. For the sake of your honor a man may not touch your holy person, but a man may fast against a king, and the king must fast with him until the dispute is settled."

She looked at Sammy with an expression full of love and pride. "So fast away, my love," she told him. "You've more meat on you than our good king here."

Sammy watched Rory's already florid complexion

go deep red with fury. He searched the man's eyes for any sign that he was going to attack. But Rory just stood rooted in place, rigid with anger. Sammy, on the other hand, felt as light as a feather and full of energy. Brianna's confidence in him made him strong, stronger than every martial arts discipline he'd ever studied.

"I love you," he told her. "I could do anything for you."

"I know," she said, and her look was as potent as a kiss. "Ours is a love like no other."

"Seen that in one of your visions, have you?"

"No. I just know it is the truth."

Brianna pried herself away from Rory's grip and went to stand beside Sean. Sammy wished she would come into his arms. But from the stiff, formal way she and her uncle stood together he got the idea that this was too ceremonious an occasion to give in to any personal urges.

First he would get her back, he thought, then they would have the reunion of a lifetime. Maybe she had a spell that would take him back to the future, but they would make the most of the present as soon as he got her alone.

He gave Rory a formal bow. "Let me know when you're ready to give up," Sammy said. He turned and headed for the door. Custom dictated that he conduct his fast while seated outside the king's door, making it a very public affair. "I'll be right outside," he called back cheerfully just before he went outside to take up his vigil in the courtyard.

Brianna was sent to bed only a few moments after Sammy left the hall. Rory's people had crept back into the hall during the king's confrontation with her husband. Most had overheard Sammy's intention, and everyone had heard Rory's howling anger in response to the challenge.

A slave slept in the room with Brianna. Uncle Sean had insisted on taking his rest just on the other side of the doorway. He was concerned in case Rory considered forcing himself on her. Before Sammy had shown up she'd been worried about that too, but with Sammy so close by she now felt perfectly safe. She had every faith that her beloved would know if she were in any danger. He would never let any harm come to her. She was so confident of her own safety that she slipped easily into sleep on the narrow bed she'd been given.

In her dreams, Sammy came to her in spirit, just as he had when he patrolled the countryside with Donal. In her dreams they danced the dance of love they'd put off too long in reality. They fell down together in a sunlit place, very like the lush, colorful land of their first dream loving. In this place he refused her nothing and taught her how a woman could please a man and a man, a woman. In the dream they soared and touched and shared, each becoming the other and then something that was a blending of them both for just a few precious moments.

It was indeed, she thought, waking briefly in the dark room, a love like no other. There was no one in the bed beside her, but that didn't matter to Brianna. She knew that she was not really alone and never would be again no matter where their separate fates took them.

Hunger gnawed in the back of his awareness, but for Sammy, fasting wasn't really a problem. Not yet, anyway. He was used to doing a three-day fast on his visits to the Buddhist ashram where he meditated twice a year. He'd been sitting outside the king's door for only a day and a half so far. He was hungry, he found the growing crowd distracting, and he kept getting rained on, but there was an up side to the situation.

The sex was great.

Distracting, but great. Every time he dozed off he had the most amazingly erotic dreams about Brianna.

The frustrating part came when he'd wake up and remember that Brianna was locked away, a prisoner, just a few feet from where he sat. He wanted to walk in, kick a whole lot of local ass, and take her home. There were times when he daydreamed about this being a martial arts movie and he was Chuck Norris, Bruce Lee, and Jean-Claude Van Damme all rolled into one, with a little Terminator thrown in for good measure. But this wasn't a movie, and he'd agreed to do it this way. He would go through with shaming Rory into giving Brianna back. It was for the best.

"But passive resistance is a real bitch, you know?" he said to Ailill, who'd shown up to keep him company last night. The kid kept pulling griddle cakes out of the sack of food he'd brought. "You haven't stopped eating since you got here," Sammy pointed out.

"Perhaps watching you fast makes him hungry," Donal joked, as Ailill handed him a griddle cake, then tossed another one to his wolfhound.

Like Ailill, Donal had come to offer his support. He kept pointing out that he'd left his wives to be by his teacher's side. He also loudly claimed that leaving his wives was worth it for his sister's sake, and that this peaceful solution was better than going after the king with a sword. Donal never sounded terribly convincing when he said any of these things. Still, Sammy was glad of Donal and Ailill's company.

Of course, most of the rest of the people in Ban Ean were here as well. They prayed a lot by way of lending their moral support. Word was spreading and people from other villages in Rory's tiny kingdom were showing up to witness Sammy's fasting vigil.

This was what Sean had predicted would happen, and the druid worked the crowd like a pro, drumming up support for Sammy and Brianna's plight. The way Sammy figured it, Rory didn't have a chance. He knew he could hold out for as long as it took, and he was willing to bet it wasn't the fasting or the disapproval of his people that was going to get to the king.

Rory had a wife he loved too. Never mind what Sammy was doing, if Rory wanted Deirdre back he was going to have to give in, give up and get on with apologizing to the one person he really cared about.

"I figure this'll be finished by tomorrow," Sammy said, closing his eyes to meditate rather than watch Donal and Ailill share any more of the griddle cakes.

Rory was more than a little bit put out by the messenger's news about the Viking ship that had been sighted in the waters near Ban Ean. He wasn't in any particular mood to protect the monastery, even though it harbored his runaway wife at the moment. He didn't suppose Deirdre was in any danger, at least not yet. The scouts he'd sent to track the movements of the raiders had seen no signs of their planning to come ashore. They would, he knew, and the prosperous settlement of Ban Ean would be their target, but he thought the village was safe for a few days yet.

Rory didn't want to think of Viking raiders just now, so he dismissed the messenger and went into his chapel to pray. He stood before the altar, as alone as he ever was, with only a few of his retainers standing in the back of the chapel. With this semblance of solitude he let his troubled thoughts gnaw at him for a while.

It wasn't the fasting that he minded so much, he'd been fasting through holy days his entire life. Being a king, with more obligations than most, he fasted more than most. It was part of his duty to preserve and protect his people, whether from invaders or the wrath of God. He was a good king, he knew it. His taxes were light, his laws lenient. He asked for very little from his people. It galled him that the one indulgence he craved, Brianna's body for himself, her children to strengthen his line, was going to be denied him.

He knew he'd lost, the moment the big outlander sat down to fast outside his door. For his pride's sake all he could do was hold out a reasonable amount of time. Three or four days of fasting was uncomfortable, but it would save face. That was the most important thing outwardly.

Inwardly, Rory knew it wasn't the giant starving himself in the courtyard that had brought about his true defeat. It was Deirdre. He hadn't realized how stubborn and strong she was until she'd left him. He hadn't realized she would go through with any threat of making him choose between Brianna and herself. His meek little dove turned out to have the talons of a hunting hawk.

"There is no choice," he whispered from his aching heart, and it sounded to him like a prayer. "It is Deirdre I truly love."

He genuflected before the altar then turned to face his followers. "It is time," he said, taking a few steps forward. "Dillon, Cormac." He gestured for the men to kneel before him. The two had been slinking around on the edges of his vision ever since bringing trouble into his house. He'd decided to deal with them at last.

"You did what you knew I wanted." He touched each of them on the head, like a benediction. "I forgive you for only trying to serve me." They said hoarse, hasty thank-yous without lifting their gazes from the floor. "So," Rory went on, "I will not exile you. I will not execute you. But—" he let silence draw taut like a bowstring before he finally pronounced sentence on the pair, "I would have you visit every saint's shrine in all of Eire to pray for me before I set eyes on either of you again. I give you horses and gold and provisions for the journey," he added kindly. "But get out of my sight."

Rory left the chapel without a backward glance at the kneeling men. In the hall he called to a servant. "Fetch the druid and Brianna out to the courtyard." Then he squared his shoulders, took a deep breath, and went outside to tell Sammy son of Bergen that he'd won his wife back.

All because Rory couldn't bear another night without his own wife sleeping safely in his arms.

Rory hadn't touched her since she'd been brought into his house, for which she was deeply grateful. Brianna was prepared to scream and scratch and bite if he did lay hands on her, but when he took her and led her to Sammy's side she made no protest at all.

She ignored his angry frown, gave him a gracious smile, and said, "Thank you, my lord."

"Go home," he said to her, placing her hand in Sammy's. To the people crowded tightly into his courtyard watching the proceedings beneath an iron-dark sky, Rory said, "I concede the justice of this man's grievance against me. I lay claim to Brianna Nariade no longer."

There was a cheer and applause and some bawdy jesting. Brianna paid no attention to it at all. She had eyes only for Sammy. His beard had grown a bit, turning into a gold fuzz on his square jaw. He needed bathing. He didn't seem to have lost any weight, but there were dark circles under his eyes, and he looked tired. Tired, and by his loving smile, happy to see her. She wanted to take him in her arms and hold him to her breast, to comfort and thank him. But not here, not now. Soon, when they were well away from Rory.

She looked at the king, and knew that this was the last time she would see him. He would no longer be a trial to her from this moment. He would be but a memory, and an almost fond one at that. Soon she would be leaving Ban Ean forever. Forever. It was her fate. All the visions of the smoking city made sense at last. Sad as she was to be going, she knew this was no longer her world.

She bowed to the king, as did Sammy. "Thank you," she said loudly enough for all the watchers to hear.

Hand in hand, she and Sammy began to walk to where the black beast stood in the shadow of the well. Rory's voice stopped them before they reached Sammy's magical steed.

"People of Ban Ean," he called, "hear me one last time."

She and Sammy turned, giving their attention to Rory along with the rest of the crowd. Rory pointed at Sammy.

"That—man," he said, "or fairy, or whatever he may be, is not welcome in my land." The crowd murmured and cast questioning looks, but Rory ignored them. "I have admitted to doing him wrong. This has stained my honor so deeply that I cannot show my face anywhere this man dwells. Since he dwells peacefully among the people of Ban Ean, I can no longer call myself the king of Ban Ean."

It was Donal who called out, "This is no great loss to us, Rory MacMurdo!" but the rest of the crowd murmured in shock.

Sean stepped forward. "What does this mean, Rory MacMurdo? When you say you are not our king?"

Rory folded his arms across his chest and surveyed the crowd. The look on his face was very close to a sneer. "It means, that when the Norsemen come to burn Ban Ean to the ground, I will not stand in their way."

Without further comment, Rory turned and strode back into his hall. The carved door slowly swung shut, leaving the people outside to ponder just what they would do without Rory MacMurdo's erstwhile protection.

Brianna didn't let herself think about it for the moment. She explained to Sammy. They exchanged a wry look, and she knew he wasn't going to worry about it yet either. They would worry about it, because caring for people was their way, but not yet. They had more important things to settle between them before they concerned themselves with the fate of Ban Ean.

"Tomorrow," he said. "I'll think about that tomorrow."

"Aye," she said, and led him to the black beast. "Let us go home and share a fine meal. Then," she added with a mischievous smile, "I am taking you to bed."

Sammy didn't need any further urging to wake up the beast and ride them away.

20

Brianna loved the rumbling quiver of the black beast between her thighs and the rush of air over her skin as they rode. She had ridden the beast only once before, and she found that she had missed the sensation though she had not known so until she mounted behind her husband to ride proudly away.

It wasn't just the power or the speed of the beast that drew her. More than these things she loved pressing herself close to Sammy, drinking in his scent, unwashed though it was at present. She loved that his back was wide and hard muscled. She loved the feel of his hair against her cheek. She wanted to do this forever.

"It is good to be with you," she said, though she knew he could not hear above the roar of the wind and the beast. "And why does it have to be such a noisy creature?"

There were many things she wanted to say to

Sammy, but they would have to wait for the beast to come to a stop. Besides, she told herself, learning to love the noisy beast helped her adjust her mind for living in Sammy's world. "Talking about your world will keep, my love," she said, her face buried in his whipping mane of curls. "Make the journey short for I would have you before the sun sets this day."

Somehow, Sammy heard her words. Or perhaps he just responded to her longing thoughts. She could tell by the laugh that even the beast couldn't drown out. Pressed close against his back, she felt the laughter as much as she heard it. It was full of relief, and wickedness. It was a laugh that promised pleasures she'd only dreamed about, vividly detailed though those dreams had been. She marveled at how Sammy's laughter could make her feel so cherished, but it did.

"Just a few minutes until we get to Ban Ean," he called back to her. "We're not stopping. We're going somewhere where it's just you and me."

The women of Ban Ean were waiting on the outskirts of the village, with Deirdre in the front of the group. Brianna didn't know how they'd gotten word that the fast was over or if they'd been waiting like this for days. No one ran away at the approach of the beast; they were getting as used to it as she was, she supposed. She wished the women would scatter before the beast like autumn leaves before the wind because she wanted to be alone with her love. At the same time she welcomed the sight of them, knowing that they were anxious on her behalf.

Sammy slowed the beast as they approached the waiting women, but he didn't stop. He wasn't going to stop, she realized. He meant what he'd said about finding privacy. He smiled and called out greetings that no one but she understood. Meanwhile the inexorable advance of the beast nudged the waiting women out of its path. She called out herself and gave the queen a big, confident smile. She saw Deirdre sigh with relief and gaze longingly toward the way they'd come.

Good, she thought, Deirdre will go home and this will all be settled. She almost pitied Rory in his upcoming, touchy reunion with his queen. Almost. The gods knew what Deirdre saw in the man.

Brianna tightened her grip around Sammy's waist, somehow, for she had been clinging like a leech already. He grunted but didn't complain at her fierce clamp on him. "Hurry," she urged. "Take me to the grove. No one will disturb us in that sacred place."

"You got it, babe," he replied. He gave one more wave to the women, and the beast sped on through the village.

"I need a bath," Sammy said as he stripped off the plaid tunic he'd been wearing for days.

Brianna had gotten supplies out of a bag in her lean-to shelter. Then she moved her potion pot away from the ashes to work on building up a fire from peat and twigs.

Sammy looked up at the sky, where clouds hung low and dark. "This is such a wet country I don't know how you people ever get any cooking done."

He noticed Brianna was singing quietly as she worked, her beautiful voice low and compelling. It made him wonder if she was using magic to get the fire started.

"Yes," she answered before he could ask. She smiled. "Fire making was the first spell I ever learned. And, no, I couldn't use magic to escape from Rory. That would have meant compelling a person against their will. I will never do that. 'Tis a grave sin." She pointed at her potion pot. "Even love philters only work on people who want them to work—whether they know it or not. People must never be forced by magic. To do so brings a curse down on the magician."

"Bad karma," he agreed. He sniffed. "I'm sleepy, I'm dizzy, and I really stink. How can you stand to be near me?"

"Your company is far better than Rory MacMurdo's. Better than anyone else's in the whole world," she added with a loving look that made him want to do anything in the world for her. She pointed past the altar. "The stream that runs past Uncle Sean's starts in a pool nearby. You bathe while I fix you something to eat."

He grinned. "And then you'll take me to bed? You promised."

"That I will. Now, hurry. And I'll try not to burn the honey cakes because my mind is on bedding you."

He hurried off, and a few minutes later came back clean and naked. Brianna looked as if she appreciated both. He'd smelled griddle cakes cooking while he washed, the scent had set his mouth to watering. He heard the herd dog barking fussily at the sheep in the distance as he came slowly up to the fire. Brianna stood as he approached. She held out a warm, flat cake that he downed without even tasting. His attention was on Brianna. His stomach registered that there was something in it at last with a thankful rumble, but he scarcely noticed that he was no longer hungry.

Because he was hungry for Brianna, he guessed, as she came into his arms and tilted her head back for his kiss. Brianna had quick hands, and they knew how to do magic. Even as their lips met and tongues entwined, her fingers were playing over his back and buttocks and thighs. He held her close and let her hands roam while peaty smoke from the fire curled around them. Thunder rumbled and the clouds threatened rain, but Sammy didn't think the sky would dare open up on them just yet. The air was charged with impending lightning, but lighting that crackled between them, not from the clouds.

Brianna had been kissed by Sammy in reality and in her dreams. This rushing, melting, aching magical feel of his kiss was a part of her and made her a part of him. It was like something she'd always known and couldn't do without.

Then he helped her undress and his touch made her forget everything but the two of them. His mouth moved to worship her breasts and then lower, to a spot she'd barely realized existed before now. The sensation that coursed through her filled her soul. Sammy conjured magic of his own and gave it to her with his caress. It was the magic of her singing and of the earth, air, fire, and water that made up all the world centering in the core of her. Sammy's touch was like all the elements and all the power that ever was, taking her over and making her new.

And being made new, she was not timid about touching him as he touched her. She found that his nipples, ringed in gold down, were as hard as hers, his reaction when her tongue teased each one in turn was as strong as hers had been.

She stroked his muscular thighs, her fingers shying away from the thing she wanted to touch. At last he took her hand and groaned with pleasure as she stroked him, her hesitation overcome by his reaction. And by the growing ache that called to have him inside her.

She said in wonder, "How marvelous it will feel to be joined with you."

Sammy had closed his eyes when Brianna's hand closed around him. They flew open as she spoke. "Oh, right. You're new at this," he said, dredging up a little sanity to deal with her first time.

"You'll not be putting on one of those things again, will you?"

He knew he should have brought a condom with him, but he hadn't. Nothing about making love to Brianna was safe. She was his wife, he loved her. She was worth every risk. "No," he said. "I won't be wearing one of those things."

She looked relieved. "Then perhaps we'll get a child this day."

He should have been terrified. Instead, he was delighted at the thought. "Yeah. Maybe we will." He drew her into another long, passionate kiss.

It wasn't easy finding some measure of control when he wanted more than anything to wallow in the building spiral of pleasure. But there was no way he was going to give the woman he loved less than she deserved. Not the first time. Not ever.

He took her hand and eased it away from his erection. Looking around he noticed that they were somehow still standing in the center of the grove. That they'd been there for a long time. He just barely remembered kneeling before her, then slowly kissing his way up to her face again. Now he lay down with her on the grass and they stretched out to kiss and caress each other for a while longer. His body was screaming for release, but he wasn't going to hurry this.

After trailing a line of kisses from her navel all the way to her chin he looked the happily squirming Brianna in the eye and said, "Let's not do this the traditional way, okay?"

The fingers of Sammy's right hand went between her thighs to stroke and tease the places that wanted to be touched the most. She hardly had any mind left to listen to his words, but she managed a tight nod. "Sammy!" she pleaded as she arched against his hand. What did he mean? "What tradition?" she asked. "Should I turn over now?"

He looked up from slowly licking the sweat off her throat. "What?"

"Like a ram with a ewe—is that your way?" His fingers stopped flicking back and forth across the spot where the pleasure centered. She grabbed fistfuls of his golden curls. "Don't. Stop."

He laughed. In the reassuring, caring, loving way that only her Sammy could laugh. "Have I told you I love you yet today?" he asked. And he started kissing her all over again, until his mouth replaced his hand at the center of her need.

"I love you," she answered him, though she didn't speak with words. She couldn't, because all words left her as she nearly drowned in a wave of pure pleasure.

When she came back into herself she was still trembling with the joy of the moment. And she was somehow perched across Sammy's stomach while he lay flat on his back beneath her. His strong hands were the only thing keeping her from collapsing in a contented heap on top of him.

"Sammy?" she eventually said as her mind cleared somewhat.

"Yeah, babe?" he asked, running his hands up her waist to cup her breasts. He began to play with her nipples. And the ache inside her began to grow again.

"Aren't you—" she had to take a deep breath before she could continue, "—aren't you supposed to tup me?"

"You're not a sheep."

"Bed me," she said, thinking perhaps they were having trouble understanding each other for the first time since he'd arrived. "Mount me. Whatever you call it."

She could tell he was keeping himself under close control. His jaw was tightly clenched.

"Make love to you," he said, his voice a low growl. "That's the term you want."

She cupped his face in her hands, stroked his fuzzy cheeks, and looked deep into his eyes. "Make love to me," she said.

He shook his head, and she saw just how tight his muscles were, that his restraint was costing him. "You're in control here, babe," he said. "You need a chance to be in control." He lifted her hips, nudging her backward until she felt herself positioned over his straining erection. "You take me, Brianna." His eyes closed. His hands fell away to his sides, where they bunched into tight, tense fists.

This left Brianna to make the decision of what to do next. Take him, he'd said. She needed to be in control. He was right. Things had gone disastrously wrong all the other times they'd come together, and Rory's abduction had left her feeling very out of control of her life. It wasn't hard for her to make this choice; she knew exactly what she wanted. And what she must do.

Slowly, carefully, she eased her way down onto him, bringing him inside of her. He let out one sharp breath as he entered her. Then he croaked, "Careful, babe. Take it slow. Ease up if it hurts you."

Brianna barely heard him, her concentration was centered on the sensations of penetration, of marveling at the perfect way he fit inside her. If there was a moment of pain, it wasn't important. This perfect joining was all that mattered.

Sammy groaned once more. His hips bucked, his hard-held control slipping. His movement sent a strong ripple of desire through her. Brianna threw back her head and laughed, wildly happy, wildly in love with this glorious giant of a man.

She knew what he wanted and needed. For her to take his gift and give him back the completion he'd already brought to her. So she moved, riding him wildly while he twisted and moaned beneath her. She gave him back the passion he gave her while her own emotions climbed in a feverish spiral once more. Her own delicious need grew with every stroke until his release rocked her out of herself and into a long, shattering moment of ecstasy.

Time ceased. She was neither body nor mind, neither Brianna nor Sammy, nothing existed but the soaring joy. They were one, complete, lost in each other.

"Oh, babe! Yeah!" was Sammy's comment on this instant of epiphany.

Brianna knew that she was herself once again, though she didn't know how long it took her to respond. And when she did, it was with a laugh. It was a weak, feeble sound, for she was utterly exhausted, but it was a sound full of love for the dear man who was so much a part of her. He did not have the language of a bard or a poet, but he had the soul of a curious, accepting philosopher and that was good enough for Brianna.

She found herself lying on his chest with his arms wrapped tightly around her. He was a hard but deliciously warm mattress. Rain was doing its best to wash the sweat of their lovemaking off her. She didn't want to move, but she didn't want to drown or freeze, either.

For it was raining very hard and a cold wind was blowing. It was dark enough to be past sunset. She was hungry again.

"Just how long have we been doing this?" she asked Sammy.

He grunted. Moving slowly, he helped her to her feet. He shook himself like a wet dog and lifted his face to the pouring sky. Lightning flashed overhead while thunder competed with the crash of the storm-driven surf. "Whoa," he said. "I wonder how long this has been going on?"

"The storm or us?"

"Both."

The ground shook as lightning grounded in the field nearby and they ran for the slight shelter of the hut she'd made. There was barely enough room for the two of them to squeeze inside, but they enjoyed the tight fit. The sheltering branches kept them dry enough, and there was a woolen blanket for them to share. Cuddling close together they made do, and despite the howling noise of the storm, they were both soon fast asleep in each other's arms.

21

The warm richness of the sunlight filtering through the oak branches told Brianna that she had slept until midmorning. Beside her, Sammy slept on. She had found out during the night that her beloved husband was a blanket thief, but she supposed not even Sammy was completely perfect. She kissed his cheek, then carefully crawled out of the shelter without waking him.

She found her dress, wrung out the wet pile of white cloth and hung it across the sun-warmed altar to dry before going to the pool to bathe. Once back in the grove she built a fire and sat down before it to cook herself breakfast while she went back to work on the most important spell she'd ever sing.

A spell that was no longer just to send Sammy home but one that would take her to the land where he dwelled as well. She had seen it and so it would be. She no longer fought against leaving this place she so dearly loved, for she would be with the man she loved most of all.

She felt that she almost had it right. Much thought and experimentation had gone into what she needed to do. She'd decided that what was needed was a combination of the summoning spell that had brought Sammy to her, since somehow that had opened a door into the future, and a song of power to control the door, so they could open and pass through it at will.

The hours passed while Brianna sang variation after variation of the spell she sought. The air around her crackled with magic, power spun, rose, and fell with the notes of her song. The magic held out promises and dead ends and hints of visions. She absorbed and learned from it all. She lost herself in her work as she drew closer and closer to the correct combination of words. Meanwhile, her clothes dried in the sun, and Sammy snored gently on.

Sammy woke up to the sound of Brianna's singing. He'd heard it through his dreams, and the dreams had been wild and wonderful. His dreams had had bits about butterflies that morphed into fighter jets, talking doorknobs like those in *Alice in Wonderland,* lots of flying clocks, camels jumping through the eyes of needles, Dr. Who's TARDIS, the nuclear-powered De Lorean sports car from the *Back to the Future* movies, and all sorts of other crazy, busy, traveling things. Time-traveling things. Even his Harley had shown up a few times. As he woke he knew the dreams all had something to do with what Brianna was singing.

The first thing Sammy saw when he opened his eyes was his naked wife. She was sitting on the ground and singing, with her eyes closed and a look of complete concentration on her face. The next thing he noticed was that she wasn't quite in focus. Her form was wavering and shifting, sort of faded around the edges. And the edges were outlined in blue light. Sammy didn't think this effect was caused by the smoke of the dying fire that was between where she sat and where he was lying.

"Totally weird," he said as he scurried on hands and knees out of the lean-to. "Brianna!" he called as he rushed toward her. "Are you okay?"

Brianna's concentration was broken by Sammy's frightened shout. He scooped her up off the ground as she opened her eyes. Within moments she was sitting on top of the altar with Sammy anxiously running his hands over her as if searching for broken bones.

"What are you doing?" she asked him. "And don't stop. It feels good."

It felt so good she wasn't even irritated that he'd interrupted her just as the spell was starting to come together. She could go back to the spell later.

"You're here," he said with a relieved sigh. "You're all here."

"Oh, aye," she said as she wiggled forward to put her legs around his waist. She pressed up against the heat of his groin and felt his manly member begin to stir. She put her arms around his neck, turning her face up for a kiss. "I'm all here, and so are you," she told him.

For some reason working magic hadn't tired her as it usually did, it had set her blood racing with need the instant Sammy touched her.

"I'm here," he agreed with her. "And I'm never going to leave. I'm going to stay right here. With you. Forever."

Jerry Park was his friend, he was innocent, and he needed Sammy to prove it. Sammy was sorry that he wouldn't be there to help his friend. But Brianna needed him. Ban Ean needed both of them. He'd finally made a commitment. He was deeply sorry it had to be at the cost of Jerry's freedom, maybe even his life. Sammy knew he'd feel guilty about his choice for the rest of his life, but Brianna needed him more. Right now, he needed her more than anything in the world. While he was making love to her, he wouldn't have to think.

Her throat was burning from all the singing, her muscles were stiff with hours of sitting perfectly still. When he kissed her and caressed her she didn't feel anything but what his lips and hands aroused in her. Sammy made her body sing, and soon he was inside her, making love to her on the altar that hadn't been used for fertility rituals for a good two centuries. Brianna had the feeling the old gods who dwelled in the rattling oaks of the grove looked on in approval as the pair of them were joined on the wide stone bed.

Sammy made love with a sure, gentle touch, controlling the great body that covered hers with the poet's skill his words lacked. He was an artist, a bard, a magician, a teacher. Brianna was his eager pupil. The lesson went on and on, but nowhere near long enough. She was greedy with loving him. It ended once more in the bright rapturous moment of completion. When she came back to herself she was left gasping for breath, so satiated she was almost melted into the sun-warmed stone.

Sammy collapsed on top of her in a heap. "Woman," he whispered in her ear, an ear he'd recently been nibbling, "what you do to me is amazing."

"Is that good?" she asked.

"Uh-huh." He rested on her breasts for a few moments more, then he helped her to sit up. "That was great," he said. "But I'm not quite sure how it got started." He scratched his head and combed his fingers through his tangled curls. "I was dreaming—or I saw you fading away. It was really weird. Then I was making love to you. I think I lost it for a while." He shook his head.

"This is heavy. Very heavy."

She put her hand reassuringly on his bare thigh. "No need to fear, my love. I like that you are heavy."

She jumped off the altar and pulled on her dress while Sammy looked at her. "Hungry?" she asked when she was dressed.

Sammy wondered if he wanted to talk about what she'd been up to. She'd only been doing what he'd asked her to do, now he was going to have to ask her to stop. He knew he couldn't leave her.

But Jerry Park wasn't just a friend, he was an innocent man.

Sammy got up and dressed before he said anything. Brianna was spooning her love potion into a small earthenware pot when he came to sit down beside her.

"You were working on a time-travel spell, weren't you?" he asked her.

"So I was," she replied. Her wide mouth quirked up in a pleased smile. "I was almost there, my love."

Sammy put his hand on her shoulder. "Listen," he said earnestly. "It's not that I don't want to go home— but I can't. I like it here. With you."

"I'll always be with you. Don't you see? I'm coming with you."

"What?" The word exploded out of him. "You can't!"

"Ah, but I can. It will be the easiest thing in the world. The black beast holds two, does it not? Though I have to admit I'm a bit worried about Ailill. Can we take him with us, do you think?"

"I'm not taking either of you with me. Babe, you don't understand. You don't have any idea what my world is like."

"Then why have I been dreaming of it my whole life?"

"You don't belong there. It's not safe. It's a totally

different world. You couldn't adapt to all the changes."

She was calm, confident, and totally sure of herself. "You'll be there to help me, to teach and protect. Oh, I fought the truth for a long time, but now I'm willing to go where my visions take me. It'll be painful, I know, for much of my heart will always be in Ban Ean, but being with you is where I belong."

"Me? You want to be a star," he said. He couldn't help his bitterness, for fate had taken one magic woman from him already. "What do your visions of fame have to do with me?"

Brianna's pleased expression turned thoughtful. "What's it to do with me?" she countered. "I just have the visions, I don't understand them."

"Oh. Right." Sammy considered her words for a while. Of course she had no way to interpret the things she saw. She didn't want to be a star, but she truly did want to be with him. He wanted her with him, too, but he knew it wouldn't be good for her. No, his way was best. He'd stay here with her. "Listen, babe," he explained, "you don't belong in my time."

"I don't have any choice," was her serene answer.

"Los Angeles is not the nicest place in the world."

"It has pretty flowers," she said. "And sunshine." She looked up at the sky. "Eire is lovely and green, but I really would like to live somewhere where the sun shines more."

"Sunshine." Sammy could understand her longing for sunshine. Living in Ireland wasn't doing anything for his carefully cultivated tan. "Yeah, we have sunshine, and inversion layers and smog so thick you can't breathe out in the Valley some days. And earthquakes and mudslides and brush fires. It can be hell on earth."

"The sea is lovely there, a bright green-blue."

"Yeah, but there aren't a lot of places left where you can swim in it."

"There are so many different kinds of people all living in one spot."

"And hating each other's guts. That's when they aren't robbing, shooting, stabbing, and suing each other. And they only have time to do that stuff when they aren't hung up in traffic. You'd hate all the noise. Everything moves too fast, and too loudly."

"Like the black beast." She gave a fond glance toward the Harley. "I like the noise the beast makes."

"You wouldn't if you heard a hundred of them all roaring down the highway." Okay, so he did, but he was used to it. Brianna was an innocent child from a pristine land in an ancient time. "You couldn't cope, babe. It's just one frustration after another. And it's dangerous." He pulled her into the protection of his arms. "I don't want anything to happen to you."

From inside his sheltering embrace she said, "You don't want me to go to your time? Is that what you're saying?"

"Yes. Yes, that's what I'm saying."

"Why?"

"I've been trying to tell you—it's dangerous."

She gazed up at him. "Dangerous?"

"Way dangerous. More dangerous than you can envision."

"Ah." She looked up at him with amusement in her trusting, confident demeanor. "So," she said, "you want me to stay here. Where it is safe."

"Yeah." It looked as if he was finally getting through to her.

She lay her palms flat against his chest. "So I am to stay in Eire, with its plagues and storms and famines. I'm to stay *safely* here while the Viking raiders come to ravish the coast. Ah, yes, it's such a quiet, safe, secure life we lead in Ban Ean, my love."

Sammy got her point, but he didn't concede it. "It's still better for us to stay here."

Brianna pushed away from him. She got to her feet to look down and shake her head at him. "You act as if there is a choice. The visions have shown me where my fate lies, and there I must go."

Sammy jumped up. "No! You don't have to."

"I do. I will."

He didn't know what he could do to shake her certainty. "Listen, babe, the future can be changed. Nothing is certain."

"This is." She wasn't angry, just unshakably sure. "You tried to make me think otherwise and I ended up lying to my father, and then all this nonsense with Rory happened. That taught me that I had better trust my visions of the truth. Everything will be all right," she assured him. "You have to believe it will be for the best."

Sammy didn't agree, but he saw there was no use trying to argue about it just now. "Fine," he grumbled as Brianna picked up the jar of love potion and turned toward the path. "Where you going?"

She looked over her shoulder at him. "Why don't you gather some of that seaweed you like and meet me at Uncle Sean's for dinner," she suggested.

"Fine," he agreed. "But what are you going to do?"

She held up the jar. "Find Donal," she said. "And have him deliver this to Lady Deirdre. If ever a woman needed help to keep her man, it's she. I, on the other hand," she added as she walked away, "have been blessed with a love like no other to last me through all time."

"Yeah, right," he called after her, not sure if he was joking or not. "Tell me that when you're rich and famous and a star." Not that she was going to be, because he wasn't going to let her risk her life in the future.

"Very well," she called back, "I will!"

"Viking raiders." Sammy spoke softly into the darkness of Sean's house. "Sounds like a football game," he went on. "Vikings versus the Raiders." He sighed and Brianna's hand came up to touch his cheek. They were sharing Sean's narrow bed and Brianna was mostly on top of him. Her weight and warmth were comforting even if he couldn't get to sleep. It was long after midnight, he knew.

Sean had left after dinner to see to a patient in Ban Ean. He'd told them he wouldn't be home before morning. So Sammy and Brianna had spent the rest of the evening making love. He'd tried to have another talk with her about how going to live in the future was a really bad idea, but they hadn't gotten around to talking, except when he was answering her questions about sexual positions. Several had gotten demonstrated during the course of the evening. It had been great, and exhausting, but he still couldn't get to sleep.

It worried him that she wouldn't discuss her plans for the future. Or, the future's plans for her. He guessed that was the proper way to look at it. Of course, by discussion he meant getting her to change her mind.

And his conscience was killing him over his decision to stay in the past. Jerry Park needed him, but Brianna needed him more, and so did her people. He knew the Viking ships couldn't be far away. He tried to tell himself he was being pragmatic, trying to do the greatest good for the greatest number. He'd just have to live with his choices and not let his guilt eat him alive. Or interfere with his relationship with Brianna. He'd made a commitment to the woman, her time and her people. He was going to stick by it.

Sammy sighed into the darkness and stroked Brianna's hair. It covered his chest like a soft black silk blanket. "It's not gonna happen, is it, babe?" he asked, his voice barely a whisper. *Forever isn't going to happen for us.*

Brianna stirred, lifting her head enough to look at him. "It's bad enough you've been talking too much inside my head," she complained. "Hush. Go to sleep." She put her fingers over his lips. He sucked gently on her fingertips. "Don't do that."

He flicked his tongue across the soft pads of her fingers before asking, "Why?"

"Feels good." She rested her head back on his chest. "Want to sleep. Don't think so much."

"Can't help it," he murmured. He didn't want to think any more than she wanted him to. He caressed her back and shoulders. "You feel good."

"Hmm," she mumbled. She rubbed her cheek against him, like an affectionate cat. "What about the Vikings?"

"I don't think they'll make it to the Superbowl this year," he answered. He was suddenly more interested in exploring all the curves and hollows of his wife's anatomy than in doing anything else.

"No," she said sleepily, "they won't make the Superbowl until 199—" She lifted her head again, sharply this time. "What are we talking about?"

"You were talking in your sleep," he assured her, taking the opportunity to cup her breasts. "Don't worry about it."

She arched up, giving his hands freer access. "You were talking in my sleep," she corrected. "You were worrying about your friend. And Vikings."

"I'm not worrying about them now," he told her. He ducked his head to suckle on a nipple. He could tell by the tightening in his groin that there wasn't going to be much more conversation for a while. "I can't get enough of you," he said to Brianna before he rolled her onto her back.

Her legs came up to circle his waist. "Or I, you," she said as he sheathed himself inside her.

The next time he spoke, it was to tell her afterward, "I can't seem to stop doing this."

Brianna combed her fingers through his hair. "Good."

He sat up and swung his legs over the side of the narrow bed. "What were we talking about?"

Brianna rolled onto her side. "The Norsemen," she reminded him. "As if you didn't already know. You're worried about them."

He nodded and gazed off into the shadows beyond where the banked fire glowed. "I'm worried about Ban Ean. And the monks out on the island." He looked back at her. "Remember your vision about them?"

She touched his arm; her fingers were cold. Her voice was sad when she spoke. "How could I forget it? Those are my friends and family I saw die."

"I think the attack is coming," he told her. "Soon."

"You've seen it?"

He shook his head. "I don't have visions. It was just—I don't know—the way Rory acted, I guess."

Brianna scooted up to sit beside him. "They're coming," she agreed. "I've been lost in loving you in the last day, but I've felt the danger in the back of my mind. I was selfish. I ignored it."

He took her hand, running his thumb across the back of it. "Me too," he said. "I wanted the world to be just you and me." He sighed. "I guess we better see what we can do now."

"And hope it's not too late?"

"Yeah." His voice was heavy with worry. "Promise me one thing," he went on.

She stiffened. "What?"

"That you won't go to the grove alone," he said. He moved to cup her face in his hands. "Remember how we met?"

She nodded against his palms. "You saved me from the Norsemen. You don't want to have to worry about doing it again."

"You got it, babe."

"Aye. I see how it could be distracting to have to keep saving me. Also," she added shrewdly, "you don't want me working on the time-travel spell until after you've saved the Culdees."

"Uh . . ."

"Then you'll use having saved the Culdees as an argument that the future can be changed."

"I hadn't thought of that," he protested.

"But you were going to."

"Don't *do* that!"

Brianna giggled. She kissed him until he didn't care if she did spooky things sometimes. "Now," she said when she had him dazed and confused, "do you want to go to sleep? Or do you want to get on with saving Ban Ean?"

"Uh," he responded. She pushed him back onto the bed. "I—" A jaw-cracking yawn kept him from finishing whatever he was going to say.

Brianna pulled up the blanket and snuggled warmly at his side. "It'll wait until dawn," she promised. "You need to rest. Sleep, and don't worry so about your friend. We'll save him too."

He decided not to argue. Somehow, her reassurances eased his mind. He needed to sleep. So he did.

22

"Is it a warrior you truly want to be?" Brianna demanded of her brother as he stepped out of the house he now shared with his wives on the outskirts of Ban Ean. She waited impatiently for his answer while he yawned.

"Is that why you came banging on my door well before dawn?" he asked once he'd gotten his mouth under control. He looked around. "Where's Sammy?"

"He went to visit Uncle Gerald."

She didn't add that she'd followed him toward Ban Ean after he slipped out without trying to wake her. She'd watched him take a fishing coracle to paddle out to the island. Then she came here to put an idea of her own into action.

"Do you want to be a warrior?" she repeated.

Donal closed the door behind him and looked at her thoughtfully. "Aye," he said. "You know I do. I am a warrior," he added sternly after a moment's thought.

"Then get your sword and get the men who'll fight organized," she ordered. "The Norsemen are coming."

He looked at her as if she'd hit him. "Where's Sammy?"

Brianna folded her arms across her chest. "I think that you have it in you to be a king, Donal son of Colum."

He snickered. "Oh, aye, of course I do."

"And why not? Rory MacMurdo has abandoned this piece of his holding. A holding he's pledged the high king of Tara to protect."

"The high king might award Ban Ean to whoever saves it from the Norsemen," Donal said thoughtfully. "It could be a beginning." He chuckled. "Perhaps I could be living in the bishop's house by the time Grandfather returns."

"Or in Rory MacMurdo's."

"That's a wicked thought," Donal said with a laugh. He patted her on the head. "A secret thought I have had myself."

Brianna didn't mind nursing Donal's ambition. Rory MacMurdo deserved a bit of trouble for abandoning the peaceful monastic community to its fate, just because of his hurt pride. "Vikings first," she told her brother. "Rory later."

"I'll do what I can. Fergus will fight," he quickly decided. "And his apprentices. They weren't happy when Father decided not to listen to Sammy. Their stone-carving tools can be used as weapons."

"Talk to them," she urged. She patted his shoulder. "There's not much time."

"What have you seen?"

Brianna looked around her as the sun came up over the horizon. It lit the village with gold. She shuddered. "Fire," she told him. "Soon." She clutched her brother's arm. "Hurry."

Donal gave her a quick hug and hurried off toward his father-in-law's house. Brianna found that she was trembling. She could feel their enemies approaching but could not pinpoint where they would strike. She just *knew* the Norsemen were nearby.

And she knew there was one more thing she had to do. It would mean breaking her promise to her husband, but she would if she must, to save Ban Ean. To save Sammy. For he was only one man, despite his skill and strength, and despite the great ally he had in the black beast.

The black beast was very much on her mind as she made her way to the sacred oak grove. It waited there, crouched in the shade of one of the ancient trees, sleeping. She didn't know if it was truly a monster or a kind of magic-powered chariot.

She knew that when its master woke and rode it into battle his foes could not stand before him, as long as they didn't outnumber him by a hundred men. She knew that this time they did. She had seen that another boatload of reckless warriors had crossed the sea to join the Norsemen who'd raided Eire all summer.

The vision had come to her just before she knocked on Donal's door. It had been too late to warn Sammy, and it would be hopeless to confide in her brother. Sammy and Donal needed allies in the coming battle. She could only rely on her memories of visions of life in the smoking city to find the help they needed.

She knew that the black beast had many brothers. It was up to her to call them forth from the future. To gather the beasts, she needed the help of the old magic that dwelled in the grove.

So Brianna went up to the top of the hill alone—as she had promised she would not do—and began to sing.

*　　*　　*

The warriors scaled the cliff just before dawn, after having crossed the whale road to join their brothers on a summer's viking. They came for treasure, to plunder gold and silver and jewels. They came to spill blood with their swords and battle-axes. Monks, they knew, were like sheep perched up on their high rocks, easy to slaughter. Taking their lives would be no challenge, but it would be a pleasant game before moving on to the rich monastery on the mainland.

The warriors knew that as the sun rose the monks would be in their little windowless chapel. Their emaciated forms would be bent over in fervent worship of their puny god. The men laughed as they approached the chapel door and prepared to make quick work of butchering the feeble excuses for men inside.

The door was heavy, but all they had to do was yank it open. Swords and axes held at the ready, shouting the promise of blood sacrifice to Odin and Thor, the Vikings rushed into the dark church.

It was empty.

The door was shut behind them while the men in the rear were still running into their stunned comrades who had been the first into the room. The windowless chamber seemed airless as well, and full of an angry god's spirit. From outside came a crow of bright laughter.

The warriors turned at the sound and rushed back toward the closed door, only to find that it would not open. Someone outside had blocked the entrance.

Outside, Sammy helped Gerald push one more boulder against the church door, then he pointed. Gerald nodded and they raced off to join the monks who were gathered on the cliff above the cove. He heard the sound of axes starting to chop through the wooden door as he and the monk reached the bend in the path that would take them around the jut of the point.

He didn't look back. He just prayed that trapping the attackers inside had bought them enough time to escape. He also thanked whatever deity was in charge of this operation that Uncle Gerald and his people had preferred escaping to becoming martyrs under the Vikings' swords.

The first thing he'd done was reconnoiter the little mountain island, looking for an escape route in case they couldn't get down the narrow path up from the bay. Then he'd arrived just as the monks were stirring out of their tiny cells. The sight of him had terrified all but their leader, who was surprisingly young and looked a lot like Donal. Sammy had some trouble making them understand the danger at first, but they'd caught on quickly enough. He'd argued for flight with what little Gaelic he'd learned, while Gerald shouted and the others dithered.

Eventually Gerald had changed his mind about staying. Sammy thought he'd decided he was going to lead a mission to preach the gospel to the pagan Norsemen if he lived through the day.

The pagans in question had been making their way up the only path to the monastery by then, just as Sammy had thought they would. With that way blocked there was only one choice left for the monks. Sammy outlined a plan with gestures and very broken Gaelic. The Culdees hurried to the spot Sammy indicated, while he and Gerald stayed behind to delay the attackers.

Most of the monks had been lowered down the cliff by the time Sammy and Gerald reached the spot where the ropes were fastened. The ropes reached only halfway down the sheer slope, but dropping from there into the deep water was preferable to being tossed to death from the top. Sammy knew that most of the monks couldn't swim, but the few that could had gone down first. They were now busy hauling their nonswimming brothers into fishing coracles. One of the small cowhide boats belonged to the Culdees. Sammy had towed another behind him when he paddled out to the island.

Looking down from the edge of the cliff he judged that there would be enough space for everybody to get away. "I was worried about that," he said as the last of Gerald's people took his turn to jump off the cliff, his robes flapping around his skinny legs. Sammy and Gerald were the only people left on the cliff.

Sammy glanced back the way he'd come. He could hear shouting. There wasn't much time. "I think they got the door down." He turned back to Gerald and gestured toward the water. "You first."

The monk nodded grimly and grabbed the rope. Gerald began to pray loudly as he stepped off the cliff. Sammy looked up, toward the mainland and Ban Ean about a mile away. In the growing morning light he could make out the buildings clearly, and the sheep-dotted meadow with its ancient standing stones beyond. The oak-crowned hill bulged up on the left. It might have been a peaceful scene, except for the second Viking longboat beached on the shingle near Uncle Sean's house.

Sammy let out an angry gasp. Behind him he could hear the raiders scrambling around the point. Dark smoke began to curl up from the common house in the center of Ban Ean. Sammy could make out a tiny lick of flame in the distance. The village was under attack.

"Brianna," he breathed on a shiver of mixed anger and dread. The first of the Vikings came running around the point.

Sammy hardly even noticed the man coming at him swinging a battle-ax as he swore and dove off the cliff. All he thought of as he passed Uncle Gerald on the way down was that he had to get to Brianna.

Los Angeles, A.D. 1993

"Do you smell smoke?"

Brother Bill MacNicol read his wife, Nellie's, lips as she spoke, but he ignored the question. His mind was on the singing. "Do you hear that?" he signed, and wasn't surprised when Nellie looked at him strangely.

"You heard something?" Nellie signed back. "Uh, Bill . . ."

"I know. I've been deaf for fifteen years. I still hear singing. In my head. It's not even the Righteous Brothers."

What he was hearing was a beautiful lilting female voice singing in a foreign language. He could only figure it was because he was remembering things Sammy had said to him on the day he disappeared.

In the time since Sammy had roared off up the hill not a trace had been found of him. Not him, not his motorcycle. The police thought Bill's explanation of Sam Bergen's disappearance was crazy. Sometimes Bill thought he was crazy. All he knew was that his friend, the friend he'd promised to do anything for, was gone, and he had no way of knowing whether Sam was alive or dead. Deep in his heart, Brother Bill believed Sam was out there, in some mysterious somewhere, doing good.

But wherever he was, he was gone. So Bill and twenty members of Holy Thunder had gathered on their Harleys at Sammy's place to give their friend a proper biker send-off. The street was full of leather- and denim-clad men and women on big motorcycles. The neighbors were all gathered in Sammy's yard, waiting for Brother Bill, with Nellie to translate, to give the eulogy. Sammy knew everybody on the block, and everybody loved Sammy.

The problem was, Bill looked down from the top of the concrete steps in front of Sammy's door and couldn't think of a thing to say to the watching people. In his head, the girl was singing louder, demanding that he pay attention. She wanted something, needed something. She was desperate. And she wanted some help.

Right now.

Bill blinked and found his gaze inexorably drawn up the hill, toward the spot where Sammy had disappeared. He was distracted from the voice for a moment when Nellie stepped in front of him. "I definitely think something's on fire," she signed. She pointed toward the hill. "I don't see any smoke, but it's coming from that way."

The girl was singing louder. Nellie, who was standing right in front of him, faded from view. Bill blinked. He saw a crowd of people, but they weren't waiting patiently for him to make a sermon. The people he saw were racing away from burning buildings. They were being chased by men with swords.

"What the—?"

The girl stopped singing. There was nothing but heavy silence. Bill was used to silence; he'd lived in silence for years. He'd stopped fearing it a long time ago. This silence frightened him.

He looked around in confusion. Everyone's attention was drawn toward the top of the hill. Engines were being started.

The girl filled up the silence in his mind with a desperate call for help.

An instant later Bill was on his Harley. By the time the girl called again all twenty members of Holy Thunder were roaring up the hill.

Ireland, A.D. 805

"And about time!" Brianna shouted as the herd of snarling metal beasts appeared in the grove. She jumped to her feet to stand on top of the altar while the beasts circled. She saw the confusion on the faces of the men and women who rode the beasts and ignored it. She singled out the one who had first appeared, knowing the big, bearded man must be their leader.

"Help me!" she called out to him, using Sammy's hand language as well as words. She didn't know why her hands were making signs. Her mind wasn't even sure what all the signs meant, but her hands knew what they were doing.

The man saw her movement and halted his beast in front of her. He planted his feet on either side of his beast and gestured a question to her. The other beast riders began shouting to each other. Brianna realized she could communicate with this man from the future the same way she'd been able to communicate with Sammy, because the magic gave her the power to do so. She ignored their confusion and explained the situation to the leader.

The spell had taken all her energy. She was dizzy, and darkness threatened the edge of her vision. She didn't have much time to get help to Ban Ean, so she pointed, used hand talk, screamed, and pleaded. Eventually the leader of the beast riders snatched her off the altar and set her behind him on his beast, and they sped down the hill. The warriors from the future thundered behind them toward the village that was burning in the distance.

Brianna clung fiercely to the leader's waist. She rested her head against his shoulder and willed herself to stay awake, to keep the sickness at bay, to keep the dizziness such as had afflicted Sammy away from the riders from the future. The day was young, and there was much magic for her yet to control. For Sammy's sake, for her people's, for her own, she had to keep going.

23

Sean punched one blunt end of his walking staff into the belly of a Norseman, then began to turn, ready to run for his life from the village square. Beside him, Ailill paused to throw a rock accurately at their attacker's head. The Norseman bellowed with fury. The wolfhound finished ripping out the throat of another Viking and leaped, knocking the attacker to the ground. Ailill darted forward, using his knife to finish the man off.

Sean reckoned that the boy and his dog were the most effective fighters in all of Ban Ean. It was Ailill who had protected him when the defense of the common house fell apart and they'd been forced to run from the fire.

He grabbed the boy by the scruff of the neck and pointed. "This way!"

Ailill nodded, and they ran as two more of the invaders

appeared in the square. Donal and Fergus were fighting off another pair of Norsemen nearby. The fire was spreading from the roof of the common house to the church. In the distance Sean could hear the rumble of an approaching storm, though the morning sky was clear—except for the smoke as Ban Ean burned.

"I knew I should have gone home last night," Sean muttered to himself as he ran. Smoke from the burning houses filled his lungs and stung his eyes. Nearer than the storm, screams and shouts filled his ears.

"There's nowhere to go!" he shouted, looking around wildly.

The boy came to a hasty halt as more of the invaders rushed from between the row of monks' houses. Sean ran into the boy, knocking them both to the ground. By the time they got to their feet more of the Vikings had rushed into the square.

"It's hopeless," Sean breathed as the big men bore down on them from all sides. Sean backed up toward the church. He did his best to shove the lad behind him, to offer what protection he could. But Ailill would have none of it.

Sean wanted to remind Ailill that he was no more than eight summers old, but age seemed irrelevant at this point. They had their backs to a burning wall and were surrounded on three sides. If they were going to die they might as well die fighting. He let Ailill dart forward with wolfhound and knife as weapons. He stood his ground, staff held between his outstretched hands. As thunder drowned out his voice he began to chant the darkest curse he could recall.

A great hairy animal of a man with an ax chose him for a victim and raised the weapon to strike. Sean flinched, waiting for the ax to cut through his staff and bury itself in his skull. The man laughed, but just then the ground shook and inhuman creatures roared out challenges from behind.

The Viking whirled to face a menace far more formidable than an old man with a staff.

Then the thunder rolled into the square and it was the Norsemen's turn to scream and take flight as the beasts threatened to run them down.

Exhausted from the long swim, soaking wet, and nearly out of his mind with fear for Brianna's safety, Sammy finally made it to the oak grove. She'd promised not to go to the grove alone, but he knew his wife. He could feel her emotions in his own soul. She'd gone to the grove all right.

She wasn't there when he arrived, though. When all he saw was the blank stone of the altar and churned-up earth where he'd hoped to find Brianna, Sammy fell to his knees, panting for breath and seized by mindless anguish.

He didn't know how long it was before he could both breathe and think a bit more easily. Time enough for warmth to begin seeping into his skin as the summer sun climbed further away from the horizon. Time enough for the exploding spots clouding his eyesight to fade. As his vision cleared he finally noticed the ground where he was kneeling. He saw the tire tracks.

Lots of tire tracks. Motorcycle tire tracks. They weren't just from his own Harley. There were numerous different treads making up the tracks, like the scale patterns of a dozen different giant snakes.

"But there aren't any snakes in Ireland," Sammy said. His inane comment echoed around the empty grove.

He got to his feet and followed the trail until he reached his own cycle. It was still parked between the dark bole of an ancient oak and Brianna's crude hut. The tracks circled the grove, then led away down the hill. Toward Ban Ean.

When that knowledge hit him all Sammy could do was shout angrily at himself, "What am I waiting for?"

An instant later he was on his Harley, roaring down the hillside.

There were dead people in the square. There was smoke and fire and the flash of weapons through the heated haze from the flames. Women were screaming and running through the curling smoke, with their children clutched to their bosoms. Some of the monks were kneeling on the ground in trembling prayer, others were trying to tend the wounded, others were fighting or chasing after fleeing enemies. The air was thick with deafening noise. Sammy barely noticed any of the evidence of battle as he rode into the square.

His attention was focused on two things. One was the sight of Brianna, pale but alive. The second was the sight of the man Brianna was clinging to—bald-headed, red-bearded, and beer-bellied, riding about a thousand pounds of chopped Harley hog in slow circles around the blood-soaked square.

"Brother Bill?"

Of course Brother Bill couldn't hear him even if the square hadn't sounded like the annual motorcycle race at Sturgis instead of a quiet Irish village that was under attack by Vikings.

"Under attack. Right. What the—?"

It took some effort for Sammy to drag his attention

away from the unexpected sight of Brianna and Brother Bill and actually concentrate on what was going on around him.

There were motorcycles scattered throughout the action. The Vikings were on the run, panicked by the appearance of the cyclists. The riders were hooting and hollering and Sammy recognized every one of them. It was Holy Thunder to the rescue, and from the way most of the invaders were running it appeared Ban Ean's problems were over.

There was still fighting on the outskirts of the square as a few brave Vikings tried to keep the retreat for the boats from turning into a massacre. Sammy almost admired the barbarians who fought fiercely on, facing what must have looked like monsters out of their worst nightmares. But he wished they'd give it up and run for their boats. He wanted this over with, and he wanted it over with now.

"All right," he said, halting for a moment to center his concentration. "Let's do it."

Brother Bill pulled up beside him, with Nellie sliding her bike next to Bill's. Several other machines fell in behind. Sammy gave Brianna a quick look. She was clinging like a monkey, with her arms wrapped around Bill's broad waist. Her lips were moving, but her eyes were closed. Singing, Sammy decided. Singing her magic spells.

Sammy looked straight ahead and revved his engine. The other bikers did the same. He gave a nod and they rode forward, picking up speed as they charged toward the fighting.

Sammy caught a glimpse of Donal and then of Fergus as the men from Ban Ean jumped out of the motorcycles' way. He saw Sean hit the ground. He saw the wolfhound worrying at the sword arm of a downed Viking. Ailill waved his knife as Sammy passed by.

Some of the Vikings screamed in terror at the sight of the many-headed monster coming toward them. They broke and ran. All but one foolhardy berserker who stood with his feet braced wide apart, sword in one hand, ax in the other.

"Odin!" he shouted. He swung the ax over his head and let it fly.

For an instant nothing seemed to happen, but then everything happened at once. As one, the cycles came to a halt. The ax struck unprotected flesh. Blood splattered as Ailill fell to the ground. Sammy roared in anguished fury as he leaped off his cycle. The berserker gave a bear's deep growl in answer and rushed toward Sammy.

Sammy would have killed the man who attacked Ailill, but the wolfhound got there first. The Viking didn't have any throat left when he fell dead on the blood-soaked earth. And then the dog was by Ailill's side, whimpering fretfully.

Sean and Sammy reached Ailill at the same time. There was blood everywhere. The boy's arm was barely attached to his body. Brother Bill helped Brianna up to them a moment later. Sean examined the wound while Brianna held the boy in her lap, crooning softly. Donal came up to pull the dog away while Sammy gestured at Bill.

Bill watched the words flowing from Sammy's quick-moving hands that told him where Holy Thunder had traveled to and how, about ancient Ireland and Brianna's magic, and about the Vikings.

"I know all that," Bill finally signed back. "The girl explained." He pointed at Ailill. Sammy didn't want to look. "We've got to get him to an emergency room."

"There is no emergency room!" Sammy shouted back, too terrified at the idea that Ailill might be dying to remember that Bill couldn't hear him.

"I can't stop the bleeding," Sean said, confirming Sammy's fears about the wound.

Sammy knelt quickly beside his wife. Her eyes were closed, the look of concentration on her face was scary. "Brianna," he said. He wanted to shake her, but thought she might break if he touched her. "Come on, babe," he pleaded. "We need a miracle here. Like you did when the baby was born. Remember?"

She opened her eyes for a moment. Her pupils were enormous, swirling with eerie shadows. "I've only one miracle in me today," she said, and went back to singing.

Sammy sprang to his feet, looking around helplessly. "He's going to die."

Bill stepped in front of him and signed, "We've got to get the kid to the UCLA medical center. It's just up the street."

"It's not up the street!" Sammy shouted back. He gestured around them. "We're not in L.A.!"

"We could be," Bill signed calmly back. He pointed to Brianna. "She brought us here. She'll have to get us back. Has to." The burly missionary bent over and scooped Ailill out of Brianna's arms. Sean jumped to his feet right behind him. "Come on," Bill spoke aloud. He carried Ailill over to his bike, confident that the order he hadn't heard himself speak would be obeyed. Sean helped settle the boy onto the motorcycle in front of Bill.

"What about the rest of these people?" Nellie shouted. "We can't just leave them here. What if the Vikings come back?"

"The raiders are sure to come back," Donal said.

"There are more dead than living." He looked to Sammy for leadership. "Where do we go? What do we do?"

It was Nellie who pointed at the cycles. "Get your survivors and come with us."

Sammy was too frantic to think about the implications of what was going on here. "Get everybody on the cycles. Hurry."

Sammy helped Brianna up as Donal began rounding up the rest of the people. Her dress was covered in Ailill's blood. Sammy didn't want to know how much blood a child could lose before it killed him. He heard Bill's engine fire to life. He held Brianna by the shoulders.

"Can you do it, babe?"

She just nodded, and Sammy helped her onto the back of his own motorcycle. "Then let's go."

Sammy saw Sean on the back of Nellie's Harley, eyes squeezed tight as he clung to the woman's waist, and started his engine. The rest of Holy Thunder gathered around them, loaded with frightened villagers, motors revving. Brianna began to sing as the cycles followed Bill up the road. Sammy swerved his machine and raced to lead the procession. Brianna's voice filled his ears, his blood and his bones and his heart. The wolfhound broke away from Donal to lope along beside them as they picked up speed.

The cycle climbed the hill while Brianna's voice rose until her song filled the world. The herd dog abandoned its sheep to chase the motorcycles up the hill. The world wavered, shrank and stretched and changed. Sammy concentrated on keeping his eyes on the rutted track even as the rest of him was caught up in the song. Still, he didn't notice the instant earth changed to asphalt.

He did look up as the hot blast of desert wind caught

him in the face. The sun beat down on his head fiercely. Traffic screeched to a halt and swerved out of the cycles' way as they sped toward the hospital entrance. Sammy heard curses from the drivers in their wake. He looked around him and took a deeply satisfying breath of polluted air.

He was home.

"You awake, babe?"

Brianna groaned again and opened her eyes. She was lying on a soft bed. Sammy was looking at her with a reassuring smile and holding her hand.

"Ailill?" she asked.

"In serious but stable condition," he answered. Then he translated. "He'll be fine."

Brianna breathed a sigh of relief, followed by a fervent prayer of thanks. Sammy helped her to sit up. "Where am I?" she asked.

"The smoking city," Sammy answered with a wry lift of his eyebrows. "Where do you think?"

"Los Angeles," she said. There was no surprise in knowing she was where her visions had sent her. "But where exactly in Los Angeles, my love?"

"You passed out as soon as we got to the E.R.," Sammy told her. "They couldn't find anything wrong with you, but kept you for observation anyway."

"E.R.," she repeated. "Observation." She looked around. "I want to see Ailill," she said as she swung her legs over the side of the bed. The bed was too high off the floor for her liking. The walls of the room were smooth, and cool blue in color. Curtains were pulled across one wall. She knew she could see the city if she looked behind the curtain.

"And I want to see the smoking city." It felt right to be here. She was home, at last. Odd, how she had fought the knowledge that she must come here. How could she not be here when it was where Sammy belonged?

Sammy helped her to stand. She kissed him, which she realized as she did so was really the first thing she wanted to do. His cheeks were smooth shaven and his mouth tasted of fresh herbs.

"Toothpaste," she said, recognizing the taste once their lips had parted. "I like it."

"I love you," Sammy answered.

Brianna was surprised to hear the anxiety behind his words. *Ah,* she thought, *now he worries that I'll leave him.*

"Foolish man," she said, and kissed him again. After they explored each others' mouths and emotions for a while, Brianna drew her head away from Sammy so she could look him in the eye. "I am your wife forever and ever," she assured him. "No matter where we may be."

His eyes lit with teasing joy. "I gotta get you home," he said. He glanced past her to the bed. "Then again—"

She cut him off with a laugh. "I want to make love, but I don't think I want to make love in this place."

"Yeah," Sammy agreed. "A nurse might walk in on us or something." Sammy frowned. "Say something."

"Where's Ailill? When can I see him?"

"Ailill's asleep right now. They've got him pretty drugged up, poor kid. They performed about ten hours of microsurgery to get his arm reattached yesterday. Doctors say he's got a very good chance of getting full use of it back. I'm hoping you can help the healing along, Dr. Druid."

"They reattached his arm?"

Sammy nodded.

"What magic your time has. Sammy, why are you looking like that?"

"'Cause you're speaking English." He chuckled. "With a sexy Irish accent. I never noticed your accent before."

"I noticed your accent when you were in Eire, but now you have none. I wonder what language it was we spoke to each other." She noticed she was wearing some sort of lightweight shift. Sammy's white shirt and faded blue trews clung to him like a second skin. "What funny clothes. Doesn't it hurt your manly member to squeeze it into such a tight space?"

Sammy looked down at his crotch. "Uh, no."

He went over to the curtain and pulled it open. Tall trees filled with purple blossoms grew outside the large window. Brianna saw the brown slopes of high hills in the distance, covered with roads and buildings but very little vegetation. The light was harsh and bright, yet full of dark haze. It looked very familiar.

"The smoking city." Brianna sighed wistfully. "And not a sheep in sight."

Sammy put his arm around her shoulder. "Afraid not, and that sheepdog isn't too happy about it. It's herding people all over Bill's shelter. Are you happy to be here?" he asked.

"Happy has nothing to do with it," she told him. "It was my fate."

"But are you happy? To be with me?"

She stroked his cheek. "Aye. For now and always."

"For now and always," he repeated. "Me too. You sure? I mean, it won't be easy to adjust. You deserve better than this world can offer you. You won't understand about pollution—and stuff."

In a fit of exasperation, she stomped on his foot.

"Now will you stop being such a fool, Sammy Sam Bergen? I know what you truly fear. I am not a holy woman like your Karen. I ran *from* a monastery, not *to* one."

He was quiet for a moment, then a bright smile lit his face. "Yeah," he said. "That's right."

"We've a life to build together." She stomped on his foot again to emphasize her point. "Forever."

Sammy didn't seem to notice her trodding on him. "Together," he repeated.

"I promise."

"I promise too." He looked at her thoughtfully. "You mean it. You won't leave me." He laughed softly. "And I finally believe it."

"After all we've been through together, you had better."

"But what about your being a star?"

"What about it?"

"Well, what kind of star are you going to be?"

"Sammy, I don't even know what being a star means! I just know what I'm meant to do."

He gestured at the world outside the window. "Stardom's out there. What will it be? Singing? Movies? Television? What about that Oscar ceremony you had a vision about?"

"I don't know." Brianna went back to the bed and sat down. Sammy came over and tossed his fanny pack down beside her. He pulled up a chair and leaned forward, with his hands clasped anxiously together.

"Lot of weird stuff in there," he said, indicating the pouch with a jerk of his head. She picked it up and emptied a stack of papers onto the bed.

"What are these?" She unfolded the top sheet of paper and looked it over. "I can read it, though it's not in my own language." She grinned at Sammy. "It's a marriage license."

"Ours," he concurred. "Also your driver's license, and your Social Security card and Ailill's birth certificate. There was stuff for other people, too. Those papers magically appeared when we showed up in the twentieth century. It's like what happened to my Harley. Some sort of magical side effect of what you do."

"Special effect," she said, and blinked, not knowing what she meant. But it sounded familiar—

"Did you know that Ailill's our son?"

"Is he now?" she asked.

"Yeah." He rubbed his jaw, the teasing light returning to his eyes once more. "That's what his birth certificate says. Only his name's Alan. Alan O'Niall Bergen. Seems I've acquired a wife and a kid and a dog—just all of a sudden."

"It wasn't so sudden," she told him. "The wedding was hundreds and hundreds of years ago. What of the others?"

"My friends are taking care of them. Bill and Nellie are used to taking in homeless people. We'll go visit them as soon as they let you out of here."

She nodded. "It would have been painful to be far from Donal and my father. And what of your friend? Did I get you home in time to help him?" she asked anxiously.

Sammy let out a sigh of relief. He nodded. "Yeah. There's still a week to the trial. Bill says another witness changed his testimony, so it won't just be my word now. Things are going to be fine for Jerry."

"You would have gone back to save him, you know," Brianna told him. "It was not in you to abandon justice just because you loved me."

He looked away from her. "I—"

"But you didn't have to make that decision, my love. It is our fate to be together."

He gave her a smile that lit her heart. "Thank the Buddha for that." He pointed at the fanny pack. "There's more stuff in the pouch for you."

"What's this then?" she asked as she picked up a small square of stiff paper. It was white with words written in bright blue ink. She knew that this was an important clue to her new life. "Brianna Bergen, it says here."

"I like the sound of that."

She flashed him a smile. "So do I."

She sensed that he finally, truly believed that she had no intention of leaving him. She had never had any fear of him leaving her. Now all they had to do was find out what fate had in store for her. She had little memory of the journey to Los Angeles.

"It was fate," she said. "It didn't seem like I had anything to do with it at all."

"I've been thinking about that a lot," Sammy said. "I see what you mean about our not being able to change this future. Since it was Brother Bill who got us here."

"*Our* future," she told him. "Together."

He waved his hands at her. "All right. Our future."

She gave a firm nod, then waved the square of paper at him. "Now, what is this?"

"It's a business card," he informed her as she turned the card over and over between her fingers. "Your business card."

"A business? Like a merchant? I have a business, then?" Yes, that sounded right. She was going to sell something to people who dwelled in places called studios.

"It has your name on it, babe."

"Aye." She blinked as a bit of dizziness sent her vision whirling. She saw explosions and strange creatures and impossible feats of illusion. All of them under her command. This was what the people in the studios wanted to buy from her. They would buy her magic.

When her Sight cleared she gave a happy laugh. "Ah, so now I understand!"

"What?"

She read the rest of the card. "Singing Magic. That's the name of my company. Singing Magic."

"So, what is it? A recording studio?"

She shook her head. "No." She lifted her head proudly. "I'm going to win an Academy Award for special effects." She narrowed her eyes worriedly at her suddenly grinning husband. "Is that good?"

He was thoughtful for a moment, then said incredulously, "You're gonna do special effects? Like the dinosaurs in *Jurassic Park,* or something?"

"Better," she replied, recognizing what he meant. "Better than Stan Winston or Industrial Light and Magic—whatever that is."

Sammy sat back and crossed his arms. "No kidding. You're gonna be a special effects artist. How?"

"Singing magic, of course. I sing. It makes magic."

"Yeah. But—"

She jumped off the bed and into his lap. Draping her arms around his neck she gave him a long, thorough kiss. Once she was sure she had his complete attention she asked, "Why not? It's all a matter of natural talent, isn't it? Isn't magic what movies are about?" *Whatever movies were,* she added to herself.

"Hon, you're a walking talking encyclopedia of movies."

"I am?" He nodded. Suddenly she knew: movies, or at least unconnected bits of movies, had been parts of her visions and dreams all her life.

He stroked her cheek and her neck and kissed his way along her collarbone before asking, "You're gonna use magic to make movies?"

"Aye. I'll be able to work on a very low budget that way."

Sammy's hand strayed to her breast. "Makes sense," he said.

Brianna ran her hands through Sammy's thick curls. "All I need is you," she told him, with a world of promise in her voice.

"All I need is you."

"And a computer," she added. "And some software to get started."

"Right," he said as he rolled her nipple between his fingers. It sent a shiver of desire through her.

"Maybe we shouldn't worry about a nurse coming in," he suggested.

"Maybe not." She put her arms around his neck as he lifted her from the chair.

As he carried her toward the bed she asked, "Sammy, what is software?"

"Later, babe," he said. He put her on the bed and covered her with his strong, powerful body. Just before he kissed her again and she stopped caring about the future, he said, "I'll explain later."

Epilogue

Sturgis, South Dakota, A.D. August 1999

"Five kids in six years. You ought to be ashamed of yourself."

Sammy was glad Brother Bill was talking in ASL, because he couldn't have heard a word over the roar of the motorcycle races circling the nearby track. Harleys were not quiet machines. Problem was, he was holding his three-year-old twin daughters in each arm, so he couldn't use his hands to sign back.

"It's not my fault," he answered, trusting in Bill's lip-reading ability. "My wife doesn't believe in birth control."

It was oven-hot out on the rolling plains of South Dakota, sweat was rolling off him in buckets, and he was plastered in the dust kicked up by the race. There were bikers at the annual Sturgis meet in their leather-clad thousands, from every walk of life and from all over the world.

Sammy wondered what people would think if they found out the members of the White Bird Motorcycle Club of Yachats, Oregon, were a bunch of transplanted medieval monks. They wouldn't believe it, he decided, even though the members of White Bird were also the residents of a very successful artists' colony.

The people they'd brought back from Ban Ean had adapted pretty well to the modern world, much to Sammy's surprise. Oh, they'd been confused and frightened at first, but Brother Bill and his people had helped ease them into the twentieth century. Pretty soon they'd even gotten back to their calligraphy and manuscript illumination and intricate stone carving.

Their handicraft skills had been incredibly marketable, and Uncle Sean had caught on to the idea of capitalism right away. They'd done so well with Sean managing their finances that they'd been able to purchase the land on the Oregon coast within two years. They'd settled down to the quiet, secluded life they preferred. Quiet, that is, except for the biker hobby they'd adopted from their time spent with Holy Thunder.

He and Brianna, on the other hand, had stayed in Los Angeles to have a family. In between babies, Brianna learned computers at the speed of light and started her special effects business. Sammy had continued to teach at his *dojang* and had just received his Master's rank. He was opening a second school soon, to be run by his old friend Jerry Park. Brianna's latest project was going to make her rich and really famous. More importantly, she was having a wonderful time creating pretend monsters and space ships and doing what she wanted to do with her life.

Sammy was the happiest man in the world, and he thought they were maybe the happiest couple in the world. He looked from one beautiful daughter to the other and gave each of them a quick kiss on the cheek. As he did Donal came strolling by, a wife on each arm. Bridget and Moira were dressed in matching skimpy halters and skin-tight leather pants. They all waved but didn't stop to chat.

Bill watched them go and shook his head. "I've never quite gotten used to the three of them," he signed.

Sammy shrugged, and the twins giggled as he bounced them. They began tugging on his hair as he spoke to Bill. "Whatever works. At least they're happy."

"And they consider it a marriage," Bill said. "Have you been to Donal's exhibit yet?"

Like his twin sister, Donal had a talent with computer imaging. He worked with Singing Magic, but he also did computer art on his own. His latest works were being shown at an art gallery in Sturgis.

"Brianna's there now. No, she's not," he said as he saw her coming toward him through the crowd behind the stands. Ailill was with her, pushing a stroller. Their five-year-old walked beside Brianna, his little hand in hers. Baby number five was a barely perceptible bulge around her middle.

"Mommy!" the twins called as they caught sight of their mother.

The twins were kind of uncanny in that they tended to do everything together. In fact they were uncanny in lots of ways. Brianna assured Sammy that they were fine, that they'd just inherited her psychic talents. He said that was what he was afraid of, but he was only joking. He kind of liked, no loved, having psychic women in his life these days.

He smiled as Brianna came to his side. Every time he saw her he was surprised by how strong his love for her was. She said that it was the same for her. Whether they were parted for minutes, hours, or days, his reaction at seeing her was always incredibly intense. She was still as beautiful as the day they'd met, and still as welcome as his soul's comfort and other half. His body always tightened with desire, and his heart with wonder. She was his. How had he ever gotten so lucky?

"Forever," he said as she turned her wide mouth up to his for a kiss.

"Forever," she agreed.

As their lips met, the crowd, the dust, the heat, the noise, all slipped away. What remained for this brief delicious moment was their promise to each other.

Comanche Magic by **Catherine Anderson**

The latest addition to the bestselling Comanche series. When Chase Wolf first met Fanny Graham, he was immediately attracted to her, despite her unsavory reputation. Long ago Fanny had lost her belief in miracles, but when Chase Wolf came into her life he taught her that the greatest miracle of all was true love.

Separating by **Susan Bowden**

The triumphant story of a woman's comeback from a shattering divorce to a fulfilling, newfound love. After twenty-five years of marriage, Riona Jarvin's husband leaves her for a younger woman. Riona is in shock—until she meets a new man and finds that life indeed has something wonderful to offer her.

Hearts of Gold by **Martha Longshore**

A sizzling romantic adventure set in 1860s Sacramento. For years Kora Hunter had worked for the family newspaper, but now everyone around her was insisting that she give it up for marriage to a long-time suitor and family friend. Meanwhile, Mason Fielding had come to Sacramento to escape from the demons in his past. Neither he nor Kora expected a romantic entanglement, considering the odds stacked against them.

In My Dreams by **Susan Sizemore**

Award-winning author Susan Sizemore returns to time travel in this witty, romantic romp. In ninth-century Ireland, during the time of the Viking raids, a beautiful young druid named Brianna inadvertently cast a spell that brought a rebel from 20th-century Los Angeles roaring back through time on his Harley-Davidson. Sammy Bergen was so handsome that at first she mistook him for a god—but he was all too real.

Surrender the Night by **Susan P. Teklits**

Lovely Vanessa Davis had lent her talents to the patriotic cause by seducing British soldiers to learn their battle secrets. She had never allowed herself to actually give up her virtue to any man until she met Gabriel St. Claire, a fellow Rebel spy and passionate lover.

Sunrise by **Chassie West**

Sunrise, North Carolina, is such a small town that everyone knows everyone else's business—or so they think. After a long absence, Leigh Ann Warren, a burned out Washington, D.C., police officer, returns home to Sunrise. Once there, she begins to investigate crimes both old and new. Only after a dangerous search for the truth can Leigh help lay the town's ghosts to rest and start her own life anew with the one man meant for her.

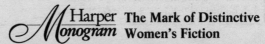